APARTMENT

IN

ATHENS

1

GLENWAY WESCOTT

APARTMENT
IN
ATHENS

GREENWOOD PRESS, PUBLISHERS
WESTPORT, CONNECTICUT

The Library of Congress has catalogued this publication as follows:

Library of Congress Cataloging in Publication Data

Wescott, Glenway, 1901–
    Apartment in Athens.

    I. Title.
PZ3.W512Aℓ6 [PS3545.E827]   813'.5'2   76-152617
ISBN 0-8371-6052-9

Originally published in 1945
by Harper & Brothers Publishers, New York

Reprinted with the permission
of Harper & Row Publishers

First Greenwood Reprinting 1972

Library of Congress Catalogue Card Number 76-152617

ISBN 0-8371-6052-9

Printed in the United States of America

813.52
W511a

To my brother's wife

APARTMENT

IN

ATHENS

1

1.

ALL THIS HAPPENED TO A GREEK FAMILY NAMED Helianos.

Nikolas Helianos was part-owner and editor of a reputable publishing house in Athens; a middle-aged man with a wife a little older than himself, and a ten-year-old daughter and a twelve-year-old son. They had lost another son of nineteen or twenty, Cimon, in the battle of Mount Olympos in April, 1941. A brother of Mrs. Helianos' had also made his home with them; but when the invaders reached Athens he disappeared or fled, they had no notion where.

The invasion of course was ruinous for publishers —the firm of Helianos had not a chance, as it was small and conservative, specializing in schoolbooks and scholarly treatises—and although Mrs. Helianos had inherited a little income, their standard of living had to be reduced to bare necessity. With the two young men gone, their dwelling in the suburb of Psyhiko was larger than they needed; so they moved into an apartment vacated by Helianos' chief printer, four pleasant but small rooms in the center of town.

Naturally they were not a happy family, but they had good hearts, and did their best to console each other in their bereavement and impoverishment.

[1]

Helianos was not quite what one thinks of as a typical Athenian, but rather like some Frenchman of the superior middle class, such as a college professor or a civil servant; soft-spoken, with a mind perhaps over-cultivated, discursive and discerning, seeing both sides of a thing. He was a small man, with sloping shoulders, with no paunch but no waistline either. He had a cheerful look, in spite of something heavy and drooping about his face. He had fine friendly eyes. Even in the lean years, 1941, 1942, 1943, he still kept his stoutness, formed by years of good nourishment and good life.

Mrs. Helianos, who had been beautiful in her girl-hood, with the wide eyes and pouting lips and strong rotund throat of the women of antiquity, suffered from heart-trouble, to which was added a certain hypochondria; and she had grown indolent and stout. A shadowy freckle had strewn itself throughout her ivory skin. Her mouth drew down tight, and her eyes protruded and had pouches under them. She was an orphan, adopted and very indulgently educated by two uncles who were wealthy merchants. Helianos, taking up where they had left off, had gone on spoiling her. It made everything more troubling and difficult for her when the bad time began. The first year of the disaster of Greece seemed to bring out only the weaknesses of her character.

Their twelve-year-old, Alex, was a bright but strange little boy. He had great over-excited eyes, a nose straight from his forehead, turned-up lips, and a precocious fixed hard expression; but if you looked at him or spoke to him, his lips parted, his eyes danced.

He had adored his elder brother, and when the war began, only hoped that it would go on a long time, until he grew old enough to enlist in the army. He had taken the news of his brother's death on Mount Olympos very quietly, but after that, when Greece no longer had a proper army, he began to talk only of growing strong enough to kill at least one German, himself, without waiting to grow up. Every few days he asked his parents whether in their estimation he had grown taller or gained weight; and many of his games were tests of his strength, experiments, for vengeance's sake.

In fact he was not strong. His father was afraid that he had inherited the mediocre health which ran in Mrs. Helianos' family. Although they had somewhat more to eat than the average household in Athens, he seemed to be shrinking, not growing; and between his sharp hipbones he was developing the little pot-belly of famine.

His ten-year-old sister Leda had the physical stamina that he lacked, but the Helianos' worried about her too, because her mind was backward. She had never been a clever child, though they had thought nothing of it until after the fall of Greece. Then in the terrible year her infant character took on a strange aspect, as if she drew all the confusion and intimidation in with her breath, absorbed it through the pores of her skin in an unwholesome damp or an icy chill.

Although she had that pearly white skin which had been a feature of her mother's loveliness in her girlhood, Leda was not pretty. Her teeth grew too far forward, and her cheekbones were too high under her eyes. But the great pity was her expression or lack of expression. Sometimes, when something went wrong, or when she could not understand what was happening, her sensitive but passive face made one shiver. It merely shrank and hung heavy like the loose petals of a large flower.

She never wanted to play with anyone except her brother, and rarely spoke, sitting and watching things without a word for hours at a time. Whatever was said to her or done for her she accepted indifferently, and gave no sign of devotion to either of her parents. Only Alex found the way to her small heart.

When their various relatives came to visit them, Helianos would remark, "Leda is more like a daughter-in-law than a daughter."

It was the kind of delicate, obscure joke that he liked to make, in his low voice with his clever smile. And there was truth in it: the delicate boy and the sleepy-headed little girl were like a bride and groom in a fairy-tale, diminutive, uncanny, one as bewitched as the other.

Chattering by the hour, Alex confided to Leda all his fantasy of taking revenge on some German, often with extreme passion, with details of childish atrocity. It frightened her but because it was he, and she so loved the sound of his voice, her dull chubby face would light up with blissful attention.

Mrs. Helianos thought that Alex should be punished for his wild talk, not only because of its bad effect on Leda but for his own sake and for their sake: his long-suffering parents! War was not for children. She wanted her children to think of it as it might be of illness in the family, or bankruptcy, or an earthquake or a flood; with no one to blame. She could not imagine where Alex got his vengeful notions. If he went on harping on the war in this way of his, daydream and melodrama, sooner or later he would feel that he must do something in fact, to make his dreams come true. And as he was not capable of anything, he would fail and be caught by the Germans and be punished in the German way. Had they not suffered enough?

Helianos only shook his head dubiously, refusing to discipline his silly son. As a matter of fact Alex's cruel patriotic make-believe did not depress Leda so much as her mother's fuss and foreboding. Children are somewhat immune to their own level of cruelty... She overheard a part of the argument her parents had about this, and started to cry in her silent, passive fashion. There was an affinity between Mrs. Helianos and Leda, somehow closer than their affection: the anxious motherly imagination reflecting itself in the little one as if it were a dark cloud over a small stagnant pool.

One afternoon in the summer of 1941 Leda had an adventure. Alex was absent, taking a message to one of his father's friends; and Leda went out and down the street to a vacant lot where he had promised to meet her and play with her. Presently Alex came back alone, asking, "Mother, where is Leda? Where is Leda?"

An hour later Leda returned, like a small sleepwalker; and for two and a half days she would not, or could not, move or speak or eat or sleep. She sat no matter where all day long, and when her mother picked her up and put her to bed, lay all night long, breathing with her mouth open and staring straight ahead, as though her eyes were of marble. The family physician, Dr. Vlakos, whom Mrs. Helianos summoned on the second day, could not explain her condition. On the third day, a chance remark of Alex's having aroused her, she resumed her poor listless existence as usual, but would never tell what had frightened her.

Although they were newcomers in that part of town and Mrs. Helianos did not know or care to know many of her neighbors, now she went among them to investigate the mystery of Leda. At last she found one whose small daughter, younger than Leda but not so sensitive or secretive, had gone along in search of Alex that afternoon. This is what had happened: another neighbor's child had misinformed them as to the direction of Alex's errand. They had strayed into a side-street near the municipal market where, earlier in the day, there had been a gathering of hungry Athenians to protest against some new ruling or new deprivation. The German military police had arrived, chosen to regard it as a riot, and fired upon it to disperse it. Eight or ten bodies lay on the pavement, machine-gunned, some with grimacing faces, all with grimacing bodies, rags of flesh in ragged clothing. There was a sickening wall against which some had been knocked, and as they fell they had soiled it, sprinkled it, painted it. Only one living being was there, when the two little girls in their confusion wandered up: a young German on sentry-duty, who paid no attention for a while, then shouted at them to run away, for God's sake!

The neighbor's child, having narrated this historic scene to her parents at the time it happened, now repeated it all to Mrs. Helianos. Leda on the other hand still would not answer their questions, or Alex's either; but Mr. and Mrs. Helianos thought it unlikely that she had forgotten it or ever would. She had a kind of placidity, never the least hysterical alarm or panic; but there was something always weighing upon her thought, oppressing her spirit, as if the thick little skull were too tight for the melancholy mind.

Mr. and Mrs. Helianos themselves could never forget the loss of their elder son, their Cimon, who from the day of his birth to the day of his death had been perfectly healthy and intelligent and promising. But, as Greeks having a natural realism and a sense of the absoluteness of death, they somewhat closed their minds to this; at least they kept silent for each other's sake. There was heartbreak enough in having to bring up the two living offspring in this evil time, poor inferior offspring; which they discussed by the hour.

There was also the troubling subject of Mrs. Helianos' brother. "Probably he too is dead," she would say; but neither of them really believed it.

"Oh, he will turn up one of these mornings, when we least expect him," Helianos would answer, "perhaps in peril, perhaps in disgrace."

He had never thought highly of his brother-in-law; a cynical and sycophantic youth, in his estimation. Before the war he had held a good government job under Metaxas, and belonged to a reactionary club where he talked the platitudes of those days, against the parliamentary form of government. Helianos, recalling all this, wondered if he might not have gone over to the enemy in some capacity. He had heard that they were eager to have some knowledgeable Greeks on their side.

Mrs. Helianos fiercely defended her brother against her husband's ill opinion; and in their fond but uneasy relationship of late, this had been the worst disagreement and the strangest issue. For Helianos felt that in her heart of hearts she would have been willing to have his worst suspicions confirmed. She wanted to believe in secret what she would not have him believe or speak of: that her brother had come to terms with the Germans somehow. She had reached that point of the sorrow of war when nothing matters except the survival of one's loved ones.

The Helianos family had always been liberals, and now two or three had become heroes with great prestige in the eyes of all the rest—notably the leader of a band of saboteurs and snipers who troubled the Germans incessantly, a cousin named Petros Helianos— and none of them had ever approved of those wealthy merchants who were Mrs. Helianos' uncles. As for her young brother, they were more than suspicious, they were convinced: he was alive somewhere, collaborating with the enemy somehow; and they half blamed Helianos for having married into such a family.

He himself was to blame in a way; he was too sedentary and philosophical for the time of war. To be sure, he would have nothing to do with the Germans or

Italians; but on the other hand he did not participate at all in the underground or any sort of organized resistence to the occupiers of Greece. He never thought of anything that he felt he might be able to do in that way. His relatives let him know how they felt, by sharp sayings in the Athenian spirit, or by a new solemnity at family gatherings, or by not coming where he and his wife were expected.

Therefore Helianos was extremely despondent when they had to take a German officer to live in their apartment. As things stood between him and his kinsmen he could see that it was bound to bring disgrace as well as difficulty and distress. It was his weakness to be timid, conciliatory, he knew that, and now in the actual physical presence of the enemy he would be less than ever able to correct it in himself. He knew how sincerely his wife hated the invaders of Greece—had they not taken her first and best child's life as they came?—but indeed it was hard to distinguish between such hatred as this, and mere fear. It was in her nature to keep imagining that things might be worse; worse and worse in spite of every effort. Doubtless the German would take advantage of this; and his cousins would misunderstand it and despise them both more and more.

Little did he dream how it was to turn out in fact; and how the heroic Helianos' speak of him today, if not as a hero, at least as a martyr.

2.

A CORPORAL AND A PRIVATE CAME FIRST, EXPLAINING
that they had been ordered to make a survey of all the
apartments in that section of town for a certain officer; followed in a day or two by the officer himself.
With an indifferent air but methodically, he requested them to open all the doors, not forgetting
the kitchen-cupboards and the clothes closets; looked
down to the street from all the windows; inspected the
Helianos' themselves no less carefully than their habi-
tation and furniture, giving them to understand that
they were to wait on him personally; said that he required a telephone, and asked one or the other to stay
in the apartment until a man came to install it; reserved the sitting room and the best bedroom for his
exclusive use; sat down on all the beds to test the box-
springs, and expressed a preference for one of the
single beds in the other bedroom; and ordered them
to have this substitution made and their personal ef-
fects removed out of his rooms by five o'clock that
evening. At five o'clock he returned with his baggage
and a boxful of books and moved in; probably, he
said, for the duration of the war.

All that day and the next day Mrs. Helianos wept
as she worked, with her husband and the children as-

sisting most inefficiently. Helianos scarcely knew how
to comfort or encourage her. He himself hoped that
they might get on well enough with this officer, who
seemed a reasonable human being; but it was a hope
so mixed with his dread of the disapproval of his relatives in case they did get on well, that he dared not
speak of it. In any event, as to the housekeeping, the
upbringing of the children, and all the detail of life
which was his unhappy wife's concern, it was going to
mean more trouble, harder work, worse hardship,
than anything she had ever known.

However, he kept telling her, just how hard it
would be depended on the individual character of the
foreigner in question, as to which they should re-
serve judgment for a while, and on their own service-
ability and tactfulness toward him. He included
young Alex and Leda in his little lecture upon this
last point, and they all promised each other to be on
their best behavior.

"Furthermore, my poor dear wife," he said, "this
is not a thing for you to hold against the Germans in
your bitter way. Every army of occupation has to bil-
let some of its officers upon private citizens. It is normal. If the British or the Americans ever came to lib-
erate Greece, they too would want the best rooms in
half the houses in Athens."

But before the week was out Helianos had begun to
feel something of the peculiarity of German occupation; and his having to try to fathom the mind and
temperament of their domestic German for some
practical purpose every day, helped him understand
the general truth and the historic matter. He warned

himself against generalizing too much from the one example, but his observations of other Germans in the streets of Athens, and the confidences of other Athenians who had them thrust into their homes, gradually confirmed him in his sense of what they had in mind, all of them. It evidently was a matter of fixed policy: in one way or another, the citizens of occupied countries were to be subjugated individually, by the individual occupiers whatever their rank, in the minutest detail whenever they got a chance.

Their occupier was a captain and his name was Kalter, Ernst Robert Kalter; they found it neatly inscribed on tags attached to his baggage. He was a man just past middle age, tall and vigorous, and handsome in his way. Evidently he was as healthy as a wild animal, although now and then he caught cold, which was his weakness. There was one thing about his face that was bound to strike a Greek or any Mediterranean as odd: a certain asymmetry, as if it had been cut out of wood and the knife had slipped at certain features. As Helianos put it to his wife, in that precise but not serious style of his, his pointed nose appeared somewhat in profile however you looked at it; that is to say, it did not point straight at you. He had a dueling scar, but not the becoming kind; it was more like the remainder of a sore than a closed cut. Although his ears were small they stood out, and his hair was cropped so as to bare them to the utmost. His chin was long and full of character, with slight dimples or puckers in the ruddy skin all over it.

The Helianos' had one advantage over many other occupied families; as a basis for good relations with their officer they had languages. In Helianos' youth, while his father was still alive and active in the publishing business, his hobby and youthful ambition had been archaeology, and then in a sort of hero-worship of old Schliemann, the excavator of Troy, he had learned German. Captain Kalter knew only a few words of practical, peremptory Greek, but having served in the campaign of France in 1940, he spoke some French. Mrs. Helianos spoke fairly good French and a little German, as became the daughter of a merchant-family of consequence.

At first they could not conceive why he had chosen their modest apartment, of all places. One would have expected a man of his rank to feel entitled to a more spacious, wealthy establishment; something like their former villa in Psyhiko, for example. But having considered his way of life for a while, they saw that it was a quite characteristic and sensible choice. He was a staff-officer in the quartermaster's corps, absorbed in his work; and doubtless it was hard work. He went to it very early in the morning and stayed late in the evening, and occasionally it kept him all night; then as a rule he came back in the middle of the day for a nap. What he liked about living with them was the convenience of it: his headquarters was in the next street. In any case, they soon found, their waiting on him meant more to him than comfort or luxury, and his power over them in little ways day in and day out more than vanity.

It was a small apartment, for three grown-ups and two children; he had taken more than half of it. They were left with the foyer and the corridor, too narrow for any use, and the kitchen and one bedroom. They remembered that Helianos' fondest old aunt had a good-sized folding cot, and persuaded her to take their second-best single bed in exchange for it, and placed it in the kitchen for themselves. This enabled them to put Alex and Leda together in the bedroom. They were light sleepers—Alex because he was so thoughtful, Leda because she was timorous and given to bad dreams—and when anything disturbed their sleep it made them high-strung and tiresome next day. There was always some disturbance in the kitchen: the captain sat up late, and wanted a kettle of hot water just before he retired; and sometimes he rang for them again in the middle of the night; and in any case they had to rise at dawn to prepare his breakfast.

Their plan was to use the children's room for a common sitting room during the day, but as it turned out they spent more and more time in the kitchen. To sit where servants sat seemed to make it easier for them not to forget all the things they now had to do. They intended to keep the cot folded and back against the wall, but before long they were using it as a couch; sitting side by side on it for the preparation of the meals and other sedentary tasks, and also when they took their ease, when they were able to take any. The bedclothes of course got irremediably soiled but they ceased to mind that.

The captain insisted upon having the bathroom and the water-closet all to himself, as a hygienic precaution. "All you Greeks have venereal diseases," he explained. Since they had to be sparing of warm water anyway, and could not afford soap, their having only the kitchen-sink to keep clean at was no great increase of hardship; but the trip downstairs and outdoors and across the courtyard to a semi-public latrine was hard, especially for Mrs. Helianos with her painful heart.

At night in the winter months the apartment often got too cold for the captain to get out of bed to relieve himself—catching colds was the bane of his life—and then he rang for Mr. or Mrs. Helianos to bring him a vessel, and made them wait while he used it. Helianos liked to think that he was the one who answered this call invariably, but he was a little deaf and his wife often rose and did it without disturbing him, and complained of it the next morning. They never knew whether as an upper-class German he was accustomed to this intimate kind of service, or whether their inconvenience and humiliation amused him. He did not smile or joke about anything, but occasionally his blue eyes appeared to twinkle.

You might not think that keeping house for themselves and this one extra man would have occupied them from morning to night, straining every nerve, but it did. The marketing was Helianos' responsibility, which took all morning; occasionally, when the nearby markets had nothing edible or when the queues were long, a part of the afternoon as well. Fuel for the kitchen-stove had to be brought from some distance, sometimes in small amounts, sometimes a week's supply at a time, requiring several trips the same day, with Alex's help. He also had to do the heavy cleaning, because of his wife's heart-trouble. While they resigned themselves to the dirtiness of their own clothes, the captain expected them to wash and iron his shirts and undergarments. Mrs. Helianos was forever sewing or mending, and there was more and more of this, and harder to do, as all the family wardrobe wore out.

One afternoon as she sat with her husband beside her on the cot, thrusting her needle faster and faster, yanking the thread until it broke, she remarked, in a soft hysterical tone, "There is one advantage in our children's not having enough to eat and not growing as they should. They can go on wearing the same old garments longer than normal children."

Helianos took the needle and thread away from her, put his arms around her, and told her that this was no way for her to talk. Unintentionally or not, it was like a parody of his own ironic speech and it disturbed him, somehow between sadness and anger. Their nerves were on edge. They were unaccustomed to everything, inefficient at everything; for which they alternately blamed one another and apologized to one another.

In the past of course they had had servants, and even in the early days of defeat and poverty, until the captain came, they were able to keep one old woman, Evridiki (or as we say Euridice), a maid of all work who had moved in from Psyhiko to be near them, and worked by the day. In the captain's opinion they had no real need of her; furthermore he took an instant dislike to her. For a German of his temperament and habit, to be waited on by Greeks at all, even the superior sort, was condescension and tolerance enough.

"None of you has any talent for domestic service,"

he said, "and this kind of ill-natured but meek, broken-down, old country cousin is insufferable."

He also complained of her having a body-odor offensive to him; and at the end of the first fortnight instructed them to dismiss her and not to engage anyone else.

Not only did this make their life twice as laborious as they had expected; for Mrs. Helianos especially, in the peculiar way she felt about everything, it was one of the bitterest of the humiliations inflicted upon them by the proud captain; all the more bitter because it was not exactly an injustice. Helianos also said that in fact they ought to be able to manage their small housework themselves. They were well aware of Evridiki's inefficient service and shortcomings of character. They too minded the musky exhalation of her old body and old clothes. But she had been around them so long that her faults were like infirmities of their own flesh, perversities of their own soul.

Some forty years had passed since Evridiki as a buxom peaceful-eyed maid had been brought from a village near Eleusis to care for Mrs. Helianos when Mrs. Helianos had been a sickly motherless infant. To have her rejected and sent away by the fastidious German after so many years, troubled the sickly middle-aged woman as if it were a curse on them all; a profanation of all that time.

And yet she did not complain of it in her ordinary, repetitious, self-revealing way. For one thing, she knew that the children, and perhaps Helianos as well, agreed with Captain Kalter about the old woman's uselessness and rough ways and gloomy temper; and

[17]

she shrank from hearing them say so. She wanted to forget all about it, and her husband wondered why; it was not like her to forget anything. The reason was that letting her mind wander back in the years she had shared with Evridiki gave her an uncanny feeling, a vague apprehension of losing her mind altogether if it went too far.

They often speculated about Captain Kalter's past, background, and family. Up on top of Helianos' desk which was now his desk he had placed three photographs: one in a leatherette frame, a placid rigid lady with her arm around a slim little girl, and two of postcard size, unframed, two boys with ideal Northern faces, disciplined and morose, the elder in uniform and the younger in a college cap.

One evening when the captain was sitting there writing, and Helianos brought him a glass of hot resinous wine to ward off a chill, the latter said, "The captain's wife, if I may make the remark, is a noble-looking, lovely woman."

"That one is not my wife," the captain snapped, "my wife is the daughter. But, if you please, it is none of your business. You are not to concern yourself with anything of mine, do you hear?"

Helianos, realizing that praise of a man's mother-in-law is never very ingratiating, sighed and begged pardon, and went into the bedroom to draw the curtains and turn down the bedclothes; and there in a mirror he could still see the back of the captain's head. He was sitting with his head lifted up stiffly, staring at the photographs, with his hands clenched over the arms of his chair. Suddenly he reached for them and thrust them into a drawer and shut it with a shove; and he fidgeted a few minutes, opening and closing books, crumpling papers, rearranging things all over the desk, before he resumed his writing.

Then Helianos fancied that he understood the captain better. That stare and that impatient removal meant that he could not keep his mind on his work with the blurry photographed eyes of the slim girl and sad boys fixed on him, wooing his imagination. It was genuine excitement, wild and miserable affection.

Greeks and other Mediterranean men have not a great many sentiments in their talk or even their thought, but they are almost all familiar with this: the feeling of family, which in extreme instances may be a positive spell in a man's blood. It scarcely applied to himself, nowadays, Helianos thought—his wife had changed so, his surviving children were such poor little things—but how well he could understand it! For a man strongly affected by it, forced away from home by the inhumanity of war, loneliness, mere loneliness, might turn his entire character into a kind of drama or melodrama. Hence, he supposed, the captain's unsociability and pride, intolerance and unpredictable temper...

It made him more conscious than ever of the coldness of his own marriage and his disappointment in his children—his own old age beginning before it was due (actually he was a younger man than the captain) —and he sighed almost enviously as he tiptoed out of the captain's room and away to his marriage bed in the kitchen.

One evening a week at the officer's club: that was

all the sociability Captain Kalter indulged in. He would return without the least look of pleasure spent, or even of fatigue. They never detected any influence or even any breath of liquor. He did not ask his fellow-officers to visit him; no one saw him in a cafe or anywhere with any sort of boon companion; there was no sign of his having to do with women. Except for his hearty appetite for his breakfast and his dinner, nothing in the way of creature comfort appeared to tempt him. The Helianos' had never known a man in the prime of life to be so systematic in his habits, so independent and ascetic and self-denying. As they were conventional middle-class people, in spite of themselves they more or less admired this good side of the German character.

His rooms had to be given a careful daily cleaning, but beyond that they were instructed to stay out of them in his absence, especially to keep away from his desk. One day while dusting Mrs. Helianos disarranged some of his papers, and he reproved her for it with all his vehemence and malice, and after that kept a dust-cloth in a drawer and did this bit of the housework himself. Every night except the club-night he wrote a long letter or letters, and then studied for two or three hours, sometimes propping a book up on his desk and copying things out of it on a block of paper or in a notebook, sometimes reading to himself aloud in a language that Helianos had no knowledge of.

Finally his Greek curiosity got the better of him. He waited until an afternoon when his wife had taken the children to visit his aged aunt—for he did not wish to set them a bad example—then crept into the sitting room and made a thorough examination of the books and notebooks on that desk at which he too, in his day, had spent so many studious hours. He found several important volumes of military history and the science of war, a topographical atlas, a handbook of meteorology, a treatise on the diet of armies. In the notebook there were pages and pages of arithmetic of some sort, as well as exercises in the unknown language. He took it to be Persian or perhaps Hindustani; it was not Arabic; he knew what Arabic looked like. For an hour that afternoon he marveled at the extent of German ambition, which reminded him of Alexander the Great.

3.

By THAT TIME ATHENS WAS STARVING. THERE WERE beggars everywhere, some of them so hungry that they were like lunatics, but too weak to do any harm. Some lay down and died wherever they happened to be. Sometimes they were people you used to know, someone's servants, or keepers of little shops, or someone's poor relations; but famine had given them such faces that you might not recognize them at first glance. Mrs. Helianos was afraid to venture out of the apartment. Fortunately Alex took care of little Leda. He understood that sensibility of hers, so mixed up with dullness, he was as trustworthy with her as any governess, and he was not squeamish. He would go down to the street alone and investigate whether any of the dead lay in their neighborhood; then return for her and take her to play where it was all right.

Of course those families who had German officers to feed were entitled to certain supplies which the occupying authorities reserved for them out of the small national production or brought from abroad. At first the Helianos' expected to be able to live fairly well on the leftovers from the captain's table, but unfortunately he had ideas of his own about that. Once a day he went into the kitchen and had all the cupboards open and considered what staples they had on hand and what new purchases Helianos had been able to make. He showed a most expert mind at this. "You see," said Helianos, "his work in the quartermaster corps is something like housekeeping, on a grand scale. There's no deceiving him. We may as well be honest."

His wife resented this pleasantry.

"You remember, my dear, how you used to keep an eye on your servants, even Evridiki. Though I suppose you never were as merciless nor as efficient; and of course they were not starving to death..."

The efficient captain never forgot a thing. He required his entire meal to be brought to the table at once in covered dishes, so that he could easily check the amount they served him against what he had seen in the larder. He was a heavy eater. Sometimes he left a bit of stew or a few spoonfuls of soup; but he smoked a cigar after eating and used his plate or the soup-tureen for an ash-tray. When he rose to begin the evening's work or to stroll around to the club, he stopped and carefully brushed the crumbs into the palm of his hand and scattered them outside his window to attract birds. It was always his way to combine a painstaking, ungenerous frugality with some little manner of lavishness. Presently an idea came to him which satisfied him in both these inclinations: the extraordinary idea of purveying to a certain major's dog.

This officer was his immediate superior in the quartermaster's corps, with whom he also played cards at the officers' club; his name was von Roesch. He occupied the salon and guest-room of an old Macedonian couple whom the Helianos' knew slightly. They had an ancient half-blind dog, an English bull-terrier of good pedigree with an alarming pink-and-white face. When the famine started their intention had been to put it out of its misery, because it required an impossible amount of food. But meanwhile their major had taken a fancy to it; therefore its life had to be spared while its owners somewhat wasted away. Now it was to benefit by the wasting away of the Helianos' as well. Whatever there might be in excess of their captain's appetite, a crust of bread, a fragment of meat or bone, a vegetable, he scraped together on his plate and ordered to be wrapped up and taken by young Alex with his compliments to the major.

After about a week of sending Alex with the little packages, the captain told them in his formal manner with sarcasm: "My friend Major von Roesch appreciates your good management and generosity in contributing your little superfluity of food to help keep his old pet in good condition. By the way, it comes of one of the best blood-lines of the breed, British stock, and has taken prizes at dog-shows.

"Furthermore, it is good for that soft boy of yours to take a little exercise after his evening meal."

Then presumably the two officers compared notes as to the exact amount of dog-food entrusted to Alex, and perhaps they miscalculated. In any case they accused him of helping himself to it on the way, and first one and then the other upbraided him; one boxed his ears, and the other whipped him. His father questioned him about it patiently and gravely. The boy's reply was that of course the dog-food tempted him—after all, what was that evening meal which in the captain's opinion necessitated his taking exercise? a cup of weak soup and a single biscuit—but he had never touched it, because he was afraid to. He quite convinced his father of his innocence. Nevertheless a few days later the two dog-loving gentlemen charged him with a repetition of his offense and punished him again.

Helianos thought it over and decided to protect his offspring by a little stratagem. "My son is a growing boy," he told the captain, "and suffers from his appetite. If you entrust the food to him he will steal some of it, alas, he cannot help it. Therefore, after this, please let me carry it to the major's dog myself."

Having to make this false confession angered him, and men of his type, passive and well-meaning, have a very physical anger. The captain observed his flushed face and watering eyes, and took them to mean that he was ashamed of his son; therefore the stratagem worked.

"You Greeks are all thieves by nature," the captain remarked. "Only an old broken one like yourself knows that he cannot get away with it."

Helianos, without understanding much about the class-distinctions in Germany, never doubted for an instant that the captain was a gentleman. His manners were extremely distinguished, and yet—it was hard to understand—they permitted him to indulge in a gross discourtesy or ugly outburst every now and then without a trace of embarrassment or self-consciousness. It was never a real fury; he himself was not deeply disturbed by it. Out of the cold dignity of his bearing as a rule, suddenly the fit would come on him. He would let himself go for a few minutes; then fall back into his ordinary composure as if it all had been a matter of course. To fly into a rage without losing one's temper, to curse and shout without getting out of breath, without any fire in one's eye or color in one's cheek: what kind of self-contradiction and false spirit was this? It seemed to Helianos somehow inhuman, possibly unhealthy.

Still he was trying to understand the German in general by this officer; and vice versa, to solve his domestic problem by studying the other officers that he saw around town, and by discreetly questioning fellow Greeks who had dealings with them. Invariably there appeared to be something self-conscious and methodical about their behavior, as if they had been instructed in it according to some new historic theory or psychological science. And they were complacent, even the young ones, as if they had every reason in the world to believe that it would work. Helianos concluded that it must have worked where they had already tried it, in France, Belgium, Holland. Sometimes this conclusion inspired in him a kind of wondrous patriotism. For he knew that the psychology of Greeks differed from that of other nations; they might withstand it better. But sometimes his heart sank, when he asked himself whether he and his family were withstanding it, and realized that he could not tell. Everything depended on how long it lasted.

He had been told that German gentlemen struck

their servants, even in peacetime, at home; but he really had little to complain of in that way. When his gentleman was indulging himself, his fists were always clenched, and as it were to punctuate his ill-tempered utterance he struck out with them or swung them this way and that, apparently not minding whether you were hit by them or not; and striding up and down, he often gave at random what certainly would have been a kick if you had got in the way of it. When you helped him on with his coat, or rendered any other such service at close range, he would elbow you or shoulder you aside so brusquely that you had difficulty keeping your feet; and when you were removing his boots you had to look out for his feet. But as a rule, if you kept withdrawing and dodging with dexterity, he seemed satisfied. He was too proud a fellow to follow you across the room to give you a beating. As it seemed the look of self-preservation and intensity of shame on your face was enough for him.

Anyway, Helianos reflected, when he shook his fist or aimed his kick, you felt that he was human, after all. The unnerving thing was the great Prussian manner, serene and abstract, almost a mannerism; with insincerity in it somehow, but combined with absolute conviction. Priests have a manner somewhat like this, because in their sacerdotal function they are more than human, and their individual lapses and limitations of soul do not matter so much. So have actors, when they are sure that the play they are in is great; and so have certain madmen, when their dream is sublime...

Without a doubt in Captain Kalter's mind, he was

the personifier and minister of a power far greater than any foreigner could be expected to understand; greater than the past, present and future of Greece; greater than himself. What he was, in his mind, what he represented to himself, was far more intimidating to a simple rational man like Helianos than anything he actually did or could do. In fact he found that the fear of him physically, somewhat relieved the other deeper uneasiness.

As for himself, he came to the conclusion that he was a coward, and he told Mrs. Helianos so; but it was not exactly physical cowardice, nor chiefly on his own account. The way to upset him was to abuse Alex or frighten his wife, and before long Captain Kalter seemed to sense this.

Furthermore, in his German opinion, corporal punishment was the thing for a boy of Alex's age, especially a nervous cowardly one. He said it was disgraceful how his parents had spoiled him, and he expected them to see a marked improvement as a result of his living with them, and to be thankful to him for it. He hated nervousness and cowardice and impertinence and idleness with a zealous hate, to say nothing of gluttony and thievery. As a rule all he did, besides scold, was to give the little fellow's bony arm a bad twist while he scolded, or to strike him on the head suddenly with only the flat of his hand; but upon occasion he took the trouble to administer a more formal whipping.

Alex never seemed to mind as much as his parents expected. He learned to leap with alacrity away from the cuffs and kicks; and when he had not leapt in time, or it was a flogging in earnest, to be stoic about it and to forget it as soon as it ceased to hurt. But Helianos and Mrs. Helianos could not accustom themselves to it. They spent hours discussing his childish conduct, analyzing what it might be that chiefly aroused the German ire; and often they themselves punished him severely, in hopes of averting the captain's punishment.

Once in a while, when they were getting into their narrow bed beside the kitchen stove, Mrs. Helianos showed Helianos black-and-blue marks on her poor pallid stout body, which at first angered and depressed him so that it was like sickness. But having questioned her each time, and grown accustomed to the captain's ways, he had to admit to himself that in a measure it was her own fault. She was panic-stricken from morning to night and therefore, naturally, nothing she had to do for the captain was well done. She never had the self-control to stand and listen patiently to his sneering and complaining. He did not actually lay hands on her. It was only that same violent gesturing with which Helianos himself had to contend: histrionic shruggings of those broad shoulders, digs of impatient elbow, nervousness of booted foot. In her dread and haste she was forever springing sideways, and thrusting herself into corners, and knocking herself against furniture, and tripping and falling; hence the black-and-blue marks.

"My poor dear," he told her, "you must remember that the way we feel seems funny to the captain. It can't be helped. Now listen to me: I forbid you to reveal your feelings to him. It's the only safe way; never let him see that you are afraid of him."

Night after night with the patience of a saint he kept trying to impress upon her these first principles of protecting one's self against a man like Captain Kalter; but she never understood one word. She merely wept and fell asleep with her foolish head on his shoulder, and rose next day in the same folly and panic. The serious aspect of all this was the increasing frequency of her heart attacks.

Meanwhile the city around them, and Greece as a whole, went from bad to worse. They were so absorbed in their domestic situation, afraid and angry, tired and hungry, that others' lives and the general plight and the long process of the war scarcely had reality for them. Indeed, some things that they heard brought a slight sense of relief, almost happiness—things happening to other people and other people's children; things they and their children had been spared. They were thankful for the small favors of fate.

A neighbor woman's baby, for example, had learned to relieve its hunger by sucking blood out of the palm of its hand, making an open sore and keeping it open. Mrs. Helianos remembered how Leda in her infancy had sucked her thumb, and they had tried everything but could never stop her; and this, the family dentist explained later, had caused the ugly protrusion of her teeth. Mrs. Helianos in her natural vanity had expected her daughter to inherit her own good looks, and long before there was any question of her not having a normal mind, Leda had disappointed her bitterly, as her baby-face grew plainer every day, pudgier.

Now as she gazed at the neighbor woman's baby with its pale mouth buried in its skinny hand, like the mouth of a rat in the neck of a chicken, she was ashamed, and said to herself, All the disappointments of our life before the war were a fool's paradise.

Helianos talked with a friend whose brother had escaped from Crete and gave a fantastic account of what happened there. Crete had always interested Helianos. In his youth he had studied anthropology as well as archaeology, and tried in vain to interest his wife in pre-Hellenic religion and custom. "The cruelest part of Greek mythology originated in Crete," he reminded her. "But listen to these new stories. They are far worse, and harder to believe than the old."

Outside a certain village the Germans established a burial ground for their sky-borne troops lost in the invasion; and the children of the village playing tag had tipped over two of the little crosses which marked the graves; and for this the Germans punished the entire community. It consisted of twenty-two men and their families. They dug a long shallow trench and lined up the twenty-two in front of it, with two officers and a firing squad of one soldier apiece facing them.

Behind the firing squad they assembled the families, the mothers and wives and little ones, with other soldiers to make them behave. Behavior meant watching the execution over the executors' shoulders with-

[31]

out impatience or insolence or outcry. Whenever a woman said anything or hid her face in her hands, or a child made a tedious sound, a soldier or two stepped forward and disciplined them. The firing squad waited until all these eye-witnesses were under control, standing in good order, with their hands down at their sides, their heads up, their eyes open.

Meanwhile four of the twenty-two tried to escape, and these were shot in the legs and left lying or crawling on the ground while the other eighteen were dealt with and pushed back into the trench.

Then the younger of the two officers made a speech. Courage was the highest virtue, he said, and the four who lay on the ground, two unconscious and one groaning and one crawling along as a broken worm crawls, were obviously cowards. Absolute obedience to the commands of the army of occupation and the will of the German chief of state was required of every Cretan. Therefore the four still alive were guiltier than the eighteen dead, who had at least faced their death obediently. Therefore he ordered the four to be laid in the trench on top of the eighteen, and buried alive; and so it was done, with the women and children obliged to wait patiently until it was all over.

Mrs. Helianos wanted not to believe this story. "Are young German officers able to make speeches in Greek?" she asked. "And what Cretan villager would understand them if they did, with their impossible pronunciation?"

"Perhaps some of it is myth," Helianos answered,

"but for the most part I believe it. I have come to the conclusion that the Germans are cruel."

She implored him not to tell her any more cruel stories, believable or otherwise, and not even to listen to them himself. "What is the good of knowing what has happened to other people? It provokes us to be rebellious, which only makes matters worse. It sickens us so that we cannot do the work that is expected of us."

It also reminded them that, relatively speaking, they were fortunate to be living in Athens instead of Crete, and that there were worse Germans than their captain. Captain Kalter was a difficult, mysterious, but, after all, prosaic figure. Whereas the others who were worse seemed to fancy themselves in some barbaric poetic drama or terrible opera from morning to night, year in and year out. Or perhaps they sensed in the war the beginning of a new religion, and as the newly religious always have done, improvised things like that episode in Crete to be a kind of ritual. Or perhaps they were simply, by nature, dreamers of such things, and the war gave them an opportunity to make some of their dreams come true...

Helianos heard worse cruelties than the subjugation of Crete; certain inquisitorial techniques applied to agents of the underground movement who were supposed to be able to give information or to betray their fellows; various tricks that were like surgery gone wrong, with little up-to-date mechanical contraptions... Naturally he did not report things of that sort in detail to his poor wife. But once in the middle of the night when something the captain had eaten disagreed with him and he kept them awake by ringing for this and that, Helianos whispered to her a tedious and terrible discourse on the subject of atrocities in general.

"I think it must be useless to report things of that sort to anyone," he said. "I'll tell you something about myself, something I'd be ashamed to tell anyone but my wife: when I hear them I am always afraid that I may giggle. I suppose it is animal instinct; rejoicing in the very simple fact that at the moment I am hearing them they are not actually happening to me. Certainly it is not that they are unbelievable. By easy stages we get so we can believe anything. . ."

"But the mind," he went on, "balks at the corresponding emotion, and it's just as well, I suppose. There is a blessed stupidity about emotion. Even my brave cousins, if they were able to feel in their hearts and in their nerves and in their bones all that their noble minds are steeled to, all that awaits them if the Germans catch them, might not be so brave. . ."

Mrs. Helianos was too tired to protest against his talking to her like this. She shed tears quietly, and pulled the bedclothes up over her head to keep from hearing all of it, until at last they fell asleep.

Thus the nightmare of Greece in general gave their particular lives a background, historical and, as you might say, anthropological and psychological. Only it seemed a distant background, out of focus and in false perspective.

Daily and hourly their own slight circumstances were nightmarish too, and, alas, of a more intense interest: hurt feelings and fatigue and aching entrails, the body sore and the soul sore, and the round and round of domestic difficulty; the tired mind moving from one little trouble to the next with a little jerk like the minute-hand of a clock.

Sometimes they thought of friends of theirs who had succeeded in getting away to Egypt or England or America in 1941. This naturally increased their distress, in the way of loneliness; a sense of separation of mind in the time to come as well as of physical fact at present. Of course after the war they would try to tell them what they had been through, but it occurred to them that they might not be able to.

It is not easy to tell this kind of domestic ordeal and do it justice, without either exaggerating it or making a mockery of it. It has to be understated or else it will be lifted by one's words above that triviality, ignominy, which is one of its worst aspects. In daily detail, they realized, it was only harrowing, not tragic. It should be told with severity, irony. But its actual effect on them was to make irony almost impossible, even for Helianos; and exaggeration a habit, especially for Mrs. Helianos.

They decided not to say much about it after it was over, if they lived to see that day. It was too far below the level of what other people recognized as courage. Their having been able to bear it would be nothing to boast of. They thought of it as having been embodied in themselves, like a disease all through them, like vermin all over them. That would be the story and they would be ashamed to tell it.

4.

BUT THE EFFECT OF THE GERMAN OFFICER'S LIVING
with them was not all ignominy and bitterness. It had
its slight silver lining. It changed the family life in-
wardly, spiritually, somewhat for the better. Mrs.
Helianos, for one thing, no longer worried about
Alex as she had done when Greece was first invaded.
The actual presence of an enemy in the house had
taken the boyish cruelty and romanticism out of him
to a great extent. Now he never breathed a word of
resistance or revenge, even to Leda. His mother was
happy to think that he was learning to be realistic,
reasonable, circumspect. In her view of life this was a
wonderfully important lesson; she hoped he would
never forget it. She could not expect Alex's father to
agree with her about this. He had the courage and re-
belliousness of his Helianos cousins too much on his
mind; they were his ideal.

At first Alex's father scarcely knew what to think.
Perhaps the high-strung little boy had become a coward. Sighing for his own limited emotions—and even
as his wife supposed, for the opinion of his brave relatives—he hoped it was not that. The more he considered it the less likely it seemed. Alex stood up to
the captain's violence well enough when it was a mat-

ter of fact, a sudden blow or a regular whipping, did he not? It was when the dread foreigner was in a better mood and he stood and stared at him, loitering in a corner of the sitting room until he was noticed and ordered out, or tiptoeing down the corridor for a look through the sitting-room door, that he turned pale and trembled and bristled.

While he watched the captain, his father watched him; puzzled at first by what he saw shining in the infantile dark eyes, breathless on the thin lips, then little by little, with all the difficulty that fathers have about sons, coming to understand it.

It was a thrilling thing, he thought: a sense of evil rather than a dread of injury; fascination rather than fright. It was the stare which even the youngest of one species of animal will give another species. Helianos trembled at it. For he knew his son's shortcomings as well as his own, and the thought did come to him that in a time like the present they must be the inferior species. But it was only a thought; in his heart it was not so.

In those moments of excitement even the looks of his poor offspring pleased him. Spindling legs, faminous belly, knotty knuckles and over-obvious joints; what did these matter? They were German work. The work of his manhood and his love, all that was left of it, he thought, was the little soul which in the presence of the captain appeared in the child's face. The look in his eyes although it was only hatred was beautiful, like a flower upheld on a bent, spindling, breaking stem.

Whatever Helianos might think, he was simply incapable of feeling that a son of his, a half-Helianos, flesh of his flesh, was inferior. It was instinct and it was a kind of optimism; as in obtuseness heart and automatic egoism, even an animal at bay or a worm turning is optimistic.

So he disagreed with his wife as to the nature of Alex's changed, chastened spirit; he told her so. It was not reasonableness and realism, he said, it was the grave reality developing for him. It was not a wise renunciation of vengeance but the natural gestation of it, getting ready for it. He had it on the tip of his tongue to point out to her that even in looks, the boy was rather like his fierce cousins, not at all like her clever vanished brother—but he refrained from that. Although he argued as gently as possible and left her brother out of it, the subject of Alex always made her cry.

Oh, he had no fatherly illusions; his Alex was an unfortunate, perverse, quivering, stunted little fellow. Still, he decided, there was life in him, life and ferocity, and he was growing up! He was a brave small boy who, when his time came, if he survived the famine, might well commit some exploit against the oppressors of Greece.

The thought frightened him almost as it did Mrs. Helianos; and it increased his melancholy realization that as an oppressed Greek, an avenger, he himself was good for nothing. But at the same time he felt a little prouder of himself, a little less ashamed of himself, as a father. It buoyed up his self-respect just when everything seemed hopeless. He ceased to talk about this to his frightened wife, but she sensed what he had in mind. She still thought him dead wrong but she did not mind, if it made him happier.

Leda, too, was fascinated by Captain Kalter, and she soon lost all her fear of him; then little by little, to her parents' dismay, began to show signs of liking him. When she heard his step outside the front door, his key in the keyhole, she would slip quickly into the corridor and stand smiling up at him, seductive, like a tiny courtesan. Sometimes she took his hand, or reached out her small grimy hand to give his fine uniform a sort of envious, luxury-loving stroke. Meanwhile she seemed to grow less fond of her brother. Perhaps she was disappointed in him, now that he no longer entertained her with terrible stories. Perhaps he had noticed her friendliness toward the captain before anyone else did, and scolded her. Mr. and Mrs. Helianos did not know what to make of it. Was there more cleverness in her retarded little mind than they had given her credit for? Was she seductive in order to be on the safe side, in the terrible vague anxiety of infancy, in self-defense? Whatever it was, to some extent, with reservations, it worked. Little Leda was the only one of them, and probably the only Athenian in Athens, the only Greek in Greece, whom the captain regarded with favor.

Before dinner, when in the weariness of his day's work he stretched out in his armchair, with Helianos kneeling and removing his boots, he would ask Leda what she had done all day. She was never able to answer but she invariably smiled. After breakfast, as they all stood at the front door to hear his last-minute instructions, sometimes he would give her a little pat on the head with his gloved hand. He never did it ungloved; and upon one occasion he called Mrs. Helianos' attention to this point and sarcastically explained it: the child's hair was in a miserable tangle harboring lice, and there were some scabs on her scalp as well. The foolish woman allowed herself to be provoked by this, bursting into tears, and giving all her excuses for not taking proper care of her children; for which in his grim way he teased her. Perhaps Leda, in her chronic daydream, did not realize what they were talking about. She took no notice of her mother's weeping but still gazed up at the sarcastic German with her blissful simple expression.

Helianos, thinking it over, decided that this new enthusiasm of Leda's was a good thing. "Of course it shocks us," he said to Mrs. Helianos, "but we must look at it from the poor child's standpoint. She has scarcely taken any pleasure or even any interest in her poor life, from the day she was born, has she? I cannot begrudge her any kind of happiness that may happen to her, according to her nature. It is a strange nature. I used to think that perhaps her love of Alex was something like incest. Now perhaps this, you might say, is a kind of treason. But it does not matter, she is an innocent."

It was his way of talking which Mrs. Helianos never quite understood. "One should not expect too much of one's children," she said, humbly.

It is true that in all our human attachments based on nothing but blood-relationship there are strict limitations, inherent disappointments. For their chief comfort Mr. and Mrs. Helianos had to turn back to that intimacy between themselves which, in the beginning at least, had been based on passionate love. In the ordinary way the Greek husband, even at the time of passion, maintains his male aloofness away from domestic affairs. But now that the housekeeping was so far beyond Mrs. Helianos' strength and competence, and Helianos had to help her more and more, and they were together morning, noon, and night as they had never been in their youth, they were like an old team of horses broken to double harness.

When Captain Kalter was at home he wanted absolute silence. Leda was naturally silent, but as for Alex, this was the hardest of those rules which the poor parents tried to enforce in order to forestall the captain's enforcement; and it was hard for them too. They could never learn to work so as to keep a regular and accustomed division of their responsibilities; the simplest task at some point required their asking each other's advice, coming to each other's rescue. The partitions throughout the apartment were thin and one of these days, if they disturbed the captain, might he not require Mrs. Helianos to do all her work alone, without Helianos? Then how would she manage? Therefore they learned to speak without a sound if necessary, and to read each other's lips, indeed to communicate a good deal by mere glances, as the inmates of asylums and prisons do.

If their so commonplace wedded life had not been engulfed in misery along with everything else, their habits broken, and normal expectations aborted, they might never have learned the extent of their affection. They were middle-aged, and felt older than their

[41]

years. Even the mortal blow of losing their first and best son had not quickened their old attitudes of mind and stale sentiments much. This hard everyday life together did. It was the autumn of their love no longer, but suddenly winter, when in fact, with illness and starvation and decrepitude, the coldest husbands and the bitterest wives often do find each other kinder than other people, kinder than nature, kinder than God.

To be sure, there was nothing erotic or sensual or even sensuous about it. Helianos was, or fancied that he was, impotent; and Mrs. Helianos' menopause had come early, in keeping with her poor health in general. Yet in the dead of night they pursued an extraordinary intimacy, as they lay wearily in a heap of one body almost on top of the other on the folding cot. They knew once more the double egocentricity of lovers, confusion of two in one. Everyone else and everything else in the world might have been shed away in the forgotten sky over Athens, and the dark turning of the earth toward next day, purposeless except to rock them, on the formless mattress and sagging springs.

The captain would ring and be waited on, or Helianos would start to snore and Mrs. Helianos would wake him on the captain's account; and then they would lie awake awhile. Verbose even when half asleep, with her lips pressed to his ear like a kiss, she would whisper the things she had not dared broach during the day, pouring her poor heart into his; and he would console and admonish her to his heart's content.

[42]

5.

IN THE SPRING OF 1943 CAPTAIN KALTER WAS GIVEN
two weeks' leave to return to Germany. When he informed the Helianos' of it, they could hardly contain
themselves for joy; but with his strong small eyes
fixed on them, they did not even have the courage to
wish him a safe journey and a good time. Then he
had to wait a week for his plane-reservation. That
was hard for them, with all their work and worry as
usual, and the added uneasiness lest they betray their
unusual excitement.

When at last the day came, and they carried his des-
patch-case and duffle-bags down to the sidewalk—even
breathless Mrs. Helianos insisted on carrying one bag,
for was it not a sort of ceremony?—and they stood
watching the army-automobile slowly start and shift
gears and get up speed and turn the corner out of
sight, they were afraid to rejoice, with unknown faces
in the neighboring windows perhaps looking down
on them. Back upstairs, they still maintained their
anxious composure, as if the furniture in the captain's
rooms could testify against them, until they reached
the kitchen and shut the kitchen-door.

Then they all danced around and hugged each
other, and the children asked innumerable questions,

and Helianos made one or two jokes, and Mrs. Helianos smiled and cried at the same time in her weak way. In spite of their heavy hearts, irremediable poverty, deteriorated health, continuous hunger, and the brevity of two weeks, they expected to have a good time.

"I remember where Evridiki's husband buried a case of my imported wine, under a ruined shed in Psyhiko," said Helianos, "and I will go and get it."

"Now we can take the children to the seashore for two or three days, which will do them good," said Mrs. Helianos.

Alex began his little bravery of imagination and boastfulness again. "When he returns from Germany," they heard him tell Leda, who smiled at him contentedly as she had not done for many months, "we will lure him out on the balcony and trip him, so he'll fall over the balustrade and into the street, squash!"

It was all imagination. The blessed two weeks did not turn out according to any of their plans. For one thing, coming like a little forecast and foretaste of the liberation of Greece, it made them impatient, self-indulgent. They had time to stop and think, and take stock of themselves, and estimate their losses; and with all the good will they could muster, the conclusion seemed to be that the two weeks had come too late; and perhaps the liberation itself when it came would have come too late.

Their loneliness for their dead soldier son began aching again, in the way of a wound when there has been a sudden change of temperature. For days Mrs.

Helianos would not or could not talk of anything else, until Helianos reproved her. If she took this two weeks' holiday as an occasion for grief, the result would be one of her bad heart attacks and no holiday at all.

He went out to Psyhiko, but either his memory was at fault or someone had stolen the case of wine. He came back empty-handed and tried to be humorous about it, but he could not keep the irony and allegory out of what he said, which spoiled the jest.

They gave up the excursion to the seashore. The children did not have the energy for anything beyond their usual routine: talk and talk, Alex doing all the talking; the same games as in Hellenic centuries past, marbles, knucklebones, played now more listlessly than ever; unhealthy little naps at odd intervals wherever naps happened to overcome them; long stations at the kitchen-door as if in a trance, waiting to be fed, never quite in vain but almost in vain.

To be sure, Helianos had more time now to wander here and there in search of food, and he fancied himself as one of the best shoppers in Athens. But, on the other hand, in spite of the captain's finicking supervision, his wastefulness at table, and his purveyance to the major's dog, they had managed to abstract a good many mouthfuls from the meals they served him; and in his absence of course they were not entitled to officers' rations. Furthermore, as it seemed to them, the famine was worse than ever. It was so bad that they fell into a vague, irrational expectation of its ceasing soon, of the supply of food augmenting soon, by some miracle. Helianos sometimes showed a weird high spirits in the morning when he set out to do the marketing. For, short of a miracle, the race of Greeks would soon be exterminated; and that, even for Mrs. Helianos with her dark mind, was unthinkable.

Poor woman, indolent all her life, now she could not or would not stop working. "This is the spring," she said stubbornly, "and in the spring I give my house a good general cleaning."

When they came to brushing and airing the beds, and observed how much blacker theirs and the children's were than the captain's, because he bathed and they could not bathe, she let herself go in angry rhetoric and senseless weeping. Helianos, in his constant anxiety about her health which he never admitted to her, undertook the hard part of everything. But it was up-hill work, make-believe work; nothing went well. The fear and humiliation and anger, in which they could not indulge when the captain was in residence, now welled up in them, and this, even more than their fatigue and undernourishment, alarm and anxiety, made them incompetent, invalid. Whatever they pretended to be doing, it served only to pass the time, two weeks, ten days, one week, then only a few days, thinking and thinking of the captain, waiting and waiting for the captain to get back; and the time passed quickly.

As they thought of it afterward, it seemed that this holiday had been the worst time; soft and unstrung and maniacal. It was the time when they had no more imagination; they could not even predicate any future betterment, except that folly of expecting to find more food in the market. And apparently their mem-

ory of the past was failing little by little: Helianos'
failure to find the case of imported wine, for example...

Mrs. Helianos, on one of her rare excursions into
the street for something—scurrying along, looking
neither to the right nor the left lest her eyes light on
some terrible beggar or terrible cadaver—encoun-
tered a man whom for a moment she took to be her
runaway brother. It was not he. Afterward she confessed to Helianos that she had come to have only a
vague idea of what her brother looked like. If he came
to their very door she might not recognize him.

Their tenderness toward each other did not fail, in
spite of hard remarks; but more than once the death-
wish arose in the midst of it, mingled with it. One
night he confided to her that he was tempted to defy
the captain, or all the occupying foreigners as a lot
somehow, to make an end of his shame and enslave-
ment, at whatever penalty or cost. She whispered back
with affectation of scorn, "You know you'd never have
the courage to do anything of the kind."

She confided to him that she was tempted to kill
herself; her health was going from bad to worse anyway. He answered very roughly, "My poor dear, you
have always exaggerated your illnesses. Anyway, you
know, with your passive womanly nature, you're incapable of suicide."

Then there were reproaches on both sides, especially for that disregard of their poor helpless children
which these temptations indicated. Which brought
their minds suddenly to the strange fact that neither
of them felt any great love for Alex and Leda. They

[47]

had tried to, but they were unable to. They blamed each other for it, but with a sense of guilt so sharp in them both that they had to stop. They saw eye to eye as to what small excuse there was for their lack of love. Peculiar little bodies of their children, morbid little minds of their children: what was there lovable about them? Even if they lived to maturity they would not be normal. Their shortcomings were irremediable and their future of no interest; and irremediability in the lives of children—being a contradiction of terms, and against nature—seems worse than what happens to their elders.

It brought these elders, Helianos and Mrs. Helianos, to a clearer realization than ever of what they had to live for, all they had: each other. With almost no surcease of sleep all that night, clinging together, as they were obliged to do, to keep from falling out of the folding cot on to the grimy floor—even in the captain's absence they were afraid to move into his room, lest he return unexpectedly—they both wept together, so that there was no consolation, no consoler. Even in their early married life which had been difficult at first, infatuated, jealous, disappointed, they had not fallen into any such waste emotion.

Next day, returning to the subject of suicide, Helianos made one of his little formal discourses: "Under-nourished people almost never take their own lives," he said. "It has been a good while since we have heard of a case. Those of our acquaintance all did it at the start, in violent imagination, before they were weakened too much in reality. It is a general rule, a platitude: hunger binds one to life. You might call it a philosophy. Stop and think how it is, even with us: we live fascinated, like animals under a spell, from meal to meal."

There was another platitude applicable to their situation of which he did not think: to wit, one can never tell from what direction betterment may come; what little change will mend matters, for a while. It is never too late for a little happiness even in the shadow of death; and death itself may come and go with fascination like a spell.

6.

AT THE END OF APRIL CAPTAIN KALTER RETURNED FROM
Germany, on a Monday morning. Next day, when all
four Helianos' happened to be gathered in his presence, he made a formal announcement and request,
with some sarcasm in his tone, not much: "May I call
your attention to the fact that I have been promoted,
with a gratifying citation for the work I have been
doing in Athens? Hereafter, will you try to remember
to call me Major Kalter?"

Their hearts sank, realizing that a glance at his insignia should have informed them of this; they had
not glanced. They were very sorry for themselves: to
think that in mere near-sightedness they should have
begun to give offense again, so soon!

But the erstwhile captain, unnoticed major, did not
appear to resent it especially. Nor, as it impressed
them, did he feel any great gratification in his ad-
vancement. Probably, Helianos thought, this was the
Prussian etiquette, cheerless and perfunctory whatever the turn of events.

Or perhaps it was because he happened not to be in
his usual good health. His naturally ruddy cheeks had
a drained, faded aspect. The whites of his eyes were
yellowish, the tiny veins in them irritated, as if the

entire two weeks had been one sleepless night, a hundred hours without a wink. His thin straight mouth was thinner than ever but less straight, with chapped lips, chafed lips. There was an unfamiliar pitch to his voice, a pinched tone and sometimes a sudden flatness, like a leak in his throat. He had grown very thin. His uniform looked loose and his neck did not quite fill his collar.

At first Helianos commented on this excitedly, hopefully, the matter of the thinness in particular. He wondered if it might not mean something, as to the course of the war. The great German minus ten pounds, perhaps more, in less than two weeks; the German with a hungry look like other people, the German in a decline... Was it possible that he had not had enough to eat in his absence? Could it have begun to be hard to get enough to eat even in great Germany? Now and then that day Helianos heaved a sigh, wanting to believe it but unable to.

Mrs. Helianos did not approve of this kind of self-indulgence in vain speculation. Also she pointed out that the major with his healthy, indeed greedy appetite, if by any chance he had fared badly upon his journey, would have returned to them as hungry as a wolf. Whereas in fact he had lost his appetite.

Once more Helianos set out all over Athens in search of food fit for an officer; once more painstakingly Mrs. Helianos prepared the simple soups and stews Major Kalter liked best. He only pretended to eat them, tried and failed to eat them, and sent them back to the kitchen almost untouched. Which troubled her, partly in her pride of housewifery and partly in suspense, expecting an outburst of his criticism sooner or later, when he got around to it. However, the hours passed, and days passed, without criticism.

Mrs. Helianos' theory about it at first was the opposite of her husband's. The major, the major! his bloodshot eyes and sallow color, his mouth turned down, so sorry for himself, and no appetite: what it looked like to her was biliousness, over-indulgence, indigestion.

"Perhaps he found the food in the fatherland so rich and copious that our wretched Athenian meals disgust him," she said. Her envy and hungriness flashed in her eyes as she said it.

Furthermore, she wondered, were there not in the tradition and usage of German officers on leave worse excesses than over-eating? Perhaps when the major was not constrained to work, he drank. Presumably in every German city there was a superfluity of young women eager for their conquering heroes such as Kalter to come home, to ensnare and demoralize and exhaust them. Now perhaps this particular conquering hero was disgusted with himself.

She had in mind a type of German womanhood to be seen occasionally even in Athens, sauntering in and out of the *Hotel de Grande Bretagne* as if they owned it: young or youngish ones with breathless mouths and flickering eyes, wearing ugly, new, sometimes French-looking dresses, escorted by fond and as a rule elderly military men. And giving Major Kalter her sideways glance, scornful of his ill appearance, she would indulge in that very natural imagination of respectable women, which is, to blame other women.

She said that he reminded her of a tomcat in the morning, the worse for wear.

Helianos did not agree with any of this, and somewhat humorously reproved her. Here Major Kalter had been living under their roof for more than a year, and still she misunderstood him and underestimated him, with her talk of wine, women and song! Fancy her having to be reminded of his German strength of character, his methodical Spartan habit!

He, Helianos, did not believe that there was a soft spot in this German, or the least vice, or any quarrel witn himself about anything. Though all of Germany were a banquet table, a carnival and an orgy, he thought, still Kalter would not indulge. Though the wide world became a German property and playground, Kalter would not play, or relax or rest upon his laurels. "As I understand him," said Helianos, "he doesn't know how."

In that first week of his return, they saw very little of him and he rarely spoke to them. He put in longer hours at his headquarters than ever, doubtless with arrears of work to make up, and new responsibilities as a major. At the end of the day he seemed tired out, and twice threw himself down on his bed before dinner and took a nap, or at least lay motionless with his eyes shut for an hour.

On the Wednesday or Thursday after dinner he went out, presumably for his usual game of cards with fellow-officers; but as it appeared next morning it had not distracted him or cheered him up. That night he would not even attempt to eat anything, and went to bed at seven o'clock; but complained the next day of not having been able to sleep. Morose and listless, yawning, breathing hard, more or less sighing, still he would not or could not spare himself. Saturday night he stayed at his headquarters at work until daybreak.

On Sunday, after dinner, when Helianos came to his room to remove the half-empty dishes, and Mrs. Helianos followed to put away one of his shirts that she had washed and ironed, he looked up at them with so abrupt a movement of his head and shoulders, and cleared his throat so loudly, that they came to attention side by side, facing him. And they saw that his eyes, instead of snapping or blazing at them as usual, were blinking uncertainly, almost anxiously; his thin lips were drawn up as if in a deliberate attempt to make a kindly expression. Whereupon he asked them, "How have things been going for you in my absence?"

It was a strange, embarrassing experience. They wanted to answer, but he had trained them so long to shrink and apologize, they did not know how, they gaped like children. They tried to make amiable faces to match his, and to look him in the eye, but their glances kept veering aside toward each other, in astonishment.

Having addressed them in German, now evidently he fancied that they had not understood him. He repeated the friendly inquiry in his difficult Greek, and still they did not succeed in speaking up.

It must have appeared to him that they were afraid. A curious mixed expression, somewhat smug, somewhat sentimental, passed over his hard face; and to relieve their embarrassment he rose and brusquely announced that he had another hour's work to do at his headquarters, and left them.

Then it dawned on them that he was a different man, a changed character. It was not only poor health, loss of weight, loss of appetite. Some part of the change evidently was between him and them, a merely human matter, an attitude of mind, a change of heart. For the first time in a year he had spoken civilly to them. It was a small matter but a miracle.

In the night they blamed themselves for not being pleasanter about it, more responsive, more forthcoming, upon this great occasion. They were afraid he might have resented their bad manners, tied tongues, startled glances. It could not be helped, he had surprised them too much. They were half in dread of their next encounter with him, next day, lest the civil inquiry turn out to have been a mere slip of his tongue, or their own ears deluding them. They tried to recall the exact German wording, syntax and inflection, and argued it back and forth until they could agree about it.

Next morning Mrs. Helianos, finding some pretext, insisted on accompanying Helianos with the breakfast tray; and then promptly enough, the anxious or uncertain look still in the major's eyes, the respectful way he said good morning, and his subsequent remarks, reassured them. It was not a delusion, it had happened.

Tranquilly he inquired what brought Mrs. Helianos to his bedroom so early in the morning; and once more they were tongue-tied. But as it seemed, he seriously intended to be friendly with them, he would not be put off.

"Welcome, welcome, in any case," he said, "for after all, you are the housewife, aren't you? Worrying about something, somewhere in the house, from morning to night!"

Mrs. Helianos stood blushing as if it were overwhelming praise.

After that there was some slight amazement for them every day; and day and night a continuous gossip and analysis of things he said and did. Whatever it meant, whatever had changed him, it had begun the very day he returned from Germany, when they had noticed nothing but his thinness, weariness, biliousness, without understanding. So now they went back over every slight evidence and minute incident; but still they did not understand, nor did they entirely agree.

Helianos wanted to accept everything as it appeared on the surface; at least to interpret everything as favorably as he could, as mere kindliness, a wonderful improvement and a great blessing. Mrs. Helianos, poor bereaved creature, was never sure. Instinctively she stood on guard against the mystery of the German. It was her nature to be mistrustful.

He was a naturally pacific, sociable man; he liked to think well of his fellow men, even an occupying German officer. It was his life-long habit to make the best of everything from day to day. Now she did not trust his judgment. She lived in dread of their making some mistake or falling into some trap. Every now and then, in the closeness of their hearts, he felt twinges of her emotion. She kept him in uncertainty about everything.

The day of Major Kalter's return, for example, that Monday evening: he sank on the edge of his bed, sighing, gritting his teeth with weariness, although he had worked only half the day. Helianos knelt as usual to remove his boots; he would not allow it. "It is a ridiculous thing for one man to have to do for another," he said, in his altered tone of voice, "a humiliating thing!"

After that there was no more boot-removing, and very little valeting or intimate waiting-on of any kind. Helianos would begin something of that sort, something he had always done; Kalter would interrupt him, saying, "No, it's not necessary, let it go, I don't want it done."

Perhaps, Mrs. Helianos suggested, it was because Helianos was not good at this work. It was her way now, pointing out every obscurity and dubiety.

No, it was to make things easier for him, or to show him due respect; Major Kalter made that clear. "After all, you're a man of the world, aren't you?" he said, "a man of some distinction, as things went in your little backwater of Athens..."

Pausing and fixing Helianos with a look of some cordiality he added, "It must be hard to be reduced to domestic service."

He seemed to have no sense of how all this contradicted his attitude and his remarks of the previous fourteen months, fifteen months. Apparently he had forgotten the martinet, the humiliator, that he had been. Somehow he had grown indifferent to the little domestic comforts, servitudes of man to man. Something had disabused him of that pride and thrill of petty overlordship which had meant more to him than comfort.

One morning, when Helianos brought in his breakfast, out of practice, he overturned the coffee-pot, and a few drops fell on the major's parade-uniform, on the sleeve just below the new insignia. That same afternoon, certain of his papers having fallen on the floor, Mrs. Helianos thoughtlessly gathered them up and put them in the waste-basket. But, dread histrionic fellow that he was—that is to say, had been—he did not clench his fists or stride up and down. Nothing happened: a mere grunt about the coffee-stains, a sigh for the crumpled papers.

Somehow his bad temper, petty tyranny, bitter fuss about everything, had shifted away like a season of the year, like a scene in a cloud. When he wanted anything at all out of the ordinary he would explain it to them, patiently and clearly. In case he did not get it he complained, to be sure, but very softly, as if they were friends, or in the sympathetic patronizing way, as if they were children. Whatever happened—a noise when he was napping, or something inedible included by mischance in his evening meal, or a bad smell exhaling from the kitchen all the way down the corridor to his room, or a button torn off a badly laundered shirt—still he was correct, calm, sometimes almost sympathetic.

That night of his going to bed early he came to the kitchen-door and asked politely for his kettle of warm water. An hour or two later Helianos forgot and

[58]

walked with a heavy tread in the corridor, which woke him; and the next morning, complaining of his insomnia, he mildly mentioned it and requested Helianos to be more careful in the future. And on subsequent nights, tiptoeing extremely carefully past his door, they heard how restlessly he slept; but he never rang for them to wait on him. Finished, that little indecent chore and midnight humiliation...

He smiled less than ever, but they did not mind that. His smile was a disquieting thing anyway, with more tooth than lip about it; too suddenly and sharply drawn in. They had never especially enjoyed being smiled at. On the whole he seemed more amiable-looking and in a way handsomer with his present long face, the slight squint and frown softening his gimlet eyes; the dead calm and the rigid strength gone from his mouth.

His voice was still rough, rapid and peremptory, even when the sense of his remarks was benign. Still upon occasion a sharp focus of his Prussian eyes, small and blue, would discourage one from presuming upon his friendship or fellow-humanity beyond a certain point. But who cared, when of his own accord every day he deigned to be a little more friendly?

Now he never bothered to inspect their cupboardful of provisions and the day's shopping. No more quartermastery in the kitchen! Although it made things easier, and also enabled them to eat a little more freely, Mrs. Helianos—accustomed to the old strict regime, broken to last year's harness,—did not really like it.

In the morning when it came time for him to depart to his headquarters, time for them to run and open the front door for him, and to stand and take his orders as usual, evidently he could not think what to say to them. There were no orders; nothing was as usual. Mrs. Helianos complained of it. Without his usual criticism, she said, she had no way of knowing whether he was satisfied with what she had done the day before, or whether what she would undertake that day upon her own initiative was the thing he wanted undertaken.

But with or without orders, criticism or no criticism, Helianos impatiently inquired, had she ever known what Kalter expected of her, or what to expect of him?

In the past, in his bad temper, she answered, at least she had something to go by; some basis for hoping that in the end, somehow, something she did might meet with his approval. Even disapproval was better than nothing, she felt. As he was their tyrant, let him tyrannize!—little by little, as a tyrant should, that they might know where they stood. How else could they be expected to give satisfaction?

For some reason, for the moment, but only for the moment, she said, he had lost interest in her housekeeping. It was not natural for him not to get his own way, it was not natural for him to control his temper, it would end badly. Indifference, inefficiency, civility: none of this was in the German nature; it would not last. Before long she expected him back at her heels with a vengeance.

Helianos supposed that she was so tired of housekeeping that she could not be reasonable about it. By her account all their work went less and less well. She served unappetizing meals; they kept the household accounts badly; their usurpation of odds and ends of food just because they happened to crave them was scandalous; and the children, that is, Alex, kept taking various liberties, now that Kalter pretended not to mind... She had a sense of guilt about all this, and she blamed the new Kalter for it. For it was his new carelessness about what they did, his indulgence whatever they did, which allowed them to grow guilty. She could not keep herself up to the mark, to say nothing of keeping Helianos and the children up to their mark. There would come a day of reckoning.

Helianos grew extremely impatient with her when she talked like this. But patiently he kept pointing out that they were better off than they had been all year. If only she would not excite herself now with vain foreboding... She never denied anything he said but, the instant he ceased to argue with her, fell back into the same flutter of anxiety and stubborn mistrust.

The major had also lost interest in his military studies after dinner. Instead he bought some ordinary cheap novels and various German and Swiss periodicals, and sat with this frivolous literature evening after evening, reading or pretending to read. If Helianos had not seen it with his own eyes he would not have believed it.

Mrs. Helianos found dust gathering on the volumes of strategy and diet, the unknown lexicon, the faraway atlas; but remembering his reproof of a year ago, she let it gather. Then one evening he complained of the clutter on his desk, and asked her to make room

[61]

for his books with Helianos' Greek and French volumes in the closed bookcase.

This puzzled Helianos as much as anything. "Now that he is a major," he said, with half a smile, "he no longer needs to study, you see. He has no further ambition..."

Helianos could always think of something to say, but now his humor turned to odds and ends, ambiguous and pointless. It was not really to amuse anyone but as it were for his own sake, hoping that his own thought might be led somewhere by it. His wife took less and less pleasure in his jokes.

7.

THERE WAS AN ODD UNHAPPY TIME FOR HELIANOS IN the middle of May, a kind of crisis. He tried to keep his thoughts to himself but his wife knew all about it. All the while he was reproving her for her anxious imagination, his own imagination was running away with him in a different sense, in intense curiosity about the cause or causes of the change in the major; and often it was a miserable and ridiculous thing.

He could jest about it but he could not help it or throw it off. All his life he had taken pride in his perspicacity, his understanding of the way other men's minds worked, even foreigners' minds; obviously in vain. A change of the German heart, and presto! his non-German intelligence dumbfounded and incapacitated by it. He felt stupider than ever in his life. Somehow the terrible spirit of the occupier lay now like a great snake scotched, depressed, paralyzed—or was it charmed? reformed? metamorphosed?—and still he, the Greek rabbit, could not move, could not make up his mind, could not think of anything else, gripped by daydream.

What was it? What ailed Kalter? Why was he so sad? Why was he kinder to them than ever before? Was it some policy or scheme or trap? Would he, one fine day, having made friends with them little by little, suddenly make some terrible demand upon them? What purpose of his could they possibly serve, except by their usual submissive domestic service? Why had he lost interest in everything, even their submission? What was this strange combination of kindness and sadness; did they normally go together in the German psyche? Was he to be trusted? How long would it last? What then? What next?

He pondered it by the hour, as the days passed, and grew tired of it and tried to forget it—for the evil of their life was still sufficient unto the day, every day— but then another little innovation, reduction of their servitude or added kindliness of Kalter's, would start his speculation, his futility of mind, all over again.

Mrs. Helianos had taken his mockery to heart, as to her first theory of the difference in their German. Now she thought of another explanation, and got up her courage one night to confide it to him.

"Helianos," she whispered, "Helianos, listen! You know, my feeling has always been that my brother is not dead. Now I think it must be thanks to him that we are having an easier time, with the major.

"O poor little brother! At last he has grown influential, wherever he is, with the Germans in high position who determine the policy in Greece; and he still remembers us. He is ashamed and wants to make amends. So now somehow, I think, the word has come to the major to treat us better."

Helianos hated to hear this. In the time of oppression, especially the last year when they had been oppressed personally, his mere scorn and disapproval of his brother-in-law had turned to detestation. He felt the need that almost everyone in a defeated country must feel,—the need of someone to blame personally, in some sort of intimacy, convenient to his mind; some personification of whatever weakness and perfidy in the country itself may have helped to bring about its defeat. In this sense for months Helianos, without a word to his wife about it, had been concentrating on his brother-in-law. That questionable, departed, perhaps deceased young man had become his scapegoat. There is a certain satisfaction in having a scapegoat. The least sense of indebtedness to him, for the improvement of their relations with the German, would have spoiled everything for Helianos.

So when in the dark on the kitchen-cot Mrs. Helianos whispered it, he lost his temper a little, snapped at her, and with that arm on which her head lay all night, shook her, and told her what an intolerable idea it was, what a fool she was!

With womanly mixed emotion she let it pass with no further argument. Once more for a day or so the shadow of the ambiguous youth came between them; and once more great matrimony, side by side all day, close in each other's arms all night, naturally overcame it.

Perhaps, too, the year of oppression had given her a new insight into human nature, and remembering various things that were wrong with her brother, considering how they might have developed into real evil by now, it seemed to her preferable to think of him as dead. Thus she avoided dishonoring him in her thought, and also avoided feeling dishonored by him.

She ceased to speak of him as alive, she mourned him as dead, then ceased mourning, then more or less forgot about him. And she continued in this forgetfulness, little fratricide of mind, even at a later time when she had desperate need of him, need of someone, anyone...

Helianos, however, could not influence her so much, as to her attitude toward Major Kalter. In it her nervousness reigned supreme; about it her talk ran on and on, foolish, bitter, and contradictory, until it tired them both out. Even in that fateful springtime, ill and fantastic as she had become, he still had the last word about most things; not about the major.

However she contradicted herself, it was intuition, instinct; now like some sprout in a dark cellar growing deformed for the light's sake; now like some primitive worm brought to light, and wriggling away from the light into a safe clod, safe darkness. It was too delicate for his male mind, and too strong for his gentle spirit.

But he kept arguing with her, pleading with her, to try to meet the major halfway; to give him the benefit of the doubt; and by appreciation of what kindness he showed, to inspire in him more kindness, for her own sake, for all their sakes. But, no, she could not, or as it seemed to Helianos, she would not.

Sometimes as it appeared to him it was a kind of patriotism. She felt ashamed to take a more cheerful view of the minor matter of their life when behind it and around it lay the Greek tragedy as a whole; for which indeed it became every Greek to mourn day and night.

He himself apparently was not the type of man who can persist in tragic mood simply because it is the historic and appropriate mood, when circumstances happen to smile around him, when the season for him privately changes... Sometimes with her uncompromising unhappiness she made him ashamed of himself.

In the course of one of their arguments she said that their dead son Cimon appeared to her in dreams and warned her. He did not know whether this was a figure of speech or a reference to particular nightmares, nor did he quite understand what the warning could be. But he did not ask her because she was not to be encouraged to dwell on her bereavement.

How she had changed in that month of May! Helianos thought. All the previous year, so shrinking and conciliatory, passive and panic-stricken, a little oldish woman—now she was like a wild romantic inexperienced girl! How she had talked against his underground cousins; now never a word; and in fact she was as rebellious as they. How she had feared Alex's spirit of revenge, and endeavored to repress it; now she was the irrepressible one! From morning to night she indulged in her sense of injustice: she who used to say that they were lucky to be alive! Oh, sighed Helianos, in his manly confusion and exasperation, who can begin to know a woman's heart?

It occurred to him then that he had not heard any news of his cousins for many weeks. In their implacability and extreme energy they were so unlike him as he was now, that he could never imagine what they might be doing; he wondered. Alex, after all, was not likely to grow up to be one of them, a rebel, a fighter, he thought; and he was not sorry. He realized then how his vicarious romanticism about all this had passed in the course of those spring months. His own peculiar life with only his wife and the children and Kalter in the small apartment had preoccupied him so; not knowing how it would turn out in the end...

He thought that it was like a little stage with painted shadows, darkened lights; the whole household somehow changing places, as it were in a vague inconsequential dance to almost inaudible music, and he could scarcely see even the dear face of his wife dancing closest to him.

But at least in the old habitual strength of his love he had imagination about her. Living with her in a certain illusion and hypothesis as lovers must, even superannuated lovers, he knew how to explain everything concerning her to himself; if not in any one way, in two or three ways at once, alternatives...

One thing, as he thought, was an effect or a result of the change in Kalter. Because Kalter seemed weak her feeling about him grew strong and reckless. His easier unhappier unhealthier spirit, his weariness and softness, encouraged her to show fight and defiance; not of course to his face, outright, but in imagination and in conversation behind his back. All her spirit was strained, as if it were a grimace at him; all her thought clenched and shaken at him, like a fist.

Another thing was her having had a holiday, in Kalter's absence on leave; a rest, relatively speaking, and a change, and a taste of independence. It had put ideas in her head. For a fortnight she had been out from under the German's heel; so now naturally—although it was not the roughshod, punitive heel that it had been—she could not help fighting wildly against being back under it. That bad fortnight, when all their little plans had miscarried, when they had toyed with the idea of suicide, when they had had a horror of their poor children—nevertheless it had done her good! Helianos marveled at this. Out of it came her present tirades, which at least gave evidence of energy; her perpetual complaints, which at least showed hope.

Sometimes he felt in spite of himself that she had grown somewhat less loveable; alas, just now, when there had been an improvement in his life otherwise. Indeed she had not an easy character, she never had had. But he had not minded her exaggeration and self-pity in the past, when this or that went wrong. What he minded was her general resentfulness and permanent mistrustfulness, now that things were going better. He hated to see her assuming a kind of despair indifferent and frivolous, as if she had ceased to take an interest in a little better or a little worse, tweedledum or tweedledee. Even when she did admit a little betterment, it was ungracious. She would always add that it was too good to be true or too good to last.

Oh, yes, it was too good to last, Helianos also felt that. No doubt the amiability of the victorious foreigner was to lead to the foreign advantage in the end, somehow. That was what victory meant; victory was the lasting thing; for the victims, nothing was intended to last. But Helianos was rather philosophical

[69]

about it. His feeling of insecurity at least quickened in his good heart a certain thankfulness for every moment while it lasted.

For the duration of the war, while the foreigners maintained their overlordship, given a kind word, a few crumbs from their particular foreigner's table, a little less mortification in their underdogship, a surcease for their nerves, a domestic truce, a hiatus in martyrdom: what more could they ask? As their Greek lives stood, the world was a prison, Greece a prison-cell. Here at any rate, for him was a chink in the wall, a door open a crack, a faint beam of daily sunshine on the floor; and there are times in life when this will serve for happiness as well as an accustomed liberty or supposed security.

One evening, toward the end of the second week, Major Kalter had intended to go out after dinner, then decided to stay and write a letter instead; and the family noticed how still he kept: not a step around the room, not a cough or sigh.

About eleven o'clock Helianos went in with his kettleful of warm water, and found him stretched out on top of his bed fast asleep, in his uniform all belted and buttoned up, with his boots on. Dead to the world, flat on his back with his hands loose on his stomach, his long legs straightened out to the foot of the bed, his heavy feet pointed up side by side...

Helianos started to wake him, then thought it kinder and wiser not to, and tiptoed across the room and stood for a few minutes gazing at his slumbering face. In the weakness, unwariness, of slumber it struck him as more lamentable than ever: the bony mask like a great fist, with the flesh drawn loosely, vacuously over the bone; his cheeks long and slack and pallid, the scar on one cheek bright pink. His lips, so willfully pressed together when he was awake, now looked as though they had grown together, like another scar.

Oh, what was the matter with this man? Perhaps, Helianos thought, it was remorse for the various cruelties of the Germans in Greece, and cruelties all over Europe for that matter: the rack and the boot and the branding-iron, the whip and the club and the thumbscrew and the wheel; whatever the terms were in up-to-date parlance, whatever the equivalents were in contemporary German practice...

This was an explanation which had not occurred to Helianos before. As the major was not a really cruel man himself, not in those terms, hearing what his compatriots were up to and brooding on it, perhaps he felt the collective guilt little by little, at last heavier than he could bear. A cumulative shock and endless regret and helpless indignation; for in fact, as a mere staff-officer of the quartermaster's corps, whatever he thought about it he could not help it...

Although he lay there without tossing or turning in his corpse-like attitude it was not a peaceful slumber. There was some constant, almost imperceptible motion in his face, now in one feature, now in another; as on the surface of even stagnant water, in a leaf or a little stick or a scum, you see or you imagine the life of the water up and down, sinking, swelling.

Perhaps it was not remorse, perhaps it was fear. Perhaps Germany had begun to lose the war and the major knew it. On his journey home he might have seen signs of it.

Helianos as it happened had never heard anyone say that Germany was losing the war. How he would have liked to hear someone say it, just for the sensation, even without believing it! He did not believe it. No, he kept telling himself, no—lest he go mad with impatience—Germany had not even begun to lose the war, not yet.

Nevertheless he had a little vision of what it would be like when it did begin, when the common people of Germany all got panic-stricken, and their foreign slaves rose against them, and their armies on the broken battlefronts began to turn and run, with the other armies, especially the Russian army, hard upon them... Was this what the major had in mind? Was this the prospect, as he had seen it in Germany on his journey home? If so, it might well have sickened him, and taken the joy out of life for him, and inspired in him a little more kindness than usual, even to inconsequential Greeks.

Helianos moved a step closer to the bed, leaned over the recumbent rawboned figure, peered into the depressed face with its soft, uneasy animation, some bad dream: it was as if he could see the flesh over the high cheekbones and around the melancholy mouth, creep. If his dream was the defeat of Germany, no wonder!

As for himself, he, Helianos, wanted so to believe it that for a moment it was like an ecstasy. He drew his breath in sips as if it were a medicine, potion, poison; and his blood in his veins, in his temples and his

[72]

throat, pulsed audibly, sh, sh, sh; and his knees shook.

But he did not believe it. After all, a man of his age and his type is never very good at believing things, with nothing but his heart's desire to go by. For a breathless, foolish moment, he could deceive himself, but it was his nature to catch himself at it pretty quickly. Furthermore the ferocity of his heart's desire shocked him a little; and his physical reaction to it—wild stare, wheezing breath, gritting teeth—somewhat aroused his sense of humor about himself. An oldish Greek man-servant at his occupying officer's bedside with a kettleful of warm water shaking and sloshing in his hand, letting himself think what he wanted to think...

Furthermore he was a civilized Greek, and he had a certain deep prejudice to the effect that this kind of imaginary violence, collective vengeance, was not becoming to him as a Greek. Even fighting for his life, even (as it was in his case) having lost the fight, hoping against hope, a Greek ought to keep that moderation and strict sense of reality which, he reminded himself, Greeks had invented in the first place.

Only one German concerned him personally, in reality; the sleeping major there before him, as it seemed at his mercy, helpless and unhappy in his sleep. And certainly whatever vengefulness he might feel toward him was moderate enough...

Just then the major shook his sleeping head, and rolled over on his side with a little grunt which sounded like waking up; which startled Helianos out of his nocturne, his foolish revery. The sleeper did not wake up but he began to snore softly, and with

[73]

his head turned sideways in a different light, his lips parted by the heavier sideways breath, his appearance changed.

It was not a remorseful face or a defeated face. Helianos sighed. No German remorse, no German defeat (yet), no Greek revenge: all that had been in his imagination, and the crisis of imagination had passed. It was a mere German face, unhappy. Sooner or later probably he would find out what caused the unhappiness—surely one ought to find out all one could about Germans—but his curiosity was not intense now. It had run its course for the time being, perhaps its entire course.

So let the proud major sleep as he was, with his boots on, in his uniform, unwashed, like a common soldier, Helianos said to himself. It was a waste of the kettleful of warm water; no longer very warm anyway. He might wash his own face with it at the kitchen-sink. The major's blessed leftovers! He was not sleepy but he was so tired that it seemed a long way down to the corridor to the kitchen; and hard work to wash, and to undress, and to get into the shaky semi-bed without waking his wife.

Would she mind if he did wake her, and whispered to her a little, not what he had just been thinking but something inconsequential to drive the wild thoughts out of his head? He realized, at moments like this, that he could not have lived without her. It was her dear female mind, with its narrow, intolerant, but tender concentration on what concerned it, that kept him in his right mind.

He poured the warmish water away, too weary to

want it, resigning himself to weariness and dirtiness as it were forever. Just before getting into bed he went to the kitchen-window and leaned out, and turned his heavy shoulders and his stiff neck around to gaze up into the dark night, thinking of the misfortune (war and defeat and vengeance) of all the common humanity of Europe of which he himself now had become just a part—himself no-man, no one in particular, certainly no one of consequence.

The common misfortune, he thought, is infinite like the dark sky full of painful stars and mad clouds. The sky is as great as we are, and the stars burn like our anguish, and the clouds shift like our insanity.

His heart quailed and shrank, there seemed to be nothing in it except pity; and he could not tell the difference between pity in general and self-pity. It was a moment of despair, but on the whole it suited him better than his impotent physical anger, like a snake cut in two; and vain defiance, like a rat in a corner.

He thought of the major also as just a part of European humanity—because he had seen him sleeping like a common soldier, a most common sleep, and because perhaps, he felt a sincere remorse, and possibly he might be defeated and be made to suffer someone's vengeance, and in any case he was unhappy about something (and Helianos was unhappy himself) —and this made him laugh softly, cynically; for surely the proud man would not thank him for it. He was not the kind who cares to be included in the common international lot, even in compassion.

Mrs. Helianos was not asleep, and his soft laugh

[75]

with its mocking or self-mocking note worried her. "Helianos!" she whispered from the cot behind his back. "Helianos, what are you doing, hanging out of that perilous window?

"Someday someone is going to slip and fall out there, and break his neck. We ought to have a railing or a bar put across it," she added sleepily.

Soon they both fell asleep, but Helianos slept badly, talking aloud, waking his wife and frightening her by what he said. Sometime before daybreak he woke and heard the major awake: his footsteps around his room, the squeak of his closet-door, the thud of his boots one after the other, as he undressed and went back to bed again properly.

When at last it was another day and Helianos was up and about, at his work, he found himself more cheerful than usual, somewhat purged of both vindictiveness and sentimentality; his war-fever abated. Of course he could not expect to be entirely happy, but, he began to believe—if the major continued in his new reformed way, and refrained from shouting at him, and kept his hands off Alex, and spoke civilly to Mrs. Helianos, without frightening her—he might be a little less unhappy if he tried, if he applied his mind to it; and he resolved to.

The major did persist in his reformation; he made progress in it, better and better. Indeed, looking back on it a week or ten days later, Helianos felt that his night in his uniform and his boots—the dream in the sleeping face, whatever it had been, whether or not there had been any scrap of truth in his own interpretations of it—had marked some good turning-point in the depressed officer's life.

He was still exceedingly melancholy but he appeared to have made up his mind to something, and not to be making it worse by straining against his will. There had been a freakish spirit even in his kindness; now it relaxed into an easier, simpler manner that you felt you could trust. As a new man, the newness wore off; as a changed man, he settled into the change with less self-consciousness, with better grace.

Even Mrs. Helianos appreciated this, and for a while she seemed to forget her anxiety and malice. For a while Helianos thought that she had come around to his point of view: sufficiency unto the day, happiness in so far as possible within one's self, and hope for the best.

8.

ONE HAPPY THING FOR THEM IN THAT MONTH OF MAY was the improvement in the children. They had no particular illness all month, and they were much easier to manage. Soon Alex would be fourteen years old, and although his poor body was not really growing, doubtless there were shadowy developments in his mind as in any growing boy's. As it seemed to his father they were all to the good.

He still sometimes lurked around the major, and tiptoed in the corridor to spy upon his changed ways, but with apparently none of his old animus; rather as if it were a joke or a game, blind-man's-buff, hide-and-seek. Once in a while he seemed bent upon provoking his old enemy, with some specific impudence, some slightly amplified noise, as if to prove to himself and the others that he was not afraid. But the major did not mind him any more.

Having gathered from his parents' conversation that they had a curiosity about every little thing the German did, Alex liked to make observations all his own and give his characteristic romantic report afterward. They did not pay much attention; he still told untrue stories. He had developed a sense of humor and would spend hours trying to make poor Leda laugh, which was hard to do.

He must have heard his father's joke about the major's having ceased to study in the evening; Helianos heard him expounding it to Leda, with great variations on the theme.

"It's what they call promotion," he said, with the crescent smile which he assumed when imagining things to please her, "it makes all the difference. Captains are ferocious; majors are kind but not so healthy or happy, they lose their appetite. They learn to remove their own boots. However, they refuse to have anything to do with the housekeeping.

"I wish we knew a general, I wonder what they're like..."

Naturally it charmed and flattered Helianos to hear this. But Mrs. Helianos, very strangely, lost her patience and cried out that he was a diabolical child, and caught him by the shoulder and shook him.

It hurt his feelings and he sulked all the afternoon, which Helianos was sorry to see. But he got over it in the course of the evening or the night. Perhaps he thought of some explanation of his mother's fury which satisfied him, or found some humor in that too.

Next morning in the kitchen, with his eye on her, for her benefit—Leda as it happened was still in bed —he repeated his little classification of the military: captains fierce, majors amiable and depressed, generals question-mark. With sparkling glances he seemed to be defying her to lose her temper about it again.

[79]

She did not, she laughed softly, then with a catch in her voice apologized to him, catching him by the shoulder once more and giving him a kiss, which pleased him.

Helianos sometimes thought that Alex wanted more physical tenderness than he got. His mother, whether in some shyness or strange aversion, or in order to appear perfectly respectful of his small manhood, rarely kissed or caressed him.

In the life of Leda, as she personally had not suffered from the major's former temper, there was less change. But she was wonderfully sensitive to the human atmosphere around her, reacting to the others' moods, as if it were good or bad weather, sunshine or sundown, like a little plant. It did her good to have her parents less nerve-racked, less anxious and indignant. They thought she might possibly be coming out of her dismay and apathy, at last. Sometimes she seemed almost innocent, uninhibited, like other children. Toward the end of the month now and then, she, the silent one, said a few words to her mother, who rejoiced in this as if it were a miracle.

Whenever the major appeared she would assume a slight strange air of triumph, seeming to remember that she had been right about him when all the others had been wrong. He, on the other hand, for some reason, did not welcome her infant affection as he had done in the past. Now that he treated everyone well enough, in a melancholy correct way, no one was his favorite. He no longer made the old distinction between Alex and her in her favor; and she may have felt this as a disgrace or an infidelity. In the old days her instinctive caresses, simple-minded glances, had tickled his sense of humor; now nothing amused him. Naturally Leda, in her plight of mind, had no sense of mockery or indignity; to her, a smile was a smile, and she missed being laughed at. Sometimes a sudden feeling of being ignored or rebuffed by him would come over her like a wild soft storm.

One late afternoon as he strode past her in the corridor, and she reached out to take him by the hand, he did not notice it or would not permit it; and she caught hold of his dear sleeve and clung to it until he jerked it impatiently out of her grubby fingers. Then she sank down in a dejected position on the floor, hiding her face in her hands, quivering from head to foot, until her mother found her and carried her to bed. Helianos had a hard time removing her smudgy, sweaty fingerprints from the major's sleeve before he went to the officers' club that night.

Upon his return he called Helianos out of the kitchen, with something to say about Leda that Mrs. Helianos might not care to hear. "I wish you to know, Helianos, that I have not been thoughtless about your little girl, or needlessly brusque and short with her. It is for your sake as much as anything!

"She seems to prefer me to anyone, as you may have noticed. But a child of that age ought to love her father best. Therefore I have decided to be somewhat more severe, do you understand?

"I may have been at fault in this, perhaps. It would have been easier to discourage her in the first place; it didn't occur to me then. I'm sorry."

Helianos grimaced and blushed and drew a quick

deep breath. Oh, could a great foreigner with careless power, victorious uniform, really steal away his dull little one's affection and then in his magnanimous fit restore it to him as it were on a platter?... He gave a slight grunt deep in his throat.

"I beg pardon, Helianos, I didn't hear you."

"Oh, sir, I said nothing."

"There's another point," the major continued, "I scarcely expect you to understand it very well. I dare say you do not know modern child-psychology. It is one of our German sciences, I happen to have read two or three of the authoritative books on the subject.

"Children of Leda's age often develop sudden attachments like this, and they are extremely important, and very passionate and physiological. Now I don't want her to get into a habit of clinging to me; trembling when I come anywhere near her; feasting her eyes on me. I tell you, I don't like it. Groping toward me, and plucking me by the sleeve, and fondling my hand! Now that it has occurred to me, I find it offensive."

Once more Helianos started to protest but stopped it because he did not know what he was saying or he did not dare say it, substituting an inarticulate cough or grunt. He was ashamed of Leda, ashamed for Leda; and he remembered things he had said about her himself, in fantasy of compassion and stoic humor, and he was ashamed of every word.

No, no, not ashamed; for he had spoken only in secret, to himself and *alter ego,* his wife, in interpretation to himself of this latest poorest fruit of their lives, remnant of their old marriage; and Leda belonged to them, to interpret as they liked; Leda belonged to them in a way that none but the parents of a shameful child could ever understand...

"As you are a man of the world, I knew you would appreciate my mentioning this," said Kalter, taking no notice of Helianos' burning face and speechless breath and resentful glances.

"You know, I feel a certain friendliness toward you, Helianos. In many ways I look back quite pleasantly upon the year we have spent together."

Helianos also looked back upon the year but with a look like a lightning-flash, recalling the other insults and injuries that he had endured with more or less good grace, comparing them with this; and then gave Kalter a look of lead, coming to the conclusion that nothing in the past had been so insulting as this nonsense about Leda; whereupon he grimaced again and exhaled another wild breath.

"Are you listening to me, Helianos? Listen! Perhaps something could be done for Leda. There is a young German physician here, who, they say, is a great genius. He has published a great treatise, endocrinology as it is connected with psychotherapy. My friend Lieutenant-Colonel Sertz introduced him to me one evening last spring.

"He is attached to one of the special services of our army, my friend's bureau in fact; interrogating political prisoners and so on, not very pleasant work, I suppose. But you know how science is, all things to all men! The same great discoveries serve both for good and evil, for punishing criminals and for healing sick children...

[83]

"I think I should speak to this young scientist about Leda. Perhaps we can work a miracle for the poor little thing."

The sciences in this proposal were something that as it happened Helianos knew little about; not to mention the ghastly mysteries of the interrogation of political prisoners. But in spite of his confusion and temper, he could tell that it was intended to be an overwhelming benefaction. What he ought to do, probably, was to fall on his knees and kiss his benefactor's hand. For he had no right to be proud, nor to be too delicate in the matter of good and evil, nor to be cowardly with regard to the special services of their army, Kalter's friend Sertz's bureau—if there was any question of making sick Leda well. Leda who had everything to gain, nothing to lose...

Meanwhile Kalter sat down at his desk and began writing a letter, dismissing the problem of the child from his mind.

Helianos stood behind him and gazed at him, with his fists clenched, and his blush so hot that his cheeks prickled, and tears streaming from his eyes because he wanted to kill him. He wanted to express his feeling in some way, and it was inexpressible.

There was no great range of attitudes for him to choose from; only the alternatives, violence or softness. Therefore he decided that he would have to take the German's remarks in the spirit in which they were intended. He set his chin firmly; he straightened his mouth tight shut; he drew his sloping, somewhat stooped shoulders back as far as he could and as square as he could; he set one foot firmly beside the other, as if he stood in the fear of God or in the presence of death, with an extreme self-consciousness. As Kalter sat there writing with his back turned toward him, he stood for a moment like that, facing Kalter's back, with all his will power forgiving him.

For he felt that it was a great decision, this forgiveness, not at all forced or against his will, but simply against his every instinct. It is a grave decision, when you take the good will for the deed; when you yield to the mistaken inhuman brain or the harmful tongue because there is a kind heart behind it—accepting things that you hate, with nothing to make them acceptable except that riddle of the spirit which has prompted them, contenting yourself with good intentions whether they are according to your morality or not, whether they are to your advantage or not.

Then Helianos started to go out of the room, and so passed beside Kalter, who looked up from his letter; and Helianos really could see shining in his tired flushed eyes the fact that he meant well. He seemed not to observe that Helianos had been shedding tears. The look he gave Helianos was one of perfect candor, a little unsure of himself, a little sentimental, seeming to hope that kindness would be repaid with kindness. He bestowed upon Helianos a short warm smile; a smile like a schoolboy's. It was obvious and unmistakable that he could not have intended to hurt Helianos' feelings by his remarks about Leda. Without a doubt he was sincere; and that, to Helianos' way of thinking, lifelong, was what you looked for above all in judging other men!

Therefore he relaxed and let it pass, smiled back

as well as he could, said good night and went to bed. It was a turning-point in his relationship with the major, and also seemed to have altered something in the balance of his own mind and heart from then on, half unknown to him. No anger had ever troubled him so much as this; but on the other hand this pardon was more wholehearted, deeper, softer, than anything of the kind in his life before. He felt the forgiving spirit through and through him as a passion, with a greater involvement than ever before of all that part of his being which went on in secret and in shadow, unaware.

He relaxed, he smiled again, he forgave, he stayed his impulse to kill, such as it was, he voided his indignation. It was an event in his soul. As a rule the soul cannot relax by halves; one way of yielding gradually induces another. It is a kind of goodness that may act as a weakness. If you forgive more than you can afford, you may find yourself impoverished in emotion afterward, with a lowered resistance to whatever happens after that.

Naturally Helianos determined not to say a word to his wife about the insult to Leda. She had not his capacity for forgiveness; and he so wanted her to live easily and calmly with Kalter, to spare her temper and rest her unhealthy heart.

But to his surprise a day or two later—it was a day of Leda's strangest incapacity, when even Alex could not imagine what possessed her—Mrs. Helianos said, "You don't suppose, do you, that the major really will do what he promised, about taking this poor child of ours to his famous specialist?"

"How do you know about that? Who told you? Oh, my poor wife, did he speak to you about it?"

No, what happened was this:—That night, after Helianos had followed Kalter into the sitting room for the consultation about Leda, Mrs. Helianos, thinking she heard the children's voices very softly, perhaps Alex whispering or laughing, perhaps the little one weeping again, tiptoed into their room to tell them to hush and go to sleep. Their closet-door happened not to be shut. The major's voice mentioning Leda by name came through the flimsy partition, and she found that by stepping inside the closet she could follow the entire conversation in the sitting room.

Helianos was greatly surprised at her not seeming to take offense at Kalter's opinion of their wretched infant. Somehow her maternal feeling was not like his paternal feeling; not so proud or so easily hurt.

When Helianos tried to explain what a tragic conversation it had been for him—his shame, his resentment, Kalter's evident sincerity, his decision of forgiveness—she smiled at the inconsistency of his feeling and reproved him for his false pride.

"My poor Helianos, you are the strangest man on earth. With all your appreciation of the major, when at last he does express a little sympathy and offers some help, you resent it, you lose your temper!

"Helianos, try to be reasonable about Leda. What can we do ourselves to improve her condition? Nothing. We feed her what food there is; we get her out of bed in the morning, and put her back to bed in the evening; we wash her, when we have time. She gets a little exercise with Alex; that is all her life. We do not understand her, we have no notion of her health or her real welfare.

"It is like keeping some little animal for a pet. Or like a bird in a cage. She is both bird and cage, and forever shut!" Mrs. Helianos' face as she said this lit up with a peculiar smile, as if she knew the answer to everything in the world.

"Now, if these fantastic Germans wanted to try some treatment to help her," she went on, "oh, let them try, for pity's sake! It is the least they can do. For they are to blame for her condition, their war frightened her into it!

"But, Helianos, try not to take things so seriously. Your blessed major talks and talks; naturally he wants to impress you, with the goodness of his heart, and now with his great knowledge of science; and perhaps he means it all. But nothing happens; he has too much on his mind now, whatever it is.

"I must say, this plan about Leda is the kindest thought that has come into his head so far. But I am afraid he'll not do anything about it. It is pleasant to have him at least try to behave like a reasonable human being. But we shall have to take the will for the deed."

Because this was what Helianos had said to himself in the very act of indulgence, it made him shiver to hear her say it.

So the weeks passed, with Kalter maintaining an entirely correct and friendly attitude, toward Mrs. Helianos especially, overlooking anything that seemed not to fit into his scheme of friendliness, per-

[88]

haps making allowances for her as a woman in poor health. This was the cleverest thing he did to convince and conciliate Helianos.

She was still very alien with him, still afraid, or indignant or proud; who could tell? Whatever he said to her, the tone of her voice always shifted key a little in reaction to his voice. Her eyes pinched together somewhat at his glance. There was still a distinct withdrawal, a sudden straightening somewhere about her thick small raggedy person, if he made a gesture; evidently it was a habit she would never overcome.

Naturally all this had some chilling, discouraging effect on him, but he appeared not to hold it against her. Not once since he came back from Germany had he really reproved her for anything. He rarely asked her to do any hard or disagreeable task. When she had done something well enough, he appreciated it and complimented her. Sometimes a day would pass without his speaking to her at all, but that too may have been with friendly intention, as she had a way of showing that she preferred not to be spoken to.

"She is not well, is she?" he inquired of Helianos one evening. "I have been noticing it, perhaps you have not, you're too accustomed to the way she is. I think you must insist on her seeing a doctor. You know, it's a serious matter..."

It was in one of his genial moods, when he paid little attention to anything Helianos replied to him. "Now, Helianos, don't argue about it. Do as I tell you!

"Another thing, Helianos. There is, as you may have heard, a shortage of all kinds of medicine in Athens. Ask your doctor about that when you take your wife to see him. If he can't get what he thinks she ought to have, tell him it can be arranged, in her case. Bring his prescription to me, I will see what can be done about it."

He had forgotten all about Leda and the psychiatrist, Helianos reminded himself. How true Mrs. Helianos' intuition was now and then! Perhaps now he was talking just to make a friendly effect; but he had to be listened to in any case.

Dr. Vlakos happened to be absent from Athens that week. The physician's daughter whispered to Helianos where he was: somewhere in the mountains where some leader of the secret Greek army lay in a fever. Helianos inquired anxiously whether it was his heroic cousin Petros; it was not.

Mrs. Helianos was unwilling to change doctors. Furthermore, she said, her health at the moment was better than it had been for months. "Tell your blessed major to look at himself in the mirror," she snapped, "and he will see which of us most needs medical attention. And tell him, if you please, to compare what he has eaten and what I have eaten in the past year, and his work and my work, and his victoriousness and our defeat!"

Helianos argued with her in vain. His anxiety about her health never ceased; as a rule she too was anxious enough. What a willful creature she was! Probably there would not be another opportunity for her to get proper medication while the war lasted. Furthermore Helianos was afraid that the proud German might resent their not taking his advice; but he did not, he forgot it.

His friendly concern expressed itself in another way. "Helianos, I think our work is too hard for your wife now. Can't you help her a little more than you do? Can't you get that old servant back to help her, the one you had when I first came? Old Euridice, Evridiki..."

"Oh, but," Helianos stammered, "we understood, Major Kalter, that you didn't like that old servant."

"It's true, I didn't, but now it doesn't matter. It will be easier to have her than to train a new one. Don't you know where she lives? Send word to her, do it right away, so Mrs. Helianos can get some rest."

With a certain misgiving Helianos did try to get in touch with Evridiki but word came back from her village near Eleusis that she was dead.

Kalter still had not recovered his old hearty appetite, and one evening Helianos asked him to suggest some improvement of their meals, or change of menu. "If I knew what would tempt you, sir, perhaps I could find it in the market; and Mrs. Helianos likes to attempt new dishes."

"Thank you, no," Kalter answered, "I can't be bothered. No appetite; no matter. Why should you complain of it, Helianos, if I may ask? There is a little left for you, as it is now, and you need it, you poor devils!"

Helianos blushed, asking himself for an instant whether this might be the beginning of a scolding in the old manner, the change again, the change back.

[91]

When they had first begun profiting by his abstemiousness, reveling in the leftovers—at the thought of his temper if and when he found them out, they had held their breaths as they reveled. Then they forgot and took it all for granted. As there were four of them the little extra was soon eaten.

Helianos blushed, but the tone of Kalter's remark was so good-natured, he almost thought it might be safe to smile or to make a jest... Then he caught his breath, suddenly reminded of something else he had forgotten: the decrepit greedy old dog, the other major's dog, the dog of the Macedonian couple. Not once since Kalter's return had he ordered anything wrapped up and taken down the street to their apartment! What a strange thing; and stranger still, his never having given it a thought: he who had done the wrapping and the taking, night after night.

He served the rest of the major's dinner, he cleared the table, without knowing what he was about; amazed at himself, with that slight streak of oblivion running back through the month past, as if it were amnesia, a tiny dark hole in his good-for-nothing brain. It worried him; he wondered what else he might have forgotten, all the while he had been flattering himself that everything was going well, what worse amazement might be in store.

He could scarcely wait to get away from the major, away to his wife in the kitchen, to ask why she had never mentioned it. She said that it had slipped her mind too. What a spell the German had cast on them! It was as if they had lost some of their capacity for knowing what happened, even their own everyday existence with its slight ups and downs, unless and until it happened to be revealed to them by the major. The assuagement of their hunger by a few more mouthfuls than usual had distracted them. Night after night they had consumed the dog's portion without stopping to think what little turn of fortune entitled them to it.

This was one of the occasions when Leda spoke. She asked what dog they were talking about. All her life she had wanted some small animal all her own, a puppy or a kitten, and could not understand her parents' refusal.

Alex said that a week ago he had seen the old beast loping along the street, with its caved-in white flanks muddy, its eyes glittering red, sniffing and drooling; and he, thinking it might be mad, had run the other way; and after that it had not been seen again. But as he told this, the poetic expression played over his face, and Helianos supposed that it was a yarn; his imagination slipping loose again, incorrigible.

Presently Helianos happened to meet the old Macedonian at the street-corner and entered into conversation with him, and leading up to the matter tactfully, questioned him. "Is it your impression, sir," he inquired, "that our major and your major are not as friendly as they used to be?

"You remember how I used to bring all our leftovers for your old bull-terrier. Our major—he was a captain then—insisted on it. It was a little gesture to please your major. Then he went home to Germany on leave, and since he got back, he has never mentioned it."

[93]

The Macedonian gentleman was exceedingly old, deaf, and obtuse; but finally gave the information that interested Helianos. Far from ceasing their friendship the two officers had spent the evening together lately, two or three evenings in fact, when Helianos had assumed that Kalter was at his headquarters working or at the officers' club playing cards.

The mystery of the dog-food was no mystery at all. The ravenous old animal was dead. It was a pity, the Macedonian felt, in view of the fact that he had the best possible British registration-papers for it, and half a dozen blue ribbons of its youth, which he offered to show to Helianos if it interested him.

These coincidences, these deaths, that of the neighbor's bull-terrier following Evridiki's, affected Helianos strangely, as it were with extreme superstition. Commonplace, inconsequential deaths; representative of death in the average and the abstract. For a long time as it had happened he had not heard of anyone's simply dying; only of people getting killed, which was another thing. Killing aroused anger, sometimes caused despair, sometimes gave hope. This was death the charmer, the changer; a continuous factor in one's life, to which one yielded.

With this generalization, and others no less farfetched and poetical, Helianos yielded (as he thought) to his life, however things might turn out for him, wherever his brighter prospect might be leading him. He ceased to worry or wonder about the explanation or the motivation of the major's better nature. He kept saying to himself that he was happy, relatively happy, somewhat losing his sense of the relativity in question, ceasing to be a judge of happiness. He no longer knew what to think, and gave himself up to small simple surprises and doubts from day to day, and occasionally to hope.

One night he had a bad dream about the dead terrier, pink-faced and blistered with eczema, covered with blue ribbons, forever dying, forever whining for something to eat; and as it impressed him it was like those heaven-sent birds and beasts of mythology which lured ancient men to their destiny or perdition. He followed the pink and sick animal, somehow coerced to follow it, fated to follow it, shouting against it the while; and his shout wakened Mrs. Helianos, who shook him until he woke. Evridiki also came into the dream somehow but when he was awake he could not remember in what capacity.

He had other dreams that same week, and was moved to various emotions by them and interpreted them to himself, as a mystery, turning their meaning this way and that, as Greeks have done from the beginning of time. He mentioned them to his wife but did not narrate them, except this one of the old dog and the old servant. Afterward Mrs. Helianos was to regret his not having told her everything that came to him in his sleep: riddle, malediction, or glimpse of the future.

9.

OF ALL THE CHANGES, THE HAPPIEST FOR HELIANOS was being allowed to pass the evening in the sitting room. That was in the third week of May.

"Why shouldn't you sit in here?" Kalter asked him, with that calm inconsistency which he still could not fathom. "Here is where you used to sit, after your dinner, is it not? There in the corner, that is your armchair, I suppose. You must get tired of that kitchen (which, I must say, your poor wife does not keep very clean) don't you?

"No, you won't disturb me in the least. I am a companionable type of man; most Germans are in fact. You like to read, don't you? When I feel like a little talk, we can talk; when I am busy you can hold your tongue, can't you? Anyway I am not working in the evening now, as I used to do."

The first evening of this new regime excited Helianos so that he scarcely enjoyed it. He went to his own bookcase and took two of his old favorite books, and it was an enchantment, fantastic; it gave him a lump in his throat. He could not really read, he could not take his eyes off Kalter as he sat at his desk reading, reading: one of his new unbelievable cheap paper-covered novels. Helianos held his own book up before him in serious manner; he felt that he had to pretend to read, lest his companion who was in a manner of speaking his host, should turn around and discover that he was not really reading, and be made nervous by his glances.

But the next evening Kalter began to engage him in conversation, and from then on, all went well enough. It was an unforgettable experience to penetrate into that German mind little by little.

On the third evening Kalter went to work again, but obviously it was not his former work. It did not require a one of the volumes, the strategy, logistics, dietetics, put away beside Helianos' dear books in the bookcase, nor the worn copy-book. Instead he brought out a bundle of legal-looking papers, which he perused for an hour; then began adding and subtracting, and apparently drafting a letter or a document, tearing up version after version, discontented, frowning and pinching his thin underlip with his long white teeth; and adding and subtracting all over again, while Helianos watched from his armchair in the corner.

Presently, at a moment when the work (whatever it was) seemed to vex the military man especially, Helianos plucked up his courage and said, "Sir, if this thing you have to do is nothing confidential, nothing military, perhaps I could help you. I was the accountant in our publishing business when I was young, when my father was alive. I know bookkeeping and my handwriting is neat."

Somewhat in his former rough way the major looked up, perhaps inclined to regard this as impertinent or too prying. But the peaceful face of Helianos reassured him. He replied a little stiffly, "Thank you, no. I am making my will, that is, re-making my will. I must do it myself. I have property, and in time of war it is hard to handle such things. There are many new laws, but I have informed myself. That is all. Do not concern yourself with it."

But an hour later he asked Helianos to prepare him a glass of hot wine, and as he sipped it, volunteered a little more information. "You see, I have no family," he began.

Helianos glanced up to the top of the desk where the three photographs used to stand in a row; they were not there now.

"I have no family," the major repeated, "and it might interest you to know how I am disposing of my modest fortune. You foreigners think of us as men of action only: as statesmen, as political leaders, in world politics too, and as soldiers. Which we are; but it is only the half-truth. You forget what we have done for civilization: philosophy, science, music."

Helianos assured him that he personally had not forgotten it.

It was a somewhat mumbled interruption and the major took no notice of it. "Music is what I love best," he went on. "Now, as I am a good patriot and a National Socialist, naturally I considered leaving my property to the party, or to a welfare organization, war widows, or something of that kind.

"But no, I reminded myself, no! If things were to go badly in the next few years and our German musicians suffered great hardship, it would be disastrous.

[98]

Some of our new young men in the government—their lives have been so laborious and exciting—are perhaps a bit shortsighted about such things.

"It would be the end of music all over the world; dead silence everywhere, am I not right? You Balkans have no music, have you? Neither have the Anglo-Saxons, and French music, what foolishness! Therefore the bulk of the proceeds of my estate is to go to a music school in Leipzig, for scholarships and for a pension-fund."

In so far as Kalter's purpose in telling Helianos this had been to impress him, he succeeded, although of course as an Athenian Greek he did not like to be sneeringly called a Balkan. What mistakes one kept making about Germans, Helianos sighed. It never would have crossed his mind that this one had any great cultural enthusiasm—the future of music, of all things!—or that he was a man of property either.

Mrs. Helianos, when he reported it to her, was not impressed. "But, my dear gullible husband, we know for a fact that he has a family. Have you forgotten the photographs: the elegant mother-in-law and the sour-faced boys in uniform?

"If he is telling you the truth about his new will, which I very much doubt, then it must be in typical German heartlessness and spite," she concluded, "to disinherit someone."

Of course she intensely disapproved of her husband's new sociability with the major, and expressed it or at least implied it every hour, every day, every hour, either in a scolding way or with strange pathos. Once or twice Helianos replied to her about it in-

[99]

dignantly. "Is it not natural for two men living under the same roof to talk things over," he wanted to know, "whether or not they like one another, with or without real agreement? You do not think that I always agree with him, do you?"

No, she did not think that. Little by little he got her to speak her mind about it, her divided mind. On the one hand, her dear husband was the most charming man in the world, in her opinion. Even a foreigner, even an enemy, even terrible Kalter, might yield to his charm, and some advantage to them all might ensue; she hoped so.

On the other hand, she had decided, he was unwise and indiscreet. One of these days, with a slip of his tongue, absent-mindedly, he might say the wrong thing; her dread of that was inexpressible. Then as a warning she gave a series of past examples of his indiscretion, which bored him, and nagged at him about it off and on until he grew resentful; and when she saw his resentment, relapsed into her pathetic brooding.

It was flattering to him on the one hand, exasperating on the other; but it was hard for him to argue with her about any such thing now, because he was worried about her. She had always had a mind of her own, but of late, he thought, it had gone too far. Agitatedly over and over she would harp on certain subjects all the day long, then suddenly shift, and fall into a kind of heavy daydream in which she would not express herself at all for hours. Sometimes she went from the one extreme to the other with a rapidity and apparent lack of sequence that startled him: up and up with her fiery spirit, in some conceited opinion, vain anger, even unexpected mirth; then in an instant down, as it were visibly into a pit, a soft hopelessness. Often when her spirits fell Helianos could see where Leda got her little scowling self-absorption, her apathy and loss of herself in emotion.

There were days when she talked to herself rather than to him. He would hear her, sometimes quite loud, in the kitchen or the children's bedroom, and at first he would think that the children were with her; then find her alone. She had never done that before, and what he heard alarmed him: little exclamatory phrases, as it were bits of some obscure poem or play, little retorts arising out of some inner argument.

In his presence of course it was never more than a tiny whisper, or soundless pantomime of her poor pale mouth. But long ago, when the major was still a captain, they had learned to read each other's lips, and he read hers now, when they were not addressing themselves to him. For the most part it was familiar subject-matter—her sorrow for Cimon, her dread of what Alex might do next, her mistrust of Kalter, her anxieties about Helianos himself—but there was an increase of the phrases he could not understand; and sometimes the soundless utterance turned to mere grimacing. Of course as soon as she noticed his anxious eyes fixed on her lips, she ceased. She talked wildly in her sleep as well, and she had never done that before.

Poor weak weary woman! Helianos had less and less confidence in her, as to her future, as she grew old. Sometimes with a desperate compassion he said to himself that if the war went on much longer she might lose her mind little by little. Or if she were to be overtaken once more by grief—his death, for example, or the death of another of their children—or by extreme hardship, as it had been before the major changed, or even by great anger, she might suddenly go mad.

His friendliness with the major of course was one of the subjects she harped on, even to herself, even in sleep; but in Helianos' opinion that was not a serious matter. Certainly it was too foolish to affect her very deeply. It was nothing but her excess of imagination and lack of good judgment.

As he was a Greek, it was not in his nature to condemn a woman very severely for a mere error or shortcoming of intellect; and as he was a good man he wanted not to wound her self-esteem if he could help it. He did not reply to her nagging about his evenings in the sitting room as sharply as he knew how. Instead, in the major's absence or in their midnight hours, to flatter her and reassure her, he told her more and more of the subjects of their manly conversations, encouraging her to protest openly and to argue with him upon every point all she liked.

Still it did not satisfy her, she did not trust him. As she lay by herself on the folding cot in the kitchen, her ears were as sharp as some old watch-dog's dozing by the hearth. Through the thin partitions she heard Helianos' voice and the dread German voice the minute they began any important conversation; then arose and tiptoed into the children's bedroom, and opened the clothes closet and shut herself in, and there among the outworn family shoes and under the ragged family garments, crouched or knelt where there was a crevice along the baseboard, and hearkened to all they said night after night.

It was young Alex who, with a flash of his love of melodrama in his dark eyes, informed his father of this. For two or three evenings Helianos was made exceedingly nervous by it, sitting with the major, but forewarned of her coming; listening, then hearing her characteristic tripping step, the opening and closing of the closet door, the creak of the floor boards. The major too might have heard it; but if he did, he must have presumed that it was only Alex and Leda. Helianos accustomed himself to it and sometimes it gave him an absurd sweet satisfaction. Dear comforting though exasperating presence; love in the wainscoting, scratching softly like a mouse, knocking softly like a ghost! The secret of a good old marriage like theirs, symbolized, he said to himself, in his fanciful humor.

Then he decided that her spying on them probably had no harmful spirit or morbid motivation; it was because she was bored and lonely. In the great days before the war she had been a most sociable little Athenian, back and forth with the neighbors in Psyhiko, and with the family, his kin as well as her own. Also she might be a little jealous; the time he spent in the sitting room was, after all, subtracted from the twenty-four hours of their dear wedlock.

Furthermore, the fond, vain husband said to himself, a good deal of the talk in the sitting room was well worth listening to; and if the major continued in his present civility, it would get better and better:

revelation of the foreign mentality, and deep and prophetic historic principle. Surely it was a good thing
for Greeks to learn what manner of world these
world-conquerors intended! He took some credit to
himself for all this. Was it not his tact and his dialectic which little by little drew the major out? The
previous year, with a chip on his shoulder, he must
not have been good company; whereas now he had
relaxed, and recovered some of his social graces of
before the war.

One evening Kalter brought home a bottle of German brandy; and after dinner gave Helianos a small
amount, and drank a large amount himself, and dis-
coursed upon the subject of the heroic aims of his
great nation, so misinterpreted in all those nations
pretending to have united against it. He himself
brought it up, a bit irritably, and succinctly at first,
merely exclaiming against the united international
error. Perhaps as he had gone about Athens that day,
someone had said something challenging to him or
provoked him by some silliness.

Then, as he sat and relaxed with Helianos, Helianos expressing an interest, he began expounding his
views at greater length in a more mellow, sententious
way.

There was no excuse, as it seemed to him, for anyone's not knowing the German purpose by this time.
"For it is a platitude among ourselves," he said, "and
again and again our statesmen and writers have explained it, with the wonderful German frankness.
Only, the rest of the world has never paid attention.
That is how wars start!"

As Helianos rephrased this to himself, with his humor, it was as if the Germans felt obliged to wage war now and then in order to prove that they meant what they said.

"The incredulity of the foreign nations is fantastic!" Kalter exclaimed. "It is one of their worst weaknesses."

Helianos detected in his enunciation some slight influence of the brandy; and he remembered that all during 1942, in so far as they could tell, he had never drunk a drop.

Now he lit a strong-smelling cigar, with sensitive motions of his fingers and his lips showing his pleasure in it; and gave Helianos a benevolent look, as if he saw in him and was pleased to see in him a less weak, less incredulous foreigner than most; and proceeded to explain something of the German purpose, in his fashion.

"Naturally the German nation is superior in actually waging a war, all other things being equal; that is, unless it has been betrayed by the internationally-minded Jews or something of that sort. In fact," he pointed out, "the nations opposed to Germany are all more or less agreed about this. Even the way they deplore it is a kind of admiration."

As he went on talking the effect of the brandy wore off, although he still took a sip now and then; the intensity of his conviction of what he was saying counteracted it. He grew extremely earnest and impressive.

"But," he said, "superiority in warfare itself is not everything. It is only one side of the greatness of the

[105]

nation, one aspect of the problem of rising above other nations. It is not always possible to win a war; there are overwhelming odds, there are circumstances, turns of the tide...

"But for us losing a war, a given war, makes no difference, do you see? It made no difference in 1918. Now suppose we were to lose the present war; what of it?"

Helianos looked at him sharply, with a little heart-beat, never having been asked by anyone to suppose any such thing. So perhaps, that night when he had watched over him in his uneasy sleep like a common soldier with his uniform and his boots on—the dream of German defeat, the notion that on leave in Germany he might have seen signs of it—had not been all foolishness!

But Kalter went on loudly, as if in answer, "We will not lose it, never fear! But let us suppose that we were to, just for the argument's sake. What would be the result? It would only strengthen us in the long run. The bitterness of defeat intensifies the spirit of the nation, increases the national aptitude for war. By the loss of old manpower, with virility of the young men and fecundity of the young women, the nation is rejuvenated. And defeat teaches us so much! We grow more and more capable, especially in propaganda..."

His next point was almost mystical, but none the less arresting for that, Helianos thought. It was that if a nation is to wage war really well, it must not be simply for victory's sake, but with a longer view and a higher ideal, for its own sake.

[106]

"Do you know," he said, "I honestly believe that most Germans, that is, the aristocracy and the new aristocracy, the leaders and governing classes, do not care whether they win or not. It is worthwhile anyway, it is the best part of life, and the ideal way to die. It is a force of nature in them, as, for example, motherhood is in women; not caring for the pain, not counting the cost.

"Of course, it is not the same for the common people, I must admit. They have so much to bear, in a defeat; naturally they want to win. But, you know, they are such a good people, with stout hearts and peaceful minds; they are naturally so happy to follow the leaders.

"Oh, the cost is great, even for the upper classes, in many ways. It takes our all, in the prime of life, to the limit of our strength. In the practical way, economics and so on, it is not so bad. In that sense, to a great extent—this is something I see for myself a little, in the quartermaster's corps—we make the war pay as we go along. And in peacetime the other nations help us. It is not just sentiment; as their economy is, as they understand it, it is to their interest to do so...

"But I do not speak of materialistic matters only; it is the imagination, the future, the ideal! We Germans are not so practical a people, after all; not as you might think. It is never a mere question of how we fight or how we live; it is why we fight and what we live for.

"Victory, yes, very well, all in due time! But if this is not the time, then no matter, we will have the future! Just so long as victory is possible, up ahead—constantly beckoning like a dream, leading on and on, as it were our hope of heaven, our salvation—it is enough! You must understand what I say, Helianos! After all, it used to mean something to you Greeks, with your winged *Nike*, didn't it?

"I know, I know, there is some slight pessimism about it, and a certain desperation, but how glorious! It is what makes men fight like angels; even silly Englishmen and drunken Americans individually, in the sordid sense, at the last moment, when it is a question of kill or be killed.

"But for us, it is not momentary, it is forever. It is not sordid, it is a vision, even when it happens to be peacetime. We are always a little in the frame of mind that you all are in, upon occasion, when the battle is actually on...."

After this long portion of his tirade the strange fellow drew a sigh, as if he were a weary schoolmaster, expounding rudimentary and self-evident things to a child. And in fact Helianos as it went on felt rather like a child. He reminded himself somewhat of poor Leda listening to one of Alex's yarns.

How it would have frightened him if he had entirely believed it! Point by point, sentence after sentence, it seemed as plain as day and in dead earnest and quite convincing and almost overwhelming—then when he tried to contemplate it in its entirety, as a whole, it fell to bits, and he felt inclined to giggle. If he had been a younger man, a fighter, or a politician, it would have been his duty to try to believe it, in order to combat it. It occurred to him that this was one point upon which he agreed with Kalter: incredulity was a weakness...

"You see," Kalter continued, apropos again, "you see how weak you are, you other nations, in your intellect. After all, all you care for is the everyday life, the fun of it, or the pity of it, as it happens to be in reality.

"Naturally, everything in reality has its ups and downs; and for you, your destiny goes up and down accordingly; but ours does not! You judge everything by results, whereas we judge by the greatness of the ambition and the undertaking. If you fail it is nothing, nothing. Whether we fail or not, it is a great thing.

"You naturally are afraid of fate. We are not afraid, because we have identified ourselves with it, we are active in it, we are it. Whatever happens, yes, we have the satisfaction of knowing that we have helped it along, with all our might, with a whole heart. If it is not what we expected we care little—it is a change, it is creative! Nothing we have had anything to do with will ever be the same again.

"But now let us try to look at it from your point of view, sympathetically," he said, in a more sympathetic, companionable, though patronizing, tone of voice. "None of you, you foreigners, can even consider the possibility of losing the war, can you? Not even for argument's sake! Naturally not. The very thought of defeat is unthinkable for you. It would be the end, the end of your world, your one-sided world in which everything has to be just so."

To be sure, Helianos thought, with his heavy irony,

[109]

all this was addressed to him as you might say by cour-
tesy, representing all the other still embattled nations
as best he could in his poor person. For of course, to
him specifically as a Greek at this point, losing the war
was not at all unthinkable, alas, and there was no
argument; in so far as his world was one-sided, certainly the end of it had come.

"You must get results," Kalter said meanwhile, in
his loud voice full of life, "for whether you amount to
anything or not depends on it: results or nothing.
You must win, or your war is meaningless.

"Nothing is meaningless for us. Everything is just
a new beginning, a fresh start. There will be another
war, always, we say to ourselves; some war or other.
It stands to reason, historically. Forever and forever
history will always give us another chance."

Which was not, Helianos said to himself ruefully,
what he called looking at it sympathetically from his
point of view. Once or twice during this discourse
he had to cover his lips with his hand, to hide what
might have been called a smile. It occurred to him to
wonder what his poor wife made of it, crouching so
close, silent and secret in the clothes closet.

"At last," Kalter proclaimed, "sooner or later, it
will work for us. That will be a great day; a Utopia
as the English call it; everything new, everything
creative! At last the world will have a world-government; and who is to govern, unless it is Germany?
What other nation is there, equal to the task, self-
confident, hard-working?"

His small blue eyes, slightly dilated, with the whites

not quite white and the eyelids irritated as they had been ever since he returned from Germany, shone with the historic vision. Helianos gazed back at him in dismay; but their eyes did not meet because the major's eyes, literally as well as figuratively, were focused over his head, far off.

Then the major remarked that actually not one of the other nations really wants the job of world-government, calling Helianos' attention to the general unwillingness and unworthiness of the non-German Western world: the Greeks, for example; and the French, what foolishness! The English have ability, he admitted, but no imagination; and the Americans are wonderfully inventive but frivolous.

"I happen to know the Americans well, because my own brother is an American," he confided. "What a frivolous people, it astounds us: always on the go, getting nowhere, drinking and drinking and making merry, talking and talking and, in the end, doing very little!

"Anyway we have taken all their inventions, and made something of them. They are wonderfully generous and free-and-easy between wars," he said.

"Then Russia! It will not have escaped your attention, Helianos, that I have not said a word about Russia. You will understand why: it is not particularly the German enemy, it is not a part of the Western world, it is the common enemy, Asia!

"You know, it has spirit, a kind of great spirit, like the other Asia. As a man of the world I appreciate it. But how different it is from the rest of us, so bestial, so simple, with the passive mysticism of its poor people. We Germans understand it very well; no one else seems to. It was made for us, our natural hinterland. It has great strength, but only a defensive strength. We should have no trouble with it if the other nations would refrain from attacking us.

"As for its revolution, I presume—as I understand that you were also a man of property in your youth—that you feel as I do. A frightful thing; but it has run most of its course now, naturally...

"Don't forget that they owe it to us Germans anyway. Marx was a German although a Jew: the spiritual son of our great Hegel. We have the true version, in our National Socialism; they have the heresy. And don't forget how well it has served our purpose, turning all the liberals in the democracies against their own governments, back into our arms, where they belong; we can almost always use them."

At the end of the evening he tried to give Helianos some idea of what the German world-government would be. It sounded well but afterward Helianos found that he could not remember much of it. He seemed constitutionally incapable of taking it all in, or at least momentarily unable. His natural skepticism overcame even his curiosity, and he let entire topics pass with little attention.

He had not the least inclination to argue with the German about anything. How bored, and perhaps vexed, Kalter would have been if he had argued! Furthermore, he thought, from his own point of view, the Greek point of view, it was better not to. It seemed to him that if he tried to meet the German on his German ground, abstract, ideal, ideological, he certainly would be lost.

Perhaps there was no argument, as such, he said to himself, with a kind of serenity and idleness in his own conviction. Then he had a momentary wonderful, tragic glimpse of what his conviction was, simply this: there were too many sick enslaved women like his wife, too many wild half-criminal boys like Alex, too many psychopathic babies like Leda... Whatever the great day up ahead might be, he, for his part, was unwilling to pay that price, today. The clever thing all Germans did was to get everyone talking in terms of the future, as if the present did not exist or did not matter; and for Helianos, with his Greek sense of the value of a lifetime and the absoluteness of death, there was something wrong about that.

Presently he grew sleepy, and it was like pure imagination, laughable, though not very pleasantly laughable: himself, as it were over against the grandeur of the German humbly personifying the international nations, and perhaps combining the worst features of each: the weakness of character of one, the apathy of mind of another, the superficiality of another, as well as the Greek faults which he knew so well.

He kept nodding his head at Kalter's every word; and this mere acquiescence seemed to suit the proud German better than his various other reactions on other occasions. The longer Kalter talked the friendlier he appeared; which perhaps was a good omen for that great day to come, if and when his kind are to govern the world. World-governor or not, he con-

[113]

cluded upon an almost fraternal note; and when at last the weary Greek departed to his rest in the kitchen, patted him on the back.

Their next night of serious talk was all about propaganda. "What makes us great in propaganda," Kalter began, with a manner of having prepared his thoughts in advance, "what helps us so much, is that the other nations have no consistent belief, no soul, no idealism, except one thing... Sympathy for the underdog, that they have! It is fantastic, it comes over them like a madness! And in the interval between wars, that is to our advantage. When we need help, then it is in the nature of the other nations to give us help.

"We are the only nation that has not a divided mind. Therefore all our culture and our art is good propaganda. Wagner, for example, invincible all over the world! You see how important that is. It is the way to make peace at the end of a war, so that we can get on our feet again. It gives us time, between wars, to learn and develop, to plan and prepare everything.

"I myself do not know all about propaganda. I always have specialized in the problems of supply, ordnance, transportation. But my friend Major von Roesch knows all about it; I have studied it somewhat with him. Of course it is not so mighty as military science but as it appears, it is a more exact science. So to speak, a weapon of lesser caliber but more accurate aim...

"As Major von Roesch tells me, our *Fuehrer* as a statesman and a general has made mistakes; I admit it. Men of action always make mistakes. For one thing, military action is directed against the strength of the

enemy, propaganda against the weakness of the enemy; so our minister of propaganda has an easier job
of it. He is a kind of artist. Nothing is a mistake for
him! He never loses a battle, not even here in Greece
where you are so savage and cunning...

"Wait and see, wait and see! Even in backward
Greece, with your pride in your burning patriotism,
you will fall out among yourselves. Naturally there
are these political diseases in any occupied country,
and if the occupying authority knows its business, it
is amazing how much can be done along that line, to
keep them from being cured, to nurse them along to
our advantage.

"Naturally there are two sides to everything, two
ways about everything; that is fate. But everything
can be fixed so that it is effective for us either way,
and that is art! Wagner understood that so well..."

Helianos was not impressed by the bit about
Greece. He did not believe that there were among
his people any great schisms or angry passions helpful
to the enemy. A foreigner naturally would misunderstand the old Hellenic quarrelsomeness, which was
essentially democratic, he thought; and flatter himself
that it could be taken advantage of.

It was the main theme of the evening that impressed and fascinated and frightened him. For one
thing, the arts, literature, music, at least Wagner,
came into it a bit, at least in theory; and he fancied
himself a little less incompetent in that field than in
political philosophy, martial mysticism. They never
forgot a thing, these Germans! It was thrilling in a
way. It bore some resemblance to parts of Plato but

[115]

of course it was more in earnest... Off and on for two or three days he kept arguing the principles of cultural propaganda pro and con, not exactly with Mrs. Helianos but in her presence, thinking out loud. It seemed to him that what he had heard Kalter say that night was the most evil stuff he had ever heard uttered.

She not only despised it, she pretended not to be able to understand one word of it. How he doted on this terrible lodger of theirs, this intellectual quartermaster, this fitful bully! It was all very well for Leda to dote, she declared, but as Helianos was a man, a man of honor and good education, he ought to be ashamed of himself.

But he could not find it in his heart to be ashamed. He knew what he was about, he said to her, and to himself. Listening to the major was a kind of education; often it was a pleasure. Sitting there in his sitting room with a strange, and now strangely amiable companion: it was the natural life for him, after all; thoughtfulness, talkativeness, philosophy and history in dialectic form. It was more like his life in peacetime—as a publisher, an intellectual, and a man of some leisure—than anything else in this world-war, this German world, this brutalized, half-dead Athens.

Whatever he reported to his wife of the themes of Kalter's conversation, she never would admit that she had heard any of it. Oddly enough, her habit of hiding in the closet had never been mentioned between them. Because of something she said he felt sure that she knew that he knew; that was all. On one or two evenings it marred his pleasure: the poor woman he loved kneeling uncomfortably a few feet way on the other side of the partition, the tremulous and faded, freckled, once-lovely face pressed close to the crack in the baseboard, fearfully listening and doubtless misinterpreting it all.

On other evenings the sweetness of having her near him, of her caring enough about him to spy upon him, of speaking up so that she could hear him— whenever the major gave him a chance to say a few words—made him forget her sadness.

Then he would draw a sigh, and probably Kalter, absorbed in his theories, took it as a compliment; an admission of the dark overwhelming German logic. It was no such thing, but rather a refutation. Helianos' mind wandering away to that poor dear female of his species where she hid, knelt, prayed, trembled: it was the working in him of a basic principle of his type of manhood: private life greater than public life, which was the opposite of German principle.

More was the pity, in a way, for if he had not been distracted by his old love, if he had paid closer attention to the major's talk, he might have detected the constant little menace to him personally in it.

One of their latter conversations surprised Helianos a good deal, perhaps was intended to surprise him. "You foreigners have a notion that we Germans all think alike," Kalter said, "but it is not so. I will tell you something. It may not be the thing to tell a foreigner, but no matter, it is what I personally think. Today there is all the talk about race, Aryan and otherwise: I myself do not believe in it much. Of course it is an effective point to make in propaganda, but it is all relative and imaginary.

"Don't you see, to be a German is nothing like that, biology, ethnology, anthropology; it is not so complicated. To be a German is simply the way we live; it is a love of government and orderliness, for one thing, and confidence in ourselves and in each other. Above all, it is a role in history, and a preparation for our role; it is an education and a belief. It is the hope of the world: the hope that one day at last the world will be well-governed, by those willing and able and worthy to govern it—not always in a mess as it is now.

"That is why a great many German-Jews are wonderful Germans. They learn from us to have a vision of the future, like their promised land. Especially between wars they are wonderful; they persuade all the world to be sorry for us, to help us, to admire us.

"On the other hand a great many Germans, when they go to live abroad, especially in America, change overnight; they become Americans. As I told you, I have a brother in New York; he has not been there long, only since 1923; and he is no more German than you are.

"How strange it is! Not only peasants go there, and not only ambitious scientists, and business men who naturally are tempted by the easy money, but all sorts, scholars, film-actresses, writers—the very class who all their lives have been giving expression to the German spirit—and in a few years, it is unbelievable! they absorb all the American education and politics and morals; even the American patriotism, if it can be called patriotism.

"I think they must be unhappy when the novelty wears off. How can they ever forget what it means to be a German!" he exclaimed.

"I will tell you. See if you, as a foreigner, can understand it! Today religion is almost out of date. So few modern people have any sense of ultimate future, of life after they die. Still, in this life, hardships have to be endured, and virtue has to be exercised. And for all this, in the way of unearthly reward, we look forward to nothing, nothing! Self-sacrifice is good, in fact it is necessary, anyway it cannot be avoided; and what is the recompense? What is there, leaving out immortal things, to make it worth while?

"Now, perhaps you think I say this all in scorn, speaking only of the materialistic foreign nations. No! If this is foreignness we have it in us too, unfortunately. We too are skeptical; I admit it, you see. How can it be helped, now? For it is modern science, modern government, modern psychology: to have no heaven.

"Only we Germans can help it; we have something else, to take heaven's place. Yes, the German also sacrifices himself and he loses heart, like everyone else; but it is only personal: the nation does not lose heart. If the German fails, he gives up and goes quietly and stoically, having wound up his affairs in good order as it may be expected of him in the circumstances, whatever they are. His responsibilities he hands over to another, another who is like himself, knowing that the faith will be kept—and if not by that one, by the next one!

"Although he dies, no matter; he lives in his fellow-German, his compatriot, his kind. For us Germans, I tell you, this is our immortality. What if one man is imperfect, still there is the type; and sooner or later the type will come to perfection. If you believe that, there is vindication and a remedy for everything. If the one man is defeated—one and then another, no matter how many!—the triumph will come neverthe-less, in the end."

10.

THE LAST OF THOSE CONVERSATIONS OF GERMAN AND Greek was the strangest. It was not exactly a conversation, but rather a little drama and a revelation in the major's own person of that private weakness and defeat—in spite of which collective Germany was to triumph forever, with German after German forever taking up the burden whenever one weakly put it down—of which he had spoken so eloquently on the previous evening.

It was in the afternoon, on the last day in May, a Monday; one of Kalter's free half-days. He had returned to the apartment just before midday. As it happened Helianos had procured somewhat more food than usual for the midday meal; and the weary officer had eaten less than usual; and the family had been able to make practically a normal meal. The children descended to the street to play. Mrs. Helianos, who was not feeling well, lay down to rest.

And then—it was about three o'clock—Helianos in a good mood ventured to the sitting room, thinking that the major might not be taking a nap and might like a talk. He had some political question or other to propound to him. To his amazement he found him at his desk with his head bent far forward over it, his face pressed in his hands, in tears.

At the sound of Helianos' coming in, he sprang to his feet, crying out, "In God's name, why must you come in here just now? There's a devil in you! When I am alone, when I need to be alone—"

The Greek apologized and started back out of the room but the tragic-faced German strode over to the door and shut it.

"It's too late now," he said, returning to his chair, pulling it around to face Helianos, grimacing to stop his tears, "it's too late to stand upon ceremony. I have talked too much already. Why, why did I have to take you, you damned Greek, into my confidence? What possessed me?"

Helianos in his astonishment, stammered, "I do not understand, sir, it must be a misunderstanding, a mistake." He apologized, nevertheless, for whatever it was; and begged to be allowed to go back to the kitchen if his presence made the major nervous; and offered to run and prepare a glass of hot wine; and wondered if perhaps the major had not fallen ill, and suggested calling a physician; and begged to be told something to do, if the major could think of anything agreeable or useful.

During which well-meaning discourse the unhappy officer, unhappier than ever or really ill, seemed not to pay attention.

Then when Helianos could think of nothing more to say, he said, "No, it makes no difference. You're a good fellow, Helianos, aren't you? Or perhaps you're not, I don't know..."

It was in a muttering voice with weakly impatient gestures of one hand. "That's the worst of it, God! I don't know, I can't judge. When a German officer loses confidence in his judgment of other men," he added, "it's the end, the end of everything, isn't it?"

Then he bared his teeth in a semblance of a smile, dried his eyes, blew his nose. "No, Helianos, sit down, I will tell you what the trouble is. I wish you to know that it is nothing dishonorable; I have done nothing. I assure you of that, for my self-respect.

"Also it is good to tell my trouble. It relieves my thinking about it, it passes the time, the deadly time."

Helianos sat down, with a more ambiguous feeling than any he could remember: embarrassment? inquisitiveness? sympathy? Added to which he half expected to feel, half hoped to feel, some sense of humor and slight rejoicing in the discomfiture of an enemy; except that one could scarcely think of a man in such disorder of mind as an enemy...

He himself was not a very self-centered man, and until the end of the conversation, too late, he did not realize that it could possibly concern him in any way. He was not thinking of himself at all, only of the German: almost his friend by that time anyway in spite of the war, and in spite of different political principles.

His friend Kalter, for all his pride of intellect and of nationality, Helianos had decided, was a poor violent emotional human being, one who doubtless needed, more than most men, to be sustained by that collected agreed organized humanity which he advocated, the state, even the world-state; one who at the moment, for some reason, needed a friend.

He was deathly pale, and now and then he drew

an extremely deep breath with a slight shudder, as he controlled himself. It was a hot afternoon, and there was sweat on his upper lip as well as tears on his upper cheeks.

Then after a silence he began, with a bit of his violence, "You Greeks, and the other foreign nations, all of you—it's your damned conceit!—think that all the suffering of the war is on your side. It is not so! War is hard, I tell you, hard for everyone.

"Listen to me," he went on. "I told you that I had to make my will, a new will. Didn't it occur to you, stupid Greek, to wonder what had happened, why my old will was null and void? If you were my friend you would have wondered; but of course you aren't, how could you be?

"This is what happened:—Just before I returned home to Germany, my elder son, who was a fighter-pilot, crashed and was killed. Very well! almost every family has to give a son for the fatherland, sometimes more than one.

"Yes, very well, but while I was on my way home, my house in Königsberg was destroyed in an air-raid; a bomb set fire to it and my wife was burned, almost to death.

"And after I got there, while she lay unconscious, my younger son was killed in Russia.

"He was a young boy, a green soldier; he had never been at the front before. He wrote us shameful discouraged letters, the way green soldiers do, the poor youngster! He had not yet received any decoration or citation, he had done nothing to be proud of, he was killed like that.

"My wife lay at death's door for days and when she recovered consciousness, she was not in her right mind. They let me see her and she talked to me like a lunatic. Helianos, it was heartbreaking. It was indecent, Helianos, with all her hair burned away, half her face in bandages; and she talked nonsense; and the doctor did not know whether she would be insane the rest of her life or not.

"Then she got better and came to herself, and for two or three days she was wonderful. She comforted me for the death of our sons; she restored my faith in the future and in Germany, and my self-confidence.

"I can't tell you, Helianos, how it was. You wouldn't understand! With your Greek morality you couldn't. We were like a god and a goddess, there in the grim hospital, with her frightful bandages, in our grief and loss. Wonderful days! Then she died."

It was a good story, Helianos thought: a commonplace of today, an epitome of war; and as he listened to it he noted that Kalter's peculiar rough grudging voice was just right for it, softened by his fatigue, with the cadences of his grief. But bit by bit, word by word, he had a sense of unreality somehow, not the story itself, which was common and obvious truth, but the context—Kalter telling and himself listening; that was like fiction.

After all, it was the last thing he would have expected ever to see in reality on earth: a German officer grief-stricken, complaining of the commonplace of war. His mind ran back over all the past, the time when this weeping major was still the terrible captain, and wondered at it: the tyranny and insults and histrionics, then the metamorphosis, and his own curiosity and misinterpretation and forgiveness and relaxation, and appalling politics, and now this...

The rough voice choked on the words, "Then she died," and ceased; and Helianos did not know what to say, simply sitting there in a kind of false thoughtfulness. He found himself falsely thinking that one could scarcely begrudge these people the mastery of the world, if they wanted it enough to pay the same price they exacted of others; if they were willing to bring the common suffering and irreparable loss upon themselves as well as everyone else. Until that moment it had never seriously occurred to him that they were susceptible to the common suffering. His half-pity when he had stood peering at the major's bedside that night had not been very serious... Now it astonished him, and he realized that astonishment was in a way a tribute to the conquering race, and a measure of the depth of his own despair as one of the conquered: it had not occurred to him that conquerors could be unhappy!

Suddenly he felt that all this, acquiescence, rationalization, was idiotic nonsense. They were not willing to bring things upon themselves, no indeed; they told a plaintive story like other men, they shuddered and wept like other men, naturally; and each of them somehow blamed someone else for everything, and in fact someone must be to blame! Suddenly Helianos' short stout weary person began to tremble with another of his angers, shushing heart and sweating hand, lump in throat and knock in knee; indignation against common misfortune and against fate, his individually, Greece's, and the rest of the world's for that matter, everyone's, even this German's as an individual.

Meanwhile this German said, "You have no idea, Helianos—you don't know anything about it, you don't understand anything—but listen: I am so weary of the war! When we suffer too much, we get too sensitive to the suffering of other people, even though we know that their suffering is nothing like our own. I can't fight any more. All I want in the world is to listen to music; to sit listening and remembering, remembering my martyred wife and my heroic boys; to pass the time, the rest of my time. I know, of course, after the war everyone will feel like this for a while. But I can't wait, I am in hell, hell on earth, I won't wait."

He paused for a moment, covering his face with his hands, then uncovering it and twisting it down like a tragic mask, clenching his hands and giving little strokes in the air before him; striving either to control his feeling or to enact it physically—Helianos could not tell which.

Then he said, "Seven weeks ago; two months will have passed in less than a fortnight; it was on a Saturday. The hour coming round every afternoon, and the day of the week, and the date of the month; and it has been worse for me every minute. God, I've behaved well, I've been good, going on at headquarters, letting everything else slide, treating you so well, just trying to pass the time, talking, talking! I know the minute, sixteen minutes before three, when it comes. Always an anniversary, every hour is a year long. Always in my mind, a huge horrible clock striking!"

Having said this, he sat in absolute immobility and in silence, and shed tears again. It was a strange thing to watch; it was so imperturbable. Suddenly his face all twisted into the ugliness of grief, and not one muscle in it moved after that; only the tear-ducts were alive and active, and his tears were not drops but a little inundation down his cheeks, all the way down to his chin. It was like seeing sculpture weep, not Greek sculpture of course; Gothic sculpture...

He was facing the window, and the bright light caught the scar and the scar-like mouth, emphasized the asymmetry of the nose, showed up the deep lines and hollowed-out places in his cheeks, where the hand of the sculptor had slipped.

Whereupon that sculpture was moved to say something more but for a moment was unable to, with every muscle straining and straightening it into shape; then said, "Helianos, listen, the reason I have been making my will, the reason you see me in this shameful unmanly grief, like a damned Frenchman or damned Jew...

"Listen to me: I have decided to commit suicide. I cannot go on. It isn't that I will not, I cannot. I am good for nothing now, my nerves are broken. I can think all right, as a good German should think, I can talk as I should—I made it all clear to you, the great cause of the fatherland, didn't I?—but it's no good, the emotion is dead. I cannot bear to go on living, I loathe living. It is a psychopathic condition."

This speech was all in a half-whisper, soft and hurried like someone in love, and singsong like a sick infant; and when he fell silent his grimacing and tears began again. The spring sunshine made the tears shine down his cheeks, streaky, greasy. He began shaking his head back and forth, back and forth.

"One night," he murmured or mumbled softly, "one night I fell asleep without undressing, without getting into bed. That night you forgot to bring me my hot water—oh, Helianos, you're so forgetful!—and I did not wake up until the middle of the night. That night I knew that I couldn't go on, I stopped trying; and, Helianos, I can't tell you what a relief it was when I decided it. I could have done it then, only I had to wind up my affairs all in order, to hand over my responsibilities to von Roesch and the others, gradually, so they wouldn't notice it; and to re-make my will, for the musicians."

So, so, Helianos said to himself, so one did find out the causes of things sooner or later. He wondered if his wife was in the clothes closet; if this plaint had softened now to the point where she could not hear it. Unmanly grief indeed, although not really like that of any Frenchman or Jew he happened to know. While Kalter was silent he listened for Mrs. Helianos, and could not detect the least rustle or mousy stir or creak of the floor-board. He hoped she was not there. For, as she was a creature of heart rather than head, with her own bereavement, and her own thought of suicide, this would be worse for her poor failing spirit than any amount of clever hair-raising explanation of the German purpose, the Germanized world, Germany forever. Whether it moved her to compassion or to rancor and scorn, no matter, it would upset her.

He was glad, too, that the children were not indoors, especially young Alex possessed of the devil.

To know that the German was in tears, heartbroken, would excite him so; and he might make some jubilant noise or impertinent remark or gleeful grimace which would irk poor Kalter unbearably.

It did not occur to Helianos that the threat of suicide was to be taken seriously; nevertheless the effect of it was to make the threatener more sympathetic to him. Perhaps any invocation of death or even mention of death does that. It is so universal and exalted a thing in itself...

But intermixed with his sympathy was also a certain uneasiness; as it were a slight revival of the way he used to feel in the old days, Kalter's unregenerate days. Now that the secret of his changed character was out, now that he had acknowledged and in fact dramatized his bereavement, might he not suddenly turn to some other aspect of himself, or turn back? The instant weakening of so powerful a creature, shameless avowal of a state of mind so shameful, and supererogation of death in the talk of killing himself—as if the deaths of a wife and two sons were not enough, to say nothing of the rest of the world delivered to death by German ambition!—it was all too strange for comfort; too sudden and incoherent for a Greek mind.

Still he could not think what to say. He thought himself stupid; the contemplation of grief always makes one stupid. And physical creature that he was, he still felt his rebellion against odious fate, everyone's fate, death, war; his tremor of knee and hindrance of speech. But at last he found his voice and said a very simple thing, "I am sorry, sir."

To which the major did not reply or respond even by a glance.

Then Helianos felt a stubbornness about it, and protested, determined to convince this self-absorbed sufferer that it really was so, he did pity him.

"May I tell you, Major Kalter," he went on, "I lost my son, two years ago on Mount Olympos. I can understand your unhappiness. My elder son; he was worth more than little Alex and little Leda. But I admit that it was not a great loss, compared with what you have lost."

It occurred to him with some bitter irony that he could scarcely say more than that! But in spite of bitterness his pity suddenly became quite real to him. It was as if he had tried not to feel it, not to mean it, but then did. Once more he was struck by the realization that Kalter was sincere, sincere at least in his suffering, sincere at last; therefore so was he.

Still, Kalter did not answer. Only his wet eyes seemed to dry up enough to focus on him; and they appeared to be ordinary humane grief-stricken eyes, like anyone else's, Helianos thought, not fierce or unfriendly; and he hung his head, he shook his hanging head as if in an effort to listen; and he began hunting in his uniform for a handkerchief. Helianos felt that his sympathy had been accepted.

"Oh, Major Kalter," he exclaimed, really meaning no harm, thinking out loud, "is it not intolerable? To think that two men, two men with too much power, fatal tragic men, should have brought all this tragedy upon us other men?"

Major Kalter's head jerked up to attention. "Two

men? What do you mean?" he demanded. "What two men?"

"I mean the Fuehrer and the Duce," Helianos answered, without stopping to think.

That was his undoing. Major Kalter sprang to his feet and stumbled over to him, in a worse rage than ever before. Helianos too sprang to his feet and tried to get away but he was not quick enough.

"How dare you, you vile Greek," the major shouted, "how dare you say a word against the Fuehrer!" And he struck the vile Greek in the face, first one side, then the other side; resounding slaps.

"You stupid subnormal brute, filthy Slav! Defy the Fuehrer, will you? Sneer at the Italians, will you?"

And this time the look of shock and mortification, the Greek mouth gaping open, the Greek eyes puckered out of sight, did not satisfy him. This time he followed him, drove him stumbling back step by step across the room, and knocked him hard against the wall, and kicked him, with imprecations—damned coward, treacherous animal, cheating bootlicking old sick thing, sickening old fool—and all the while Helianos kept trying to apologize and he continued shouting, damning him, and accusing him of things.

"We'll pound it out of you, the nonsense! Damn you, damn you! You'll not speak of the Fuehrer again, we'll fix you," he threatened, with untranslatable curse-words, at the top of his voice; his voice breaking on the top-notes, in the worst insults and worst threats.

Away in the kitchen, meanwhile, Mrs. Helianos had heard the first shout and come scurrying to her post in the clothes closet; and there beneath the clothes and amid the shoes, when the slaps and kicks began, she began to weep, reaching up and drawing the hem of one of her dresses and the cuff of a pair of Helianos' trousers over her face, to muffle the sound of her weeping. Thus she heard all the major's insults, from which she gathered that Helianos had said something insulting about the German chief of state; the major alluded to it in every other shout.

"Whatever possessed Helianos, oh, whatever possessed him!" she cried, as softly as she could. "I warned him, what madness, whatever shall I do!" she lamented, stuffing the hem of a dress into her mouth to hush her cries, in order to hear more.

Then the major somewhat relaxed his angry effort, and the woman in the clothes closet heard her husband's softer voice apologizing, in unutterable regret and confusion; her husband sobbing softly and hiccoughing, stumbling away and sinking into a chair and still apologizing, which was heartbreaking for her to hear, shameful to hear.

And from what Helianos said—still, by way of apology, offering his vain condolences—she gathered that the major's wife and two sons were dead. It explained the German sadness and gentleness all month, which Helianos, poor accursed mortal, had so tormented himself to understand; it made the German violence of the moment more beastly. The major himself alluded to it in his diminishing shouts; his very natural sorrow for himself resuming at the end of his anger. . .

His shouts and his blows abated suddenly. His voice sounded normal, perhaps even quieter than usual, but still clear and with a little regular official martial rhythm, saying, "You poor rascally old Greek, I thought you were more intelligent than the others. I thought you knew better than this. You know what comes next, I presume. I now telephone the military police to come here and take you in custody."

He paused a while, to let that sink in, then said, quieter still, "I am sorry for you, you fool, but it cannot be helped. It is what has to be done in such a case."

Mrs. Helianos, in the clothes closet, hearing this, trembled so that it seemed impossible to get to her feet. She crawled out into the children's room on her hands and knees, and there quickly gathered strength, and hastened down the corridor, in despair but in hope; hope of preventing Helianos' arrest somehow, by protesting, arguing, imploring.

But when she reached the sitting-room door it opened, and there stood the major with his pistol drawn, pointed not at her but sideways at Helianos; and he snapped at her, "You unfortunate woman, your husband is under arrest. Go away!"

He slammed the door and locked it. There she stood a moment twisting the doorknob, pressing against the door, and through it she heard him repeat, still in the calm but percussive voice, the marching little rhythm, "Sorry, it must be, you're a fool, it's my duty..."

Then she hastened back to the clothes closet, knelt again and heard him quietly and concisely telephoning, and could not endure it. She stood up, and got her head entangled in the coats and skirts, which came down with a clatter of a couple of coat-hangers; and as she came through the children's room she caught a glimpse of herself in the mirror in that accidental, incongruous garb, like a madwoman, veiled with a petticoat, cloaked with trousers. She felt faint, and as fast as possible crept to her bed in the kitchen, shedding the old clothes behind her, and in her impatience, afraid of fainting away before she got there, tearing the bodice of her dress down off one shoulder as well.

She did not faint away; but her heart was so sick that she could only lie still, helpless, a long time— sweating and salivating, wringing her hands, biting her fingertips, listening to her blood ceasing, and starting again with a little thunder, and ceasing again —until after the soldiers had come and gone with Helianos, until Alex and Leda returned from wherever they had been all this time.

They came up the stairway from the street just as Helianos went down, between two soldiers—young, impassive, even good-natured fellows, for whom this was all in the day's work—followed half a flight up by Major Kalter, formal and portentous. The children saw their father before he saw them; instantly sensed what the escort of Germans meant; and turned and fled back down to the street.

Thus the last Helianos saw of them was their springing, skipping, fleeing away two steps at a time, as if they were afraid of him. He called after them, "Wait, your mother is ill! Alex, Leda, your mother has had a heart attack. Go and get the doctor for your mother!"

11.

THOUGH ALEX HAD NOT DARED TO TURN AND ACKNOWL-
edge his father's last instruction, he had heard it. To
be quick about it, to run all the way to the doctor's
and back, his problem was what to do with Leda in
the meantime, where to leave Leda. The street-corner
would not do, the vacant lot where they played would
not do. She shrank from passers-by, and when by herself, was apt to be panic-stricken if she had any sort of
open space around her or distance stretching away
before her. She preferred enclosures and hiding-places
and shadows.

Then Alex remembered a quiet shadowy place, adjacent to their playground, where they sometimes
took refuge in the middle of the day when it was hot;
and where they went for their loneliest games on certain of Leda's bad days when she did not care to play
with other children, or other children did not care to
play with her. It was in a portion of the masonry of a
fallen building; an empty door-frame in a tumbledown wall with half a stairway up inside it and a little
caved-in cellar underneath, which made a kind of
nook. It was a place Leda liked.

He led her there by the hand and seated her in it,
blinking and mystified; and he explained what he had

to do and how soon he would come back to her. But twice she climbed out, and came running down the street after him, whimpering his name. Twice he re-seated her, and as it were hypnotizing her with the fiery eyes she loved, stamping his foot, and chattering at her like a worried little monkey or a vexed bird, tried to persuade her. Then he gave her a great stick to hold, to defend herself with, as he told her; and that seemed to reconcile her to being left. Her appearance in the odd niche of broken plaster and stone pleased him: her confused head crowned with her shaggy black locks, and the way she bore the stick formally before her like a scepter. Although his heart was heavy with his father's peril and his mother's illness, he gave a little laugh at her to show his admiration, and that pleased her.

Then he ran, and fortunately found the family physician's daughter in his office; and she knew where he had gone, and promised to go after him and send him to the Helianos apartment before long.

Leda was waiting in the ruin when Alex returned to her, but not happy. Before he got over the fence and around the broken wall where he could see her, he heard her murmuring his name, "Alex, Alex, Alex." She was standing up in the niche, facing into it with her forehead and her hands pressed against the plaster, the way sleepwalkers do when they have strayed into a corner or behind a door.

Then they returned to the apartment, and because their mother seemed extremely ill, Alex refrained from talking and Leda from weeping.

The doctor followed shortly, and although he did

not have the requisite medicines, his visit did Mrs. Helianos good, and she fell asleep and slept the night through, in exhaustion. That night the major did not return until midnight, and he arose early next morning and slipped out without their seeing him, without any breakfast.

Mrs. Helianos was obliged to stay in bed several days, with the children waiting on her; Kalter taking his meals somewhere in town. He came to the kitchen to see her on the second day. His temper had passed as if it had never been, as if he had forgotten it. In a grave, correct manner he expressed his good will toward her and his concern for her recovery.

What little he had to say about Helianos seemed to her encouraging; at any rate it was not ill-tempered, or calamitously prophetic, or overtly vengeful. "You know, Mrs. Helianos, do you not? that your husband spoke to me in the most defiant manner, about the German chief of state and about our allies, in insulting terms. As you are a far from stupid woman, you understand that this could not go unpunished. Now a rigorous investigation of him, and all his friends and family, will be necessary.

"But for yourself, Mrs. Helianos, do not be alarmed. You will not be blamed for his folly. Be patient," he added, "and if he is reasonable, perhaps it will all be over before long."

Mrs. Helianos' eyes were bright with hatred, her dry lips whetting one another, her body restless with hatred shaking the old kitchen-cot. The major took no notice of any of this. Actually it was somewhat superficial emotion; it did not cause her to have a serious heart attack. The shock of her husband's arrest had brought its own remedy for the time being, a kind of reduction of body and soul: not enough energy for real hatred or grief or fear; only poor wandering thoughts, a stupid optimism, and a loneliness so absolute that it did not even evoke lost Helianos in her mind very clearly. It seemed a good thing to stay in bed and have a rest.

She was optimistic but not really stupid. With that little intuition of motive, slightly cynical, which is in women more than men, she sensed that the alternative of having to eat in restaurants or looking for another place to live, another family to live with, worried the German; and therefore at this point, with her illness, he genuinely regretted the arrest of Helianos. She thought how to take advantage of this, and made a plan, a little womanly plan: she would get well as quickly as possible, and work hard to make him more comfortable than ever; then fall ill again, or threaten to fall ill. This might stimulate him to have Helianos released as promptly as possible, for his own sake.

He sent a German doctor to see her on the third day. Because he came unexpectedly and in uniform, frightening her, he found her heart in its disturbed condition, and to please Major Kalter took her case seriously. He was a sad gruff little man; but he had a valiseful of medicines, and he impressed her with his air of science, and she liked him. It was the first time in her life she had ever really liked a German; now that it was too late, now that, in her poor natural womanly opinion, for good reason, they were all hateful! . . Among other remedies he gave her certain pills

[139]

to counteract undernourishment, and admonished her not to waste them on her children, but smiled kindly when he saw by her expression that she meant to disobey him in this particular; which in fact she did.

Then she got up and resumed her life and house-work and motherhood more or less as usual. The hard work, without Helianos' help, with all the tasks neg-lected during her illness, and her little plan of influ-encing the major by good housekeeping, and especi-ally the care of the children—more troublesome than ever—these things were Mrs. Helianos' salvation for the time being; keeping her from thinking, grieving, or even hoping. Leda was having a little new sort of weeping fit daily or every other day, sinking to the floor with her arms crossed over her face, and every breath a tiny moan almost inaudible. Alex had re-verted to all his former wildness, Germanophobia and melodramatic fancies. He apparently took the darkest possible view of his father's situation, and he would talk to his sorrowful sister about it, sometimes with an excitement verging upon enjoyment, exaltation; for which at last his mother felt obliged to scold him severely.

A day passed, two days, and a part of the time Mrs. Helianos too felt a kind of exaltation, stoicism, and indeed a saving sense of humor. One morning, almost midday, alone in the apartment, she stood at her kitchen-window, looking out in the direction of the Acropolis. She could not remember when she had last looked; perhaps not once in the entire year of the major's lodging with them. So long as she tried to do her housework as he expected and Helianos recommended, she had had no leisure for any such thing. Her plan of influencing Kalter was failing, she thought; he was too tired and sad to notice, grieving for his dead wife and sons. She fancied that he was lonelier than ever now, without Helianos to keep him company; perhaps that would influence him.

In any case, now, a fig for housework! she said to herself. Powerful evil lodger and dear foolish husband had no more mastery over her. Now for a few minutes, until the children came home for their midday crust of bread, she would relax and loiter and look out over the rooftops of Athens all she liked.

In spite of her narrow mind and emotional intensity, Mrs. Helianos was not the simple, Balkan type of Greek woman; not at all. She sometimes reminded herself of this distinction, proudly. She had European culture enough to know in what esteem ancient Greece, ancient Athens, was held everywhere; how everyone in the world was indebted to it for something, and acknowledged the indebtedness. Up there, over modern Athens, there it stood: the chief national treasure that foreign sightseers by the thousand (including Germans) came to see—Parthenon on Acropolis; a building that no amount of warfare had been able to obliterate so far, in the cloudless blue, on the timeless rock that even the might of the Germans could not alter; remnant of past upon portion of eternity. Looking at it inspired in her a certain grandiloquence and blissful stubbornness.

Then as she stood and looked, she assumed an attitude which in physical sensation corresponded to her thought, her spirit. It was an attitude prompted perhaps by unconscious memory of ancient sculpture that she had seen all her life (although without caring for it especially), or perhaps merely exemplifying a racial habit of body from which that style of sculpture derived in the first place—a classical attitude: her fatigued thickened torso drawn up straight from her heels and from her pelvis; her head settled back on her fat but still straight neck, her soiled, spoiled hands lifted to her loose bosom, through which went just then a little of the bad thrill of her palpitations, anginal pain like the stitches of an infinitely strong and invisible seamstress.

"One of the Fates," she said to herself aloud, "the frightful trio;" but she did not mind the thought. The time of not minding her personal destiny had come.

The minutes passed, she was still looking up at it: the citadel in ruins and the empty temples, the one like a vast box with a broken lid and the other smaller, less broken behind it; bright stone, although it was not pure white; the desiccated flat-topped hill which served as their platform or pedestal, with its steep slope darkling even at this time of day in the sunshine; and all around and far beyond, other hilltops and other slopes—because they were her homeland, she could conjure them up, even those out of sight—the large embracing forms of Greece as a whole with the sunshine sliding over them, rousing the extreme summer in them, and casting pale purple reflections.

In the old days it had been Helianos' pleasure to go

up there on Saturday or Sunday afternoons in winter when the wind was not too piercing, or after the evening meal in summer, to stroll about and clamber up and down, in general admiration. He had always taken her and the children along, because he liked to express himself and felt the need of an audience. She had never exactly shared his enthusiasm for the stony, vertiginous site or for the bare broken old edifices themselves. It had vexed her to see a monument so glorious in men's minds left in such dilapidation— how futile and unreal men's minds were, and how they talked and talked!—but she had listened to everything Helianos had to say, patiently, more or less agreeingly, as a wife should do.

She remembered his telling her that he wished it had acres of olive-orchard around it, to furnish it with a garment of the interweaving, wavering branches from top to bottom, just as the human body is furnished with its sensitive nerves and infinite little blood-vessels from head to foot; and the ground all the way up strewn with the mouth-puckering fruit; and the air oily in one's nostrils; and even on top against the sky, the summit and the temples themselves clouded with the pale thin lively foliage, flickering, like an unreal thing, like moonlight in the midst of the sunlight.

Mrs. Helianos wondered how his olive-orchard could have flourished upon that seamed and blasted summit. Had there been a soft bosom of earth up there, lifted to the sky, once upon a time? With her somewhat disrespectful although loving mind, she occasionally thought that Helianos' knowledge of the past was not all he pretended, or that he made things up.

Anyway, now, she preferred the great summit as it was, naked. Nothing but rock, rock, with no nerves, and no flesh on its bones, no soft vulnerable bosom, and no veins or arteries. It seemed more appropriate to 1943 as it was; an omen, a good omen, as good an omen as one could expect in 1943 in Greece. The worst having happened to it for centuries, still there it stood! It was a small comfort, but Mrs. Helianos took comfort in it.

She remembered other things Helianos had told her. Somehow her loneliness for him touched a part of her mind which had absorbed long passages of his talk like a blotter, almost word for word; even things she had not understood one word of at the time, such as the dark pre-historic mode of life and cruel mythology, and bygone foregone philosophies. His theory of ancient Greek architecture, for example; that old temple of Athena vacated and broken open against the sky over Athens especially. It had a more human character than any other architecture, he told her. That was the beauty of it, in his opinion: a kind of comfortableness to human mind and human eye.

"They made it to fit us," he said, "the way a chair or a bed fits when one is tired. The way a man's embrace fits the soft woman he is embracing; do you remember, when we were young? The way a mother's arm fits her child's weakness, and her breast fits the greedy mouth; do you remember, when the children were babies?"

[144]

She used to laugh at him when he talked like that, and chide him, and not admit remembering any such thing. But now, prompted by loneliness, with the memory of his voice as distinct in her mind as it ever had been in her ear, she remembered.

"But, you know, beauty is not only sentiment," he said, "it is mathematics and psychology. It is because the sight of the Parthenon matches the experience of our other senses, and our other sentiments; everything enters into it. We see its proportion, and at the same time we feel the proportion of our own bodies, and it corresponds; and therefore our eyes enjoy themselves, just as when we are dancing our feet enjoy the music.

"In a dance we feel the sound, we hear the motion; and architecture, our Greek architecture, is like that. Looking at it, even from a distance, we respond to it as if we were touching it, because, by similitude and ratio—ratio is a wonderful thing!—it intensifies our awareness of every part of ourselves touching every other part."

"Ratio is a wonderful thing" was one of his favorite sayings; he would raise his soft voice in a louder exclamation upon that than anything else. His discourses on architecture were always the least comprehensible, the ones Mrs. Helianos felt most inclined to laugh at. On the other hand, he most enjoyed delivering them, with special illumination of his fine eyes, slow choice of his abstruse words, vibrant utterance of the best phrases; and she had never laughed in fact.

Their dead son Cimon had also loved hearing his father talk, but as he had confided to his mother one day, it was on account of the brightness of eye and the dear voice and the charm of rhetoric; he understood no better than she did. They used to joke about his always saying "we"—"we feel and we respond and we believe"—when they scarcely knew what he was talking about. There had been a fond tacit agreement between her and Cimon; good-natured Cimon, gentle as a woman. He had loved her best, and he would sometimes say, "You are the intelligent one, Mother. In Father it is education and eloquence."

No, she thought now, doubtless Helianos was right about everything; and perhaps as a natural woman no stupider than another, she had felt all these things, as he said it was human nature to feel them, as he expected her to. Perhaps what made it all obscure and nonsensical for her was not what he said but the way he said it, as if he intended to sweep her off her feet rather than to explain anything in earnest. Whether or not architecture danced, certainly, this way and that, his phrases did.

Or perhaps it was nonsense: a mere man's make-believe, typical of men; a kind of game that the idle, over-educated male brain played for the fun of it.

No matter now! For remembering it now gave her a sense of importance and intellectual outlook, which was the pleasantest thing left in the world for her, the only remarkable part of her life left. Was it not remarkable, she exclaimed to herself, in a great agreeable agitation of spirit, for an ordinary woman of Athens, in circumstances like hers—a woman with nothing to look forward to, defeated and bereft, weary and unkempt, fat although famished, ailing, with heart-trouble, aching from head to foot, hot and sweaty and dirty—to have in spite of everything a mind full of abstruse luxurious words, resounding in memory: her dear husband having uttered them long ago?

For a moment the little vanity of intellect charmed her, as if around the self-conscious unfortunate dark figure of herself, the kitchen-window had developed larger, with a finer ratio of height to width than it had in fact; and a sweeter breath of air than the actual exhalation of the accursed Athenian streets; and a better heat than the midday. Then with a sigh she turned around to her dirty kitchen and patiently resumed her work.

That night she lay awake on the kitchen-cot—almost comfortable, now that her dear stout man was not on it with her, comfortable and terrible—trying to think what she ought to be doing about him, to get him out of prison. He had been in prison more than a week. In the first few days she had done her weeping, palpitating, fainting; then for a day or two she had been like an empty shell, thoughtless and helpless; and now another day spent, in the recollection of what a fine man he was and what great obscure profound things he said. Tomorrow would be the seventh, no, the eighth day, and she felt capable of doing something, if only she could think what to do.

Should she go and explain to the Germans that her Helianos was a good law-abiding man, not at all like his cousins of the same name; a man who had yielded to fact and to force and to fate, not only of late as the German yoke obliged him to do, but all his life, according to his nature; a harmless, learned, but on the whole foolish man, past his prime furthermore and not worth the trouble of their indictment and trial; and a good servant, houseman and valet, trained by Major Kalter, who (if Major Kalter no longer wanted him) would know how to make some other German officer comfortable? It was true enough. But she had grown too proud to say it, too proud or too passive or too something.

Perhaps, she thought, in a bitter moment of self-criticism, turning her aching head from one limit of the old cot to the other, worrying the pillow with her fists, beginning to fall asleep—ashamed to sleep while Helianos lay in prison—perhaps she had grown too lazy! She did not admit to herself that she was growing hopeless.

Another thing she did not do: she did not think of her brother or make any plan of trying to discover where he was, and if he was in touch with the Germans, appealing to him to help Helianos. Because Helianos disliked him so, she really had decided to think of him as dead. He appeared to her in vague dreams but when she awoke she interpreted them as having been about someone else.

She woke with a start, with another question for herself. Should she go and see the Helianos cousins and ask them to help? Though doubtless they despised her husband—angry conceited quixotic heroic men that they were—they might help, blood being thicker than water. But the very thought of them made her shiver. Probably by this time they had been driven to illegal and even criminal violence, wild miscellaneous destruction by bombing and burning, even assassination, for their good cause. It was the way of the underground, as Helianos had admitted to her long ago in spite of his family affection. She heard the shocking rumors herself, now that she had to go out and mingle with other Athenians, marketing. They scarcely shocked her any more.

Now there was a worse rumor, to the effect that with one anger leading to another, the men of the underground were beginning to quarrel among themselves. She blamed the Germans for this. One night in the clothes closet she had heard Kalter warning Helianos that they intended this to happen... In any case the fighting Helianos' could not help her peaceful innocent one in his present plight, accidental incarceration. If any of them, or anyone like them, were to be mixed up in his case, that would be the end of him. It would only prove to the Germans that he was an angry quixotic heroic man too, who deserved his arrest and imprisonment, and worse: so much worse that the thought of it shook her and the kitchen-cot trembled under her.

Whereas, as things stood, she assured herself, she had no reason to think that in a day or two the Germans would not release Helianos and let him come home. It would make them ridiculous in their own eyes if they did not. But what if they did not? What if he never came home? With sudden pangs through and through her unhealthy bosom, fear would pass through her mind, very real, but passing quickly, taking some semblance of outer reality: gloomy wraith of the midnight, evil odor of the kitchen-bedroom. She shook her head and blinked at it, and it was not there. She blew her nose, turned her pillow over, drew the coverlet up over her head, and ceased to sense it.

It was ridiculous. The conquering Germans were not gods, were they? to stop and do things for no reason, merely to astonish mankind, to make a good story. They wanted their great conquest to last and to work, didn't they? and if they made ridiculous mistakes such as misunderstanding a man like Helianos, arresting poor men for the slips of their tongues, nothing would come of it!

Thus her optimistic imagination arose once more, then merged into a dream, then woke again with a start; but waking or sleeping, thinking or dreaming, told her what she wanted to think, for one more night.

12.

Another day or two passed. Often her imagination worked the other way, not for her but against her; not in self-deception but demoralized and uncontrollable. There came a midday when, standing and resting at the kitchen-window, she could think of nothing but the ugliest matters of fact in the painful present tense. Her mind could not, or would not, take refuge in any remembrance of the past, and it had no capacity for the future.

What had she, outworn and ailing, to do with the time to come? The only time she minded was the day or two, or the week or two, she still had to wait for her Helianos to come home. What had she ever understood of the past, ancient history, Hellas? Nothing, nothing except a pretended interest for his sake. The past was his hobby, and his weakness, she thought, half spitefully, with nervousness increasing and increasing; and apart from his poor dear sentimentality and pretensions to scholarship, what did it amount to? Tumbledown temples, dead religion, obscure dramaturgy, foolishness and cruelty of myths. The myths of today, as she remembered his saying, were worse.

No help for it, no refuge from it: her Hellas was contemporary Athens, and what did that amount to, what had it been reduced to? Dust, stench, fatigue, disgust, fright, constant fright, and beggars and cadavers. She was unable to think of anything else to think about, worth thinking about. The worst of it was what was happening to the children. How much better off her wild one and her subnormal one were than the average child! They were not a really poor family. How fortunate they were in having a German major living with them! Therefore as regularly as clockwork every day of their lives they had something to eat. They did not have to depend on the Red Cross.

The Red Cross did not have milk enough or medicine enough to go around; therefore their policy had to be to select the healthiest child in each poor family, and concentrate on it, the child most likely to survive. Therefore in the really poor families you saw an unprecedented injustice and inequality: one lucky chosen child, amid brothers and sisters with abysmal eyes, loose distended stomachs, lank arms and legs, drying up and dying. It could not be helped. They could not afford to waste anything on the unchosen. The rumor was that they preferred girls, because after the war one male might serve several of them, to repopulate the country.

There had been a strange poor woman standing in a queue in the market place ahead of Mrs. Helianos that morning. A second poor woman had come and jostled her out of her turn; and she had tried to drive her away with imprecations, but suddenly changed her mind and controlled herself and stood back humbly, explaining to everyone within earshot that she never jostled nor even permitted herself to get angry when others jostled her, because she was a religious woman.

She was young but old-looking and might have been a gypsy, with unsympathetic lurking eyes, and dark skin drawn so leanly over her nose and cheekbones that it was like copper. She wore a ragged dark scarf, in antique fashion: not over her forehead but draped from the top of her head loosely down the side of her face away from her cheeks, and gathered up and pinned on one shoulder, with a sharpened stick instead of a pin.

"I am a religious woman. I pray, every day, for my little children doomed to die," she had said, turning around and addressing Mrs. Helianos. "I pray for them to die faster."

Mrs. Helianos had expressed her sympathy and rebuked her not unkindly for her desperation.

To which the woman had answered that death was the only prospect that seemed to her probable enough to be worth praying for.

She had spoken in a cracked voice, in oracular manner, staring away into space this way and that, forgetting Mrs. Helianos and turning her back on her.

"I have one who is not doomed," she had announced then, somewhat more cheerfully, to no one, to the space in front of her, "my younger son, who gets milk and medicine from the Red Cross. He is a tough little thing, a fighter, he does not need praying for."

Then she had fallen silent and concentrated on her marketing until she got it done. But evidently remembering Mrs. Helianos' word of sympathy, she had

[153]

come back with her little purchase to show it to her, having had better luck than usual.

"You know, it's a nuisance when I have luck, when I find something fit to eat," she had said, "because then I have to feed my Red Cross son separately, because he is so much stronger than his elder brother and sister; he takes more than his share."

With that dread of the future which is peculiar to mothers, which is sometimes the only imagination they have, Mrs. Helianos asked herself: what will they be like as mature men and women, these tough ones, the milk-drinkers and vitamin-eaters, whom a terrible favoritism and fratricidal appetite have kept from starving? It was the survival of the fittest in the worst way in the world. But they had no choice in the matter, the Red Cross had no choice, Greece had no choice. A little new generation had to be brought up like this, a minority of little murderous pigs at the Red Cross trough, little wolves fattened upon carcass of wolf—or else there would be no new generation at all, no more Greeks.

Meanwhile, Mrs. Helianos reflected, the men and women of her own generation finished out their lives as best they could: good Greeks becoming slaves, and brave Greeks, outlaws and firebugs and bomb-throwers and assassins. Helianos was the only man in Athens, so far as Mrs. Helianos knew, who had been able to steer a middle course; and now like a pack of fools they had arrested him, even him!

However, in a day or two they would have disciplined and investigated and reprimanded him to their hearts' content; then they would release him.

Poor soft aging man, it was an extreme hardship for him. Fortunately, he was no longer unaccustomed to hardship. He would get over it; there was nothing really tragic about it, as tragedies in Greece in 1943 went; it would soon be over: so Mrs. Helianos insisted to herself, keeping up her courage. Nevertheless she would hate the Germans for it all the rest of her life.

It was often at the back of her mind, hatred: something she had never experienced before, something mumbling and snarling and talking to itself—it was her own mind of course, one half of her mind; she herself was thinking what it said but it seemed distinct from the rest of her thought, at a little distance from the rest but louder than the rest, and it went on incessantly, and she could scarcely keep up with it or exactly understand it. It was an indictment of the Germans not only for what they did, had done, were doing, but for what they were, and even for the way they looked.

The *Herrenvolk*, the hateful half of her mind said —it was full of German words, the words of the clothes closet, Kalter's big words reiterated like incantation, plugged into her mind by his hammering tone of voice through the partition—the *Herrenvolk* had strong jaws because they kept gritting their teeth, and somewhat shapeless and chapped mouths because they kept licking their lips. Their sharp noses were not exactly centered in their pink faces between their flat cheeks. Their small blue eyes were not in the least like a pig's but they were like some other small animal's. The smallness of their eyes would have given

[155]

their countenances as a whole a melancholy and humble aspect except for the glory and cruelty shining and snapping in them. Look out for glory and cruelty, *Achtung,* look out! the wild half of her mind said.

It filled her memory up with hateful details, such as the busy way their jaws and lips and tongues worked when they were eating, and the way they mouthed and jawed their words in eloquence whenever they expounded their world-government, *Weltanschauung,* or boasted of their superiority in warfare, *Wehrmacht,* or made pathetic reference to their hard vain fate, *Schicksal,* or thrilled to their German immortality, *Ewigkeit.* Which for a weird moment made her think of strangling one of them. Her hands rose in front of her as if it were a reflex action, the fingers rigidly curving and the thumbs rigidly hooked, straining like a pair of pincers; and she looked down at them and was disgusted at their small violent energy wasted on the empty air.

It led her to make foolish observations of traits of the national German character, such as their wish to be feared and loved at the same time (and they were, too) and their determination to be scientific and mystical at the same time (and they were, they succeeded).

It deluded her senses with unpleasant impressions, such as their peculiar body-odor, a whiff of it at the moment even there at the open kitchen-window, Kalter's body-odor; and whereas in the old days Evridiki's body-odor in the kitchen had been musky, his now was lardy, and it made her sick.

It gave her a certain morbid contaminated feeling; so that she turned away from the window and went to the sink, and wet her nervous hands and her hot face, and rubbed and scrubbed them exaggeratedly. Then as she had only a few towels for the children, she went back to the sunny window and held her head back and her fingers spread out, to dry in the sun. The lardy smell was still in her nostrils and she still felt sick.

Actually of course it was not the Germans in general or Kalter in particular that sickened her, for none of this was a reality; she knew that. What sickened her was her own hatred, and weariness of being dominated and reminded and misled and disgusted and made a fool of by hatred; and it was all so foolish and childish, and it went so fast, that she could only recall a small part of it afterward.

She tried not to let her mind go on like this. She knew what it was; it was the voice of the time we live in; "the *Zeitgeist,*" she said to herself aloud, mispronouncing the word with a hiss. Until this moment, this bitter week, she reminded herself proudly, she had been a good woman. Her mind had never prostituted itself like this before; no accursed *Geist* had ever taken her for its mouthpiece before! She was ashamed of it and afraid of it. She preferred the passivity, the self-pity, which was her ordinary mood. She thought that she preferred misfortune itself, which was at any rate a real thing; whereas this hateful voice of one-half her mind sounded mad, and it was against her will. When it rose to its high pitch, she could not repress it, she had to listen to it, her whole heart joined in it.

And her heart also reacted and rebelled, in revulsion against it, with almost the reverse of it. In her fatigue, with the imaginary evil odor and imaginary contamination, the tears came to her eyes in a flood and the breath up through her mouth in a sob; and she stood weeping in the hot sunshine at her kitchen-window.

She was as ashamed of weeping as of hating. Fitful emotion, hysterical Germanophobia with the hysteria suddenly breaking, fit following fit, in fact one fit bringing on the other: it was a waste of time and energy while her Helianos lay in prison and nothing was done. Besprinkling of tears and soft bemoaning, it, too, was the *Zeitgeist!* It was another German trap and German spell, which probably everyone the world over fell into for a moment now and then. But, shaken again by indignation, drying her tears on her dirty sleeve, and trying to stop her little hiccoughing sobs by gritting her teeth and holding her breath, she resolved not to fall into it herself again. Not another tear would she shed!

What use was it? It had no influence on the imprisoner, it was harmless against the enemy, it was no hindrance to the oppressor. As it seemed to her, even Germanophobia was to the German advantage somehow. Perhaps a German like Kalter could keep that kind of temper up—against international Jews, against Asiatic Russians, against vile Greeks—but if you were a naturally good Greek woman you could not. Suddenly it broke and you were ashamed of it and it made you sick; you wept about it until you wore yourself out, in a stupor; and still Helianos lay in prison unhelped.

It was no solution. Of course as a simple emotional

woman, she did not know, or did not yet know, what solution there might be; but she felt sure that emotion was not it. Kalter was not hurt by it or even inconvenienced by it. Kalter, she thought, would not begrudge her her moment of letting herself go at her kitchen-window; he might even feel flattered by it. What if she did gibber for a few minutes in helpless animosity, what if she did whimper away the next few minutes in revulsion and confusion, did it help Helianos? As she looked back on it—looking back on it, to be sure, before it was quite over—it seemed to her that she had lost all her self-respect.

Lonely, lonely, lonely for Helianos she tried to look up to the desiccated flat-topped rock and the indestructible old temple once more, because they were what he loved—the national treasure of Greece, Athens' trademark, the tourists' delight as well as his—but as she had not yet succeeded in not weeping, they were only a phantom and a smudge; which left her lonelier than ever.

It was early in June but it was mid-summer there in the sun—the summer slid down the steep of the Acropolis, slightly green with slight purple shadows, the summer tickled her in drops of sweat on her forehead and her upper lip, the summer evaporated the shameful tears off her cheeks—and yet she was as cold as a stone. Her tedious old heart had almost ceased to circulate the blood in her veins. How long, ten or fifteen minutes (she could not tell how long), she had been standing there staring at the slightly verdant and empurpled hill without seeing it, blinded by her desperate thoughts, half-thoughts. Not only had she been weeping like a fool, she had been talking to herself out loud, and already like a fool she was forgetting what she had heard herself say.

So she turned away, with no more patience with herself, and angrily pulled the curtain across the window, and went to work in the shadowy kitchen, warming up some soup (more than half water) for the children's midday meal; then sat on the cot and dully waited for them to come up from the street. So well had they learned their lesson of enduring hunger that a good deal of the time they had not much appetite...

It was Kalter's fault. Suddenly then she remembered how when he had arrested Helianos he had locked her out of the sitting room, her own sitting room; and in a more irrational temper than ever she sprang out of the kitchen and went running and stumbling down the corridor, and took the key out of that door and brought it back to the kitchen and threw it out the window.

Her mind and her life shrinking away to this silly gesture, vain ritual and symbol, childishness! The instant it was done she was ashamed of it, and in spite of her weariness and her weary heart resolved to go down to the street after it and to put it back where it belonged. She leaned far out of the window in the hot sunshine for a long time, not knowing where it had fallen, trying to locate it on the sidewalk and the pavement, in vain, with the shadows in her eyes from the cruel blaze and the swash of blood to her head from leaning out.

The children returned from their play then, and

[160]

she was ashamed to mention the key to them, and forgot to go down after it herself.

Major Kalter rarely locked the sitting-room door. ("Only when he arrests people," as Alex said to Leda...) But the next morning by some chance he noticed the disappearance of the key and it displeased him.

Mrs. Helianos, in the kitchen, heard him in the corridor, irritably accusing Alex of having taken it to play with. At it again, the supposedly reformed character! she said to herself, with her nerves quickly contracting as if she were about to cry or to laugh. It was his bad voice, his voice like a chisel with a temper behind it like a hammer; it was insufferable!

She came out into the corridor. There was the gloomy officer facing in her direction, towering over the small boy who had his back to her. She could tell at a glance that it had begun again, their old tedious, perilous antipathy: the German's neck thrust forward and little explosive eyes, and the rigid back of Alex trying to maintain his equanimity, protesting his innocence—which for once in their lives Mrs. Helianos knew to be genuine. As she drew close to them Alex glanced hopelessly to her over his shoulder. Down at the German's side she saw his large hand agitating and beginning to come up in a fist.

In six long steps she was there, threw her arm around Alex, thrust him aside, stepped between them, and faced the major with her arms spread out, her entire person spread out, like a hen between her chick and the hawk; and for the first and last time, she addressed him with real vehemence.

"Major Kalter, Major Kalter, do not shout at Alex! What if you have lost your key? The man of the house is gone now, thanks to your fury and folly. Naturally things go wrong, things get misplaced. None of us has touched your blessed key, I tell you. If you have lost it, I am sorry, we shall find it or replace it; but meanwhile do not shout!

"Please remember, sir, that it is my property, this key you say you have lost; you shall not accuse my son of stealing it. This is my house, and I will not have any brawl or roughhouse in it, between you and Alex."

It was a fearful, freakish moment. Roused by her sharp voice, Leda came to the bedroom door panic-stricken, and tumbled over the threshold with a ghostly cry. Alex pulled away out of his mother's grasp and thrust himself back between her and Kalter, to ward off the German blow, due to strike her now if ever. Naturally she too shrank from it; even with the words on her lips she had realized that she deserved the worst that might happen.

But nothing happened. Breakdown of her common sense, fit of nerves, height of imprudence and impudence; but to her amazement it worked. She saw the German's face turn red, she saw his fist relax and go down, she saw his German authority and his manly strength hesitating and hanging in the balance for a second, and failing. He did not even say anything. He gave her a somewhat sheepish smile and turned on his heel, back into his sitting room.

As he departed Mrs. Helianos took Alex by both shoulders and turned him around, and ordered him

[162]

to pick Leda up and go for a walk with her, to be out of harm's way, and to calm her. Alex was all a-tremble; but evidently he had observed the strange surrender of the major, and perhaps with his sixth sense knew that there had been something no less questionable in his mother's outcry about the key. As he and Leda went out the front door, he turned and gave her a flashing grin from ear to ear. A few minutes later the major also departed to his headquarters with a quiet, "Good-bye, Mrs. Helianos."

It was a miracle, she said to herself. But with an ill-natured shiver she remembered how, when Kalter first came back in his bereaved and exhausted condition with a kind word for them and a little better demeanor in general, she and Helianos, fools that they were, had called that a miracle; whereupon in a new fury he had given Helianos a beating and packed him off to prison!

Well, she would not trust him now. But still, she fancied, this had a little more reality than that. A large part of that other miracle had been Helianos' bewitched and doting gentleness, and Helianos was the most charming man in the world. Whereas there had been nothing charming about her behavior: spiteful naughtiness of some little child, and dishonesty worse than any of Alex's, and the hue and cry of a common market-woman!

Upon which strange terms the force of her spirit somehow had prevailed over Kalter's tyranny and physical force. Somehow the great vile fellow's spirit really was broken, his ego undermined, his state of mind unhealthy, his energy waning. This perhaps had

[163]

been the point of his final brutality and injustice to Helianos: a last flaring up of his temper, a burning out of his evil, a kind of fierceness which took all the strength he had left. Now it was for her to pursue her little advantage. Now apparently the time had come for a change of policy and practice in what, just then, she had so proudly proclaimed to be her house. All the rest of that day she could not think of it without a slight smile.

So she resolved, from now on, to make some little scene whenever she saw the least sign of Kalter's misbehaving, a daily scene for a while if she could find pretexts enough, little by little, feeling out his weakness. Then, having saved up her energy for two or three days, having thought everything out in advance, she would stride into his sitting room, and with hysterics and histrionics, demand the liberation of Helianos! It might work; perhaps it was what the strange German was waiting for; it would work! Planning all this made her happy for two days, dreaming of Helianos' homecoming.

The episode of the key so enchanted Alex that at the sight of her, the enchantment would come on him again and he would give her the same happy grin. She did not like it. She was afraid of his feeling that her defiance of the major somehow authorized him to do likewise. Or he might guess, or perhaps he had guessed, what a shrew's part she intended to play with the crestfallen Kalter. If he should decide to take a hand in it, all would be lost!

More than this, it vexed her on her own account to have him leering at her like a fellow-conspirator or little evil genius. She was his mother, and a woman of a certain dignity, most of the time; and as it struck her, there was incongruity and mockery in this kind of boyish admiration. With all the shame and the humor of her behavior about the key, she kept an odd, intense self-respect about it. She respected the desperate nervousness which had inspired it all unconsciously, and brought it to pass.

There was a strange little test of strength between her and Alex—it was on a Friday night, the second Friday in June—as she put him and Leda to bed. There once more, once too often, was the mocking expression on his face on the pillow; and she lifted her hand, tempted to slap him. The joyousness died out of his grin but he held his lips in it stubbornly, and for a moment their glances were fixed on each other in bitter emotion, will against will; his then somewhat pathetically failing.

Even as he grimaced and she stared him down, she noticed with a little pride what perfect teeth he had. Poor little devil, with his calamitous physique, yellow-skinned, lean but soft and paunchy, with arms and legs that reminded her of sticks loosely put together with thongs—but with this one perfection, matched like a string of pearls, whiter than any pebble!

As it happened, as their lives were, in a spell and a snare around Kalter's life, this was the last occurence of her maternal bitterness against him, disappointment in him. Presently she would have to forgive him for everything, once and for all.

13.

THE NEXT DAY WAS ONE OF KALTER'S FREE DAYS, AND his presence in the apartment made Mrs. Helianos uncomfortable, irritable. He still had not made any reference to her tantrum about the key and she was afraid he might; she was not in a mood for it. He had said that he was not feeling well and declined to eat anything in the middle of the day. He had asked her to keep the children quiet, intending to sleep, but evidently he was not sleeping. She could hear him inexplicably walking around his room a while, then at his desk pulling out drawers and noisily pushing them shut again, and repeatedly clearing his throat, blowing his nose. She was so tired that she did not want to hear anything and so nervous that in spite of herself she kept listening and hearing everything.

She went to her kitchen-window once more, with her odd un-Greek notion that the midday sunshine did her good, and sank to her knees with her elbows on the window sill. She had sent the children to play outdoors, on the major's account, but they had returned for some reason. Their piping little talk came to her from the bedroom, and she wondered if she ought to go and scold them, before they disturbed the major. She could remember when with less provocation he would have shouted the house down...

Then there was a pistol shot, resounding through the apartment. She could tell by the sound exactly what part of the apartment it came from: the sitting room, his room. Just for an instant she thought that Helianos might have come back and taken his revenge; but she knew his step so well, even on tiptoe, even all the way down the corridor or at the front door she would have heard him come; therefore she instantly dismissed that thought, as she scrambled to her feet and ran out of the kitchen toward the sitting room. There was no one in the apartment except herself and the children and the major, she thought; there was no one in the sitting room where the pistol shot had come from, except the major; had she not been listening, nervously listening to everything in spite of herself? Therefore she thought she knew what had happened, she hoped it had happened, as she listened outside the sitting-room door—it was silent, not a voice, not a breath, not a footstep—and tried to see through the keyhole, in vain; then ran to the children's room.

Leda was trying to come out into the corridor, Alex was holding her back with both hands on her shoulders. Leda looked as if she had lost what small mind she had; her fleshy features out of shape and fixed in a grimace. Alex was transfigured, with his beautiful face loose and white like a handkerchief and his morbid eyes shining, and his unreasonable lips apart, panting, saying, "Mother, Mother, something has happened. Tell me, is it Father? Has Father shot him?"

"You know better than that," Mrs. Helianos answered, "your father is not here, your father is in prison. Now, listen to me, you must behave well, Alex, like a grown-up man."

She took Leda and sank into a chair, drawing the stricken infant body tight in her arms, and the pudgy face clenched like a fist against her breast; at the same time with some difficulty holding Alex by the wrist as he pulled and wriggled away from her. "Mother, let me go," he begged, struggling to free himself.

She had no notion where he was going or what he wanted. Then he drew his face down to her hand which held his wrist, and for an instant she fancied that like a little animal in a trap he was going to bite her, but instead he kissed her hand and rubbed the tears out of his eyes on her wrist. "I'm afraid, Mother," he cried, "Mother, aren't you afraid?"

No, she was not afraid, she was happy, thinking happily that there was no one in the apartment now except herself and the children. There had been no one in the major's room when the pistol shot had sounded, except the major; and therefore she kept hoping that there was no one in the major's room at all now, nothing except the major's body with the pistol shot through it; and his body, she thought almost gleefully, hysterically, was nothing to be afraid of. Her hysterical heart was throbbing faster than she had ever known it to throb, but she did not mind it because she was beginning to have confidence in what she hoped, and she could scarcely wait to go and see if it was so. But first she had to get these poor children out of the way.

Oh, she needed Helianos more than ever in her life,

and here instead she had only Alex, still holding him by the wrist: this half-Helianos, poor flesh of their flesh, small body deformed by the war, small dæmonic mind perverted! But with Helianos away in prison, in her very womanly spirit habit-bound by her relationship with him, now there was a vacancy which in these circumstances had to be filled, by someone; and it was Alex or no one!

She drew him by the wrist around where she could look at him; and looked at him as it were with strange eyes; and for a wonder, for the first time in a long time, did not mind his undersized spindling paunchy body, and was moved by his strange face—the morbid light in his eyes sparkling wet with tears, the indefinable expression of his lips, the smile that was no smile —and neither feared him nor feared for him; and decided to take him into her confidence. She had to have someone in her confidence, someone to help her, especially with Leda.

"My little boy Alex," she said softly, "I think I know what has happened. There was no one in the major's room except the major. He has shot himself, that is what I think, what I hope..."

Alex gave a soft exclamation deep in his throat, and stopped struggling, so that she did not have to hold him by the wrist any longer. The pain in her heart was not a bad pain, only a fast pain, but she was glad not to have to hold him.

"Alex, will you do something for me? Will you do as I tell you?"

"Yes, Mother, I will."

"Then, Alex..." She was trying to whisper, just in

case she was mistaken about there not being anyone else in the apartment, but when she tried to whisper no voice came at all. "This is what I want you to do. Take Leda down to the street and stay with her until this is over, until I come for you."

"No, Mother, I won't," he answered loudly. He could not whisper any better than she could.

Meanwhile Leda lay in her arms as quietly as if she had fallen asleep, with her face like a bad dream.

Then she had an inspiration about Alex. Next day she was to ask herself if it had been mere cowardice, but surely it was not so simple... There came into her mind a wave of singular pity for the vengeful little boy who had never had a chance for vengeance, and a wave of greater affection for him than she had ever felt before. In the past she had denied him her affection because his vindictive spirit displeased her; now it did not displease her. Suddenly she saw how she could compensate him for the long denial, and at the same time make use of him, for Leda's sake, to get Leda out of the way, and for her own sake: so that she could postpone everything for a moment and sit here with Leda for a moment and rest.

"Alex, do you hear me? It is for Leda's sake. You love Leda, don't you? She will never get over it if she sees what has happened."

He only stared at her, shaking his head.

"Alex, you hate Major Kalter, don't you? If I let you go by yourself, to see what has happened to him, then will you take Leda down to the street?"

"Yes, yes, please let me, Mother. I want to see what has happened," he said.

It was a cowardly inspiration in a way, cowardly
and clever. For if what she hoped for had not happened, if instead he interrupted some evil deed of the
German's, or terrible exploit of Greeks against him,
what harm? They would give him a cuff or a kick,
that would be all! They would blame him only as one
blames children, without any further suspicion; he
was too young to be blamed in earnest, or suspected
or arrested.

She grasped him by the wrist again and made him
wait. "I don't think the door is locked, I took the key
away—"

"I knew you had taken it, Mother," Alex said as
quick as a flash.

"Don't interrupt me, Alex, listen to me. Tiptoe to
the door, listen outside it, peep through the keyhole.
Open it only a crack at first, quietly, to be on the safe
side. If the major is dead or badly hurt, go in. Go as
close to him as you like and look at him.

"I will wait here. When you have seen whatever
there is to see, you can tell me about it. You can tell
Leda too, but not now! Someday, when she is old
enough..."

"Let me go now, Mother," he cried in a high painful voice which made her ashamed of herself.

"Don't touch anything," she called after him as he
scampered out of the room.

It was a wicked thing: letting him go, sending him,
and she only half understood it. It was the last effect
of her having been spoiled by Helianos all her life:
in unreasoning excitement she required someone to
do something for her. Even a semblance of help was

[171]

better than nothing; a ghostly-faced wild feeble manikin of a son better than no one. It was her nature. It occurred to her that Alex with his wild nature might be better than his father at this kind of thing; a manikin better than a man, in the circumstances.

She lifted Leda away from her bosom, looked at her, and gave her a little shake, to which she made not the slightest response, and kissed her grimacing cheeks. Perhaps the fright of the gun had done her the same harm as the massacre of the municipal market: stupefaction, mind and body. Perhaps this time it would last longer than three days; all the rest of her useless life she might be like this, like a heavy fleshy doll. With distracted tenderness, all the foolish gestures of mother-love, she fondled and rocked the hopeless small body as she might have done if she had been Leda's age, and Leda in fact a doll.

Then Alex came back. Evidently whatever he had seen had done him good; his cheeks were no longer dead white, his eyes no longer starting out of their orbits, and he had regained control of his voice. "He is dead, Mother," he announced quietly.

"I know, I thought so." She shut her eyes for an instant, imagining the proud powerful German figure fallen on the floor or down under the desk, and his evil changeable soul flying out the window with the pistol shot, whistling away, fading, in the silence after the pistol shot...

"No one was there," Alex added. "The front door was locked, the sitting-room window was latched on the inside; so no one could have been there, could any one? The sitting-room door was not locked, I went in and looked. Don't you go, Mother, please, don't you look!" he begged.

"Very well, I won't. Now take Leda, as you promised..."

Then he drew himself up as tall as he could and with an expression of obscure old drama, said, "I killed him, Mother."

"No, you did not, Alex. Remember, now you are a grown-up boy, you must not tell lies."

"I know, Mother. Don't scold me," he said. He started to cry but quivering in every nerve, stopped it.

"Now take Leda. If she can't walk, or doesn't want to, you'll have to carry her. Don't stay in front of our door, go away down the street, because the Germans are coming. Take care of Leda, play with her, talk to her, tell her anything you like, but not what you have seen.

"I won't be long. I must telephone the Germans to come and get him."

Leda could and did walk, very softly, as if in her sleep, clutching her brother's hand. For an instant, as Mrs. Helianos followed them down the corridor, watched them down the stairway, bolted the front door after them, her tired spirit lost its sense of direction: she felt some of the emotion of not expecting ever to see them again.

Then she wanted to see Helianos so badly, and needed his advice and help so badly, that she gave a little whimper, but in the empty apartment the sound of it distressed her, so she hushed. It was no time for sentiment. It was time she did something about getting the major's body out of the apartment, unadvised and unhelped. She had been given hard tasks and shameful tasks since the Germans came to Greece; this was the worst.

Alex had closed the sitting-room door, so she could put if off a few more minutes if she chose to. By that time the jerky unwilling beating of her heart had begun to frighten her, but gradually, as it seemed by exercise of will power, she was able to control it. "It is God's mercy," she said to herself out loud, "I am not going to have a heart attack."

She stood there in the corridor holding her breath, conscious of the seconds, the minutes, wasting them, pretending to concentrate on what had to be done. "Thank God," she said, "for the major's telephone." It was there in the closed sitting room with his body.

Once more her absurd voice in the still apartment making these remarks to herself, distressed her. This habit of talking to herself had been one of her reasons for fearing that someday she might lose her mind. Now she realized what self-indulgence that fear was; what spoiled hypochondria! In fact, all things considered, even in this tragic farce which had come upon her, she marveled at what good sense she had, and quietness of brain, even amid her habitual chatter.

Then, when she kept quiet, hearing only her own heartbeat—gradually beating better, though with a wet beat, as it were a sodden squeeze—it was fantastic, it was a little world in which everyone else was dead; and the silence, and absolute loneliness without the children, without Helianos, without even the major, half distressed her but half pleased her.

She went back to the kitchen and looked out the window; leaned far out, and saw Alex and Leda a little way down the street walking up and down, talking: the brave small boy pulling the automatic little girl along by the hand, and doing all the talking, telling her some long but apparently not terrible story, not the truth. Leda was walking not quite straight forward, with her fond face turned sideways toward him.

She felt, just then, a pang or a twinge of suicide; the merest hint to herself that it would be agreeable, suitable, to fall down out of the window and lie there face-down on the sidewalk forever. For there around her in the kitchen she noticed the slight stench, as of death—actually it was the bad food she had been cooking, the soiled folding cot, her own neglected body, her old clothes—whereas the breeze brought from outside a whiff of sweet smoke exhaled by someone's chimney, and a scent of wild herbs from some hill on the outskirts of town.

It was life, on the one hand, there inside the kitchen and behind her back, her life, deadly and disgusting; to say nothing of the corpse in the sitting room to be looked at and looked after. It was death, on the other hand, out the window in the sweet air and down on the sunny street, lively and attractive death! Things were in reverse; and her mind got mixed up for a moment: change of the metabolism of the mind which indeed is one of the causes of suicide. Furthermore one suicide may somewhat prompt another.

But in her mind it actually amounted to nothing;

it was just a possibility, and a self-indulgent idle game of her imagination in danger. For, in so far as she could tell in the confusion, the mad things done and the maddening things to do, she was happy. Everyone was not dead, far from it. Helianos would be back now before long. For only his enemy was dead; blissful good fortune! Now there would be no one to testify to what he had said when his tongue slipped.

So she turned away from the kitchen-window once more and with an ordinary busy step, as if it were a household task like any other, went down the corridor and into the major's room.

The proud tall body had not fallen on the floor. It sat in its usual place at the desk; its weight all toppled forward on to the desk. One arm he had flung out across the desk toward the wall, where it hung down; and the other he had drawn up under him. It was a wonder that his toppling forward had not thrust the chair out from under him and brought him down. Mrs. Helianos understood why this had not happened: the floor was not waxed, and the chair was Helianos' father's heavy old armchair, with no casters and no rug under it. He had kicked one leg far out on the right side, perhaps in a reflex effort to get up out of the armchair.

In a row on top of the desk she noticed the photographs of his family, which had not been on display since he returned from his leave: the proud mother-in-law, the puny wife, the bitter schoolboys.

There was a slight stench in this room too, and at

first, fancying that it was blood she shrank from breathing it, with her nostrils palpitating. But it was not blood, it was gunpowder. She looked at the body only enough to make sure that it was all over. The blood all came from his mouth and nostrils, and some of it had run down from the desk into his lap. It was running down his chin and down his neck. He had shot himself up through the roof of his mouth. It was a disgusting sight: the barrel of the gun still pointed toward his mouth as if it were a bottle; as if he had been drinking out of a bottle and his death was drunkenness. All except the butt of the gun and one half of the hand that had pulled the trigger were in the pool of blood on the desk, with his no longer human face resting beside them.

Mrs. Helianos imagined what it must have meant to Alex to see this, and the thought made her sick at her stomach.

But only for a moment. Sickness was not what it meant to her. Strange! with regard to this dead man, in the year of him, she had felt a variety of emotions, each overpowering at its height—but this was her first moment of anger.

Quickly she looked back and saw the order of her experience, quite clearly: fear first; then suspicion and resentment—so incessant and nagging that for a few bad weeks Helianos had almost ceased to love her, she remembered that—followed by despair, when they first took him to prison; and then in her meditation in the midday sun, seized by nightmare (only it was day-mare), hatred. All these emotions relatively

[177]

facile, in the circumstances; no true anger until now. She sensed very strongly how far superior to hatred in the moral order anger is.

She was the type of woman for whom it is hard to be angry, with all it entails in emotional exhaustion, and all it leads to: unwomanly action. She was one of those women who are not angry with men whom they respect; and most of these emotions she was reviewing seemed to her somehow respectful. Fear certainly is; and as for hatred, there is a vague spirit of damned worship in it! But now as she contemplated the man lying there dead, that is, sitting there dead, she no longer respected him, she despised him, he disgusted her.

She felt very little other emotion; this purged her of all the rest. After anger, she supposed, next in order and in cause and effect came fury; fury, to be avoided or at least put off! How much she had to do first, in anger; she and Helianos, when he got home, which would not be long now. She could not imagine where anger would lead them. She knew only that there was something she did not know.

Then with a gesture of her hand before her eyes to brush her vain thoughts away, with a kind of effort she brought her mind back to the frightful matters of fact before her. At the back of the desk, not in the blood, lay a large unfolded piece of paper, a document or a letter. "What a blessing, I can read German!" she cried, still aloud in her bad habit; coming closer, stepping over the outstretched leg, and looking over the shoulder.

It was a letter, beginning with a formal German

salutation, but in spite of the formality an intimate letter, to the dead major's friend, the other major, the dog-loving major, von Roesch. She reached and took it over the shoulder, and half read it and then— realizing that it absolved her and Helianos from any blame for his death, acknowledging to herself what she had refused to acknowledge until then, suffering in one breath the peril and terror of their being blamed, letting herself go in her sense of relief—she fainted away.

When she came to her senses, lying on the floor, it was with the strangest happiness, deliverance from peril and happy ending; but naturally for a moment it was not clear and not real. It was like a religious experience, or the crisis of an illness, or something in a fantastic book. Then with troubled eyes gazing along the floor, seeing where she was, suddenly coming to the outstretched leg of the major's body, she remembered everything: what peril and what deliverance, exculpation.

Where was the letter? It had fluttered away under the bookcase. As soon as she was able, she got up off the floor and recovered it and re-read it.

"I need not tell you my story, dear friend von Roesch," it read, *"you have heard it. My breakdown of character and courage, and this act of self-destruction: you will understand it, although you cannot sympathize with it, thank God.*

"When I told you that my mind was failing, and it would eventually come to this, you could not believe it, and I scarcely could myself; but today it is the simple truth.

[179]

"When a soldier loses hope, then he must give up, get out! If they had not refused to send me to the Russian front, into active service—you remember my telling you that I had requested it—a damned enemy would have done this for me; and it would have been more honorable, more dignified, don't you think?

"You understand, it is not the same as other suicides. It is with objectivity about myself. My intellect is one thing, my changed character and broken heart another thing, and so I can judge myself. I am incapable of living, I am unfit for the responsibility I bear as an officer, I pass judgment, I sentence myself to be shot, I shoot. If my present knowledge of myself had been brought before an army tribunal, I tell you, what I am doing now would have been done to me. I am saving you the trouble!"

As Mrs. Helianos painstakingly read all this, her angry disdain of it moved her so that she could scarcely concentrate; it rose in her throat with a catch like nausea, with a lump like self-pity. To think of him sitting there composing and inscribing these sentences of pompous pathos; then proceeding to do to himself what he had done!

"Arrange things as honorably as you can," the well-composed epistle went on; and in that paragraph recommended something that Mrs. Helianos did not understand, some arrangement with one of the special services of the army of occupation, with a particular officer, something the dead major wanted done after his death. It also gave the names and addresses of lawyers in Athens and in Königsberg who had his various business papers and his will in safekeeping.

"I do not care for my own dishonor," it concluded, *"now that my sons are dead, my family extinct. I personally have no hope—you remember my telling you how it was, like a disease, unbearable and incurable—but faith in the superior will and supreme destiny of the German people, and confidence in our leader, of course I still have.*

It closed with one of those French words which Germans like to use, *Adieu,* and only the family name, *Kalter.*

She went to the kitchen-sink for a drink of water: the water of unwholesome Athens with its deathly odor and disgusting taste! and as she sipped it, at last she was able to think. She decided that the clever thing to do was to notify, not the municipal police or the army of occupation or any general authority, but the dead major's friend in person, the other major whose name she had forgotten; whose name, praise God, was inscribed at the top of the farewell letter.

So then she returned to the sitting room and did just that. It was not easy: she had almost no voice, for one thing, and she had trouble with the name,—she pronounced it wrong, and spelled it out to two different quartermaster's underlings, v o n R o e s c h, and learned to pronounce it from them—but the trouble and delay and impatience distracted her from the corpse sitting so close across the room, steadied her nerves; the lesser nervousness steadied her against the greater. She kept crying the name of Major Kalter and the word *tod! tod!* and the name of Major von Roesch, who answered at last; and then kept dialoguing back and forth with him in confusion until sud-

[181]

denly he understood, lowered his voice to a grave husky note, promised to come at once, and instructed her to lock her door and not to let anyone else in upon any pretext until he got there.

While waiting for him she sat in the kitchen, and fell into a revery, so that she did not notice the passing of the time it took him to get there. Shocked and tired, her mind fled away from everything immediate and important: the corpse in the other room, the trouble of removing it and tidying up after it, the unknown dog-loving major on his way. It was like a sleep, a sleep in which all the unimportant small realities around her were the dream, this and that in the kitchen: the stove, rusted in one place, an old rag of a shirt of Helianos' which served for a wash-cloth, her pair of shoes that she wore to market, a table-spoonful of rancid oil in a cup, a bedbug (she absent-mindedly destroyed it), a bucket.

Then she found herself thinking about herself: how she resembled Alex and Leda and Helianos, all three: the likeness to Leda in momentary flights away from reality at times like this, sleeps of soul; and the likeness to Alex in other ways, in excitement and verbosity, and in lively interest in trouble to come, and in increase of energy and good sense when at times like this it did come...

And as for Helianos, certainly in the early days of their marriage she had not been in the least like him —a liberal family and a reactionary family, a healthy male and an ailing wife, a scholar and an ignoramus, a humorous long-suffering intellectual and a plaintive bourgeoise—but in the last year how she had drawn close to him, been influenced by him!

So that as it seemed to her she was a different character, with a re-educated mind; and when it came to enduring fatigue and discomfort and in recuperative power, a rejuvenated body; and a new heart. From pessimism to optimism (of a sort); from hypochondria to a certain energy in spite of poor health; from womanishness and narrow-mindedness and bourgeoisie to a certain spirit, and relative knowledge of the world—what an improvement! And without any self-discipline, without even a conscious desire to improve; driven to it by the force of circumstances, for the most part evil circumstances...

She gave one more disdainful thought to the dead Kalter, and to the famous change in him, from the day of his return from Germany to this day of his death: it was nothing, nothing, compared with the change in herself! For he had no real intelligence—a preachment upon propaganda and make-believe world-government was not intelligent, a sophisticated suicide-letter was not intelligent!—and unintelligent or unintelligible change was of no account, she thought.

Oh, she reminded herself, doubtless she herself would never be intelligent enough to suit Helianos. But, she fancied, she would not be able to be really unintelligent again, not even if she tried; so much having happened to her. Thus she saw herself, lifted up above who she was and what she was, in the increase of drama in her life—the wealthy merchants' spoiled child, the clever young publisher's bride, the benefactor of her country to the extent of one hero fallen on Mount Olympos, the long-suffering mother of abnormal little Alex and subnormal little Leda besides, and now the imprisoned anti-Nazi's wife, the corpse's landlady, what next!—and it was as proud as a mystic vision.

Though with no false pride; evil circumstances keep one from false pride... For in a sense she owed it all to the Germans. She had risen to the occasion indeed, but the occasion was German. It was their intervention in her common circumscribed, stagnant, passive existence that had aroused her. But she did not, she would not, thank them for it. It was a good thing; and to admit that a good thing has derived from an evil thing is to bend the knee to evil to some extent. In her uneasiness and exalted sentiment—a lone Greek woman in a kitchen with a German corpse in another room, waiting for the police—she did not even thank God for it; she thanked her Helianos.

All of which passed in her mind in the little time; in less time (as she herself thought) than it would take to tell it.

14.

Then there they were, the police, the germans, ringing the doorbell and knocking on the door. They startled her, and for a moment her intelligence, her proud new-found intelligence, failed her; she suffered one more moment of panic.

What if they suspected her of having shot the major, or of knowing who had? They wouldn't, they couldn't, for there was his farewell letter! She ran to the sitting room and picked it up off the floor, and returned to the kitchen with it pressed to her bosom, as if it were her only safeguard, affidavit or license or identification-paper; then trembled to think that perhaps now her fingerprints were on it—as a woman of leisure in the old days she had read certain detective stories, *Fantomas* and Edgar Wallace—and ran back to the sitting room and slipped it back over the corpse's shoulder to the desk where she had found it in the first place. Then she opened the front door and let the impatient Germans in.

There were two of them, one in front of the other. The one in front said, "I am Major von Roesch. Where is Major Kalter? Are you alone in the apartment? Who has been here besides yourself? Why did you take so long to let us in? I thought you had run away. Speak up, for God's sake!"

Major von Roesch did not shout; his voice was quick and low and husky. Mrs. Helianos had expected him to resemble his friend the deceased; and there never were two men less alike. He was somewhat fat and a little old, he was dark-haired and sallow-skinned, with eyes of bright hazel and ugly drooping lips. It was a kind face except for the lips, a clever face.

The other one accompanying him was a lieutenant —after their discourtesy of not noticing when Captain Kalter became Major Kalter, the Helianos family had learned to look at insignia—a youngster with a blank, modest, introspective face like a young priest.

Without waiting for an answer to their question, they came straight in, as if it might be only natural for them to step indifferently on Mrs. Helianos or over her. She backed away from them down the corridor to the sitting-room door, and pointed through it, and slipped in herself and shrank into the corner by the bookcase.

Major von Roesch entered the room with an easy step—a healthy stout man in a hurry, light on his feet —and stood in the center of the floor an instant with that perfect stillness which in a brave man is the equivalent of trembling; staring at his dead friend's back with one hand out before him, like a great bird-dog pointing.

Then he stepped to one side of the desk, bending a little to see exactly what had happened: the gun pointing to the mouth, the hairy wet hole in the top of the head, the bloody desk. Then he sniffed hard, and with lively motions went over to the window and unlatched it and opened it wide.

The younger officer followed, step for step, almost gesture for gesture, like a large and solid shadow; but alert, as if any moment might be the moment for him to stand at attention or to salute, which was his nature. In spite of this, and in spite of the fact that he was so much younger and only a lieutenant, Mrs. Helianos noted that the major treated him with a certain deference.

The lieutenant belonged to a section of the secret military police which, among other things, looked out for occupying German officers in their individual relations with Greeks; so officially he was in charge of this investigation. Whereas Major von Roesch, as a staff-officer of the quartermaster's corps, and the friend of the deceased, had a limited competence and informal authority. However he appeared to be a clever willful man, and he meant to have his way.

Having seen the condition of the body, they began asking questions again, the major especially with a strain in his voice, "Who did this? What happened? Speak up, for heaven's sake."

For some reason just then Mrs. Helianos forgot her German; answered in French, in a faint voice, "*C'était lui, lui-même,* he did it himself," pointing to the dead man.

Then she gave a little gasp because she did not see the farewell letter on the desk where she had put it over the dead shoulder; and looking around nervously, she found it on the floor where the draught from the open window had carried it, and pointed to it; and as the two officers seemed not to see, she sprang across in front of them, and stooped for it, and handed it to Major von Roesch. *"C'est pour vous,* it is addressed to you. I read it," she added with a slight apologetic note, "to find out what had happened."

The old major looked at it a moment, then looked up over it at her soberly, appraisingly. "It is my friend's handwriting, yes. Fortunately for you, Mrs. Helianos!"

His knowing her name amazed her. It was her reward for having gone hungry evening after evening when Alex or Helianos took the leftovers in little packages down the street to the old Macedonian couple's apartment for his dog.

"Furthermore, it refers to conversations between Major Kalter and myself," he added, "conversations at which no one else was present. Please note that fact, Lieutenant Frieher, it is a point in evidence."

He cleared his throat and accelerated his voice. "Now, my good woman, will you please show us into another room? It is perhaps an infirmity—you know, Lieutenant, in the quartermaster's corps, we do not have this kind of experience every day—I am not comfortable about dead bodies, unnecessary dead bodies."

Mrs. Helianos who was not comfortable either, led them not to Kalter's adjoining bedroom but away down the corridor to the children's room.

"Also I have something to say about my dead friend that I prefer not to say in his presence," Major von Roesch explained as they went along.

He sat down on the children's bed and re-read the farewell letter in a rapid whisper and mumble; stood up suddenly, and stood in intense reflection, with squinted eyes like gold and a bad twist of his thin lips downward; then turned to the younger officer and read a paragraph aloud.

It was the paragraph that Mrs. Helianos had skipped over because it made no sense to her; the paragraph of what Kalter wanted done after his death: —*"Arrange things as you wish, my friend, as honorably as you can. Speak to the political bureau of the secret service about it: Lieutenant-Colonel Sertz. Perhaps he will have some method of explaining the circumstances of my death, to serve their purpose in some way, in the checking of the Greek resistance. Thus even in death I may still serve a little useful purpose, for the fatherland."*

Major von Roesch cleared his throat again after this reading, and asked, "Lieutenant Frieher"—the lieutenant stiffened attentively—"do you understand what this part of my friend's letter means; what he wished us to do?"

"Yes, I think so, Major von Roesch, yes, I understand."

Mrs. Helianos did not understand but, as the manner of both officers was portentous, she stood trying to, leaning forward a little, holding her breath in order not to miss one of the major's words.

"Very well then, Lieutenant," he said sharply, "please give me your careful attention. It is not what I wish, not at all! My view of the matter is this: in the moment of his death, writing this letter, my poor friend did not have his normal understanding, do you hear? I should like Lieutenant-Colonel Sertz to do nothing about it, nothing."

He paused, narrowing his yellow eyes again, then said, "I do not care for certain of Lieutenant-Colonel Sertz's methods. I think he has got them all out of those English books that used to be sold at railroad-stations, by the Jew Oppenheim and the Jew Wallace."

Mrs. Helianos blushed, because of the coincidence of having been reminded of those books herself only a few minutes ago. She began to be extremely nervous.

"Furthermore, in this damned land of Greece the methods I refer to have not worked well," he added.

Mrs. Helianos observed that the lieutenant was blushing too, staring straight ahead with almost no expression; only a look of not taking sides in this difference of his superior officers, whatever it might amount to.

Major von Roesch scrutinized him; he gave Mrs. Helianos a keen sideways glance as well; he sighed. "The true cause of my friend's death, I am sorry to tell you, Lieutenant, was his own cowardice. Wait, don't misunderstand me, not military cowardice! It was a purely personal misfortune. His mind became deranged as a result of the loss of his two sons in service, and the loss of his wife, burned to death in an air-raid. The three deaths in one week; a coincidence!

"See for yourself, Lieutenant. He puts it very well in his letter."

He handed the letter to the younger man, who looked at it, then looked back and forth from it to

this old outspoken quartermaster as if unable to believe his own eyes and ears.

"You see, do you not, Lieutenant? Major Kalter
was an excellent officer, promoted only a few weeks
ago with a good citation for his ability and hard work
here. We shall miss him in the quartermaster corps.
Actually he worked too hard; that was part of his
trouble.

"He was a sensitive man. He tried to bear his misfortune like a man but it was impossible for him. In
all his way of life, I may say, there was no preparation
for misfortune. Which is a great spirit in a nation,
they tell me; but sometimes, for the individual, impossible...

"For example, except for his wife whom he had
the misfortune to lose, there were no women in his
life—unless we count his poor landlady here, Mrs.
Helianos!"

Whereupon he smiled at Mrs. Helianos mockingly
but not unkindly. He took out a large handkerchief
and whisked his forehead and his nose with it; for it
was a hot afternoon. "Ah-whh," he sighed, "I may tell
you that I feel a certain scorn of my dead friend at
this moment. Only we ought to respect him simply
because he is dead, do you not think?"

Now the lieutenant was no longer trying to keep an
inexpressive face. He looked bored, shocked, and perhaps angry. No doubt Major von Roesch noticed this;
he quickly resumed his sharp scrutiny and authoritative tone.

"Joking aside, Lieutenant—I say, when a man is
dead that is the end of it, let him go! For me, to turn

this case of my friend's death over to Lieutenant-Colonel Sertz to be misrepresented and manipulated for purposes of political warfare would be as unpleasant as to give his corpse to a hospital to be practiced upon by students."

"I understand, sir," the lieutenant mumbled, with a blank bewildered look.

Mrs. Helianos could not abide her bewilderment any longer. She took a step closer to the two officers, pleading in German, her worst German, "Please, for pity's sake, please! What does it mean? Is there something you do not understand about the death of Major Kalter? Has it anything to do with me?"

She took Major von Roesch's wrist, meaning to cling to it until he gave her an answer; but as this reminded her of Leda's way with the dead major, she let it go.

"You must be more patient, Mrs. Helianos," he said. "Please do not grasp my hand, because it makes me nervous. You do not speak German very well, do you? and I gather that you understand it even less well. What a pity! You have missed a wonderful opportunity, with my friend in your home for more than a year."

His yellow eyes wandered back to the lieutenant again. "I may tell you, Lieutenant, that the late Major Kalter was one of the best talkers I have ever known. It was a waste of talent, our keeping him in the quartermaster corps. By temperament he was not exactly an army-man anyway; he should have had an important post in the ministry of propaganda."

Surely, Mrs. Helianos thought, this was the most

[192]

discursive old fellow on earth! He was playing with her as a cat plays with a mouse. She made another appeal to him for information: "Tell me, I implore you to tell me, what is happening, does it concern me?"

He ignored it. "Lieutenant Frieher," he inquired, "do you know French?"

The lieutenant blushed, "Only a few words, sir. I was in France, but only six weeks."

"Then I must ask you to excuse my speaking French for a moment. I wish to make all this very clear to Mrs. Helianos. If she understands the bad trouble she is in, I think that we can count on her for cooperation in the future."

He turned briskly to her. "I will tell you exactly what is happening, Mrs. Helianos," he said in French. "It concerns you most certainly."

Then he told her, quickly, cutting his correct French phrases off short, with a certain flourish in his low husky old voice. "My friend's intention, as expressed in the paragraph of his letter to me which I read aloud, was to have you and your family held responsible for his death."

Mrs. Helianos' blood ran cold, her heart pumped no more, she saw her blood in a shadow over her eyes; and she reached out and caught hold of the foot of the children's bed, to steady her.

"Unless Lieutenant Frieher and I testify that it is not so," he went on, "it will go on record not as a suicide but as a political assassination; and you will be made to suffer the extreme penalty of the law, and I dare say, a certain number of your relatives and friends along with you."

So this was the meaning of the paragraph that she (the more fool she) had skipped over. So this was the argument of the officers; the plot that evil Kalter had devised to be carried out against her after his death by proxy. It was unheard of: as if a man were to imbue his body with poisons at the last moment, in order to kill off poor dogs after his death. So this was to be the end of her life...

For the moment it did not distress her more than she could bear. Anyway she must keep her wits about her; for she would not have anyone else caught in the plot along with her. Helianos at any rate could not be caught in it, Helianos safe in prison in incontrovertible innocence! There was happiness in that thought, enough to go on with.

The old major was still talking, still in French. "It is a blood-feud between you two somehow: an eye for an eye, a tooth for a tooth, your death for his death. It does not seem very reasonable to me in the circumstances, I must say, but there you are: it was his plan, his wish, in the solemn last moment."

She decided that she did not care. She was able to keep from shedding tears. Her lips twitched in what was practically a smile: a slight smile at herself, as an encouragement and a challenge to be at her best. But she must not let the old fellow know her carelessness; she quickly raised one hand in front of her face to hide her expression. Her bravado was not as perfect as she wanted it to be; her other hand with which she was holding on to the bedstead and her tired legs were shaking, so that she had to turn around sideways and sit down on the edge of the bed. She was almost ashamed of sitting down, thinking with a kind of humor that one ought to stand up to be sentenced to death.

But after all as it appeared it was not a sentence of death, not yet. The good major said, "Do not distress yourself, I beg of you, Mrs. Helianos. Justice will be done, Mrs. Helianos, strict German justice!"

He was a strange old fellow. Now he was making a sort of joke of Kalter's evil purpose and her plight. "This, yes, Mrs. Helianos, this is your death-warrant," he said, waving the farewell letter so that the paper crackled or rustled a little.

"How you must have hurt my friend's feelings, you Greeks! He was such a sensitive fellow. This is his vengeance; the worm turning; the recompense post-mortem. What a fighter he was! Still going strong, you see, posthumously!"

Half closing his thin lips, with what looked like a drawstring in them, he gave a small chuckle at what he was saying, chuckle or semblance of chuckle, with his breath in and out of his clever mouth, in and out, fast. As it seemed to Mrs. Helianos he must have disliked his dead friend intensely.

For one wild instant she was tempted to tell him the thought that had come to her a moment ago: of the man poisoning his own dying body for the dogs after his death. It seemed to her cleverer than the things he was saying. In her terrible nervousness she gave a great sigh. For she did not know whether his promise of strict German justice was a true promise or merely another of his jokes.

"But, you see, Mrs. Helianos," he went on, "this

kind of plan has a way of miscarrying when one is dead. My poor Kalter should have stayed alive to look after the matter himself, as he wished it. Unfortunately for him he has left it to me to arrange and I have ideas of my own about it, I am going to make a quite different arrangement. I am on your side. You may count upon me. I will protect and take care of you."

This, then, was her acquittal or at least her reprieve; apparently it was not a joke. In her profound sense of relief and gratitude she thought of kneeling like a simple peasant woman and taking his plump dark hand and kissing it; but he had made it clear how he felt about such gestures. She stood up but she did not approach him. "Thank you, thank you," she said in a faint voice; and she would have said more if the quick hard look in his eyes had not stopped her.

He turned away from her then, and faced the lieutenant, and resumed speaking in German. "Now I will explain it to you, Lieutenant Frieher. I feel sure that you will agree with me. After all my friend does say in his letter that I am to arrange it all as I wish, does he not?

"As to this Greek family with whom my friend lived," he began, waving his hand back in Mrs. Helianos' direction as if she were a number of people, an entire family, "it might indeed suit Lieutenant-Colonel Sertz to hold them responsible for his suicide somehow. Let us suppose that he should wish to proceed along that line...

"Very well then," he said, suddenly speaking in an

[196]

odd light decisive voice, and as quick as a whip, "in that case I shall be able to testify to the proper higher authority that it is not so!"

Evidently it was a threat of some consequence; the young officer looked confounded by it.

"You may, if you like, Lieutenant, inform the lieu-tenant-colonel of my attitude," the old officer added as an afterthought.

Then with his voice low and husky and slow again, as it were a whip drawn back idly on the ground, he said, "Now let me give you a little of the background of this family, Lieutenant, which as it happens I know very well because of my frequentation of the late major all the time he has been living here; which you can incorporate in your report if you wish, to give it verisimilitude.

"The facts are these: Mrs. Helianos, here present, is a respectable woman; my friend used to tell me all about her. A docile creature, timid and dutiful... She used to give me what food she could spare," he added, "for my old bull-terrier, until he got so old that I had to shoot him. After their evening meal she would send it in a neat package around to my apart-ment. It was extremely kind of her."

This idle comment upon her as if she were not there, troubled her and vexed her; but she really had no reason to believe that he meant it unkindly. The point of it appeared to be to tease the lieutenant, to pass the time with the lieutenant, and whatever the threat in the whiplike sentence had been, to let it sink into his thick young head. Now apparently it was his turn to be played with. In spite of herself Mrs. Helianos was amused by it, and she could not help liking the old major a little.

Another likeable German! she thought. Now she had met two: the little wise gruff doctor who had come to see her after Helianos' arrest and this old humorist, both in the same fortnight, which was a coincidence; when practically speaking it was too late, when she had decided upon an eternal anger. Another good German; she had always heard of good Germans but of course in the last two years she had begun to doubt their existence. Evidently this was one: insolent but smiling, slightly sinister but scrupulous, playing his games of cat-and-mouse with her and the lieutenant for love of justice, and—as he evidently expected her to believe and she herself had no real reason to disbelieve—for her sake.

He seemed inclined to stay here chatting all the rest of the afternoon. The significance of his chat kept changing terribly, or seeming to change, from moment to moment. Now he said in his careless way, "The husband, Helianos, as you may know, is in prison at this moment. He is and always has been a malcontent, or at least an intellectual, a rather bad type. The exact opposite of this docile, dutiful Mrs. Helianos!

"A bad family, the Helianos', all in the underground agitation, they tell me. He has not yet been condemned; I presume he is giving us valuable information. It may seem advisable to deal with him with our utmost severity, in due course."

At this Mrs. Helianos did kneel almost like a peas-

[198]

ant woman, protesting, "No, no, no." Now that the fearful matter of Helianos' possible condemnation had been brought up—whatever the major's intentions were in the way of strict justice—she could not keep her tears back any longer. "Not my Helianos, not Nikolas Helianos! He is innocent, innocent, innocent," she said softly and stubbornly, over and over.

The worst of it was her not knowing whether she was really in despair or only playing a part as the major intended; whether it was a tragedy or a comedy. Oh, whatever his scheme was, she thought, there could be no harm in her saying that Helianos was innocent. Perhaps he knew it, perhaps the tragic opinion he gave was only to confuse and appease the young lieutenant, for her sake, Helianos' sake, justice's sake. How could she tell? His every word had been ambiguous from beginning to end; only he had promised her that in the end there would be no injustice. She had nothing else to trust to; therefore it seemed sensible to believe in this more or less, for the time being. She had no other defender; therefore she hypothetically accepted this strange old man.

She held her arms out to him in a gesture of intercession but she did not agitate them. She shed tears, but a minimum; she wept, but as quietly as she could, in order not to interrupt his further discourse. She listened to it as if it were far away, the vicissitudes of another family.

"They have a son," he said, "young Alex, evidently a true Helianos, a bad one, but there is no harm in him as yet. He is very young and not at all healthy. We had to give him a whipping sometimes, because he stole the dog-food; didn't we, Mrs. Helianos?"

He smiled down at her with apparent kindliness.

"No, no, Alex did not steal it," she protested without any real vehemence.

Over her soft confused voice he raised his voice a little for the lieutenant's benefit. "Well, now, Lieutenant, I think I have told you all I know about this family. You will of course do your duty, make your own report, as you think best. I realize that, strictly speaking, this does not concern us quartermasters. It is a personal matter. I personally shall be grateful to you for not stirring up Lieutenant-Colonel Sertz about it."

He concluded with a few more whip-sentences. "If he will stir himself up, in spite of our good offices—if he really feels that it is his duty to entangle this unfortunate Mrs. Helianos in connection with Major Kalter's demise—ah, well, Lieutenant, I shall not be altogether sorry! It will give me an occasion for making a report to the high command that I have had on my conscience for some time.

"There has been a little peculation, Lieutenant, taking of bribes and waste of army property, here in Athens. What a pity! Some of that does lie within our jurisdiction. I shall feel that it is my duty to have it investigated if the occasion should arise. Explain all this to Lieutenant-Colonel Sertz, will you? and tell him how anxious I am not to embarrass him in any way.

"You know, Frieher, there is a certain rivalry among the services in our army. It is only natural and very healthy and, on the whole, fun."

Lieutenant Frieher looked unhappy but extremely impressed.

"Let the case of Helianos proceed in the ordinary way. Let justice be done, with no trimmings of a murder-mystery. Leave the corpse of my poor friend out of it. I suppose your bureau will want some sort of written report from me besides this, won't they? I will send it around for you to see first, so that you can corroborate it in detail, if you care to."

The lieutenant brought his heels together and bowed and murmured, "Oh, yes, sir, as you think best."

Major von Roesch gave a considerable sigh, as one relieved of a great anxiety or responsibility. "Even in the game of war it is better to play according to old rules, Lieutenant. You can take my word for that; the word of an old officer, an officer past his prime in fact, but the lasting kind.

"You know, Kalter was more brilliant than I, but I have been able to bear my misfortunes and I have lasted. I was a captain in the last war, and I expect to be a lieutenant-colonel, perhaps a colonel, in the next! I can tell you, Frieher, the National Socialist Labor Party did not make Germany up out of whole cloth.

"Thank you very much. Do not bother to come down with me. Your men are waiting in the street, I presume. I will tell one of them to come up here for your orders."

They saluted each other, and with his graceful stout step the major turned toward the door, pausing an instant as he passed Mrs. Helianos, bending slightly, and giving her a little stroke or fillip on the shoulder with his heavy gloves.

During the last part of his bullying of the young lieutenant, although it was for her sake, evidently he had forgotten her presence in the room. As she knelt there listening, amazed, it reminded her of the nights in the clothes closet with the other major beyond the partition trying to indoctrinate poor Helianos in his super-German faith. There was no such exaltation in what she now heard this better-natured major say. Perhaps he really believed that she did not understand German. Or perhaps as it seemed to him she was so helpless and hopeless, so entirely dependent on him, that her overhearing this or that was of no consequence; as if she were an old pet dog merely restless at his feet while he schemed and argued.

Looking up at him with her wet tired eyes, she saw that his yellow eyes were kind still, or kind again, although the expression of the rest of his face was peculiar: an intimate, dreary, envious expression. She went on shedding tears. But she did think that he was sincere in his good will toward her; so perhaps justice would be done in Helianos' case in due course.

"Do not distress yourself too much," he said. "I think that you are a naturally good woman, Mrs. Helianos. See that you keep good, quietly here at home with your children, and obedient. We shall meet again, you know."

"Thank you, sir, thank you," she said.

"And tell that little devil of a son of yours that we have treated you well," he called back from the corridor.

As soon as he had gone she recovered her composure and ceased her weeping. After all she had heard, she felt a kind of comfortable indifference to Lieutenant Frieher. She asked his permission to go outdoors and find her children and bring them home; they had had nothing to eat at midday.

What she feared was that in despair of her coming as she had promised, they might return alone, and perhaps meet the corpse when the lieutenant's men took it out, the corpse lurching and sagging down the stairway; and Alex might not think to cover Leda's eyes while it passed.

The lieutenant did not like to let her go; he shook his goodlooking head a great deal; it was an irregular thing, perhaps a risky thing; but because she was a friend of Major von Roesch's he gave his permission.

The children were waiting at the street-corner near the playground, sitting on two stones. Leda was all right; Alex had done a good job of distracting her. Hand in hand they followed her back to the apartment. The ambulance or the hearse or whatever the vehicle might be in a case of suicide, had not arrived yet. Hearing several voices in the sitting room, they hastened down the corridor to the kitchen. Mrs. Helianos offered the children a dish of yesterday's soup but they refused it.

"Leda is not going to mind what has happened to Kalter," Alex announced, "I asked her, and she said not."

"Sh-sh, Alex, we must not talk while the Germans are in the apartment. Sit down beside me on the cot, we will just wait here, all three of us in a row."

There once more on the cot waiting for Germans—waiting for them not to come but to go this time, with at least one who would never come back—she indulged in a little daydream of how it would be when the war was won (if the Germans did not win it). There would be days, weeks, months, when one would not see any Germans or even hear of them; perhaps one could forget that they existed. But it seemed as remote as heaven and it brought tears to her eyes again. She had the wit to turn her head before the children saw them. She resolved that, for one thing, after the war, she would not read or speak any more German.

Meanwhile what a blessing it had been to know it fairly well; to be able to follow the long obscure dispute of the officers about herself, to read Kalter's farewell letter! She happened to close her eyes just then and to her surprise, found that she could see the letter in her mind's eye exactly and entirely: the shape of the paragraphs on the paper, the forceful but jerky German script running down hill, even a blot or two, as if he had shed tears upon the ink when it was wet. She re-read it like that, imprinted or as it were photographed in her mind: word for word, beginning with the absurd formality, *Much esteemed friend and fellow-officer,* including the fatal paragraph that she had been a fool not to read in the first place, ending with the French word: *Adieu.*

She re-opened her eyes, shook her head, did not like it; but still there it was: not a daydream or a delusion but a type of memory, a new faculty that the terrible day had developed in her. All spring, especially in Helianos' absence, she had been amazed at the retentiveness of her mind, increased now by this little silly miracle.

How she despised that letter! Even her thirteen-year-old Alex had never dramatized himself as the tragic major did in it. She imagined him sitting there composing the stately false phrases; then laying down his pen and taking up his pistol and with his own blood instead of the ink-pot, writing his eternal damnation so much more plainly. Sitting like Almighty God in judgment upon himself with Helianos' father's old armchair for his judgment-seat; spilling his life's blood all over Helianos' scholarly desk as if it were an orgy, drunk on his death-wish; leaving himself as a mess for other people to clean up... She was the cleaner-up, it then occurred to her. She would put that off until tomorrow, and she would need someone to help her.

Whereupon in spite of herself her imagination wandered in a kind of funeral march for that insolent creature in whose death she had every reason to rejoice. It passed for a moment very muffled and shadowy in her thought. Then she realized what it was: it was the sound of her own heavy pulse and weary breath and throbbing headache. However, because death is the only absolute equality among human beings on earth, even the ignoblest and the most welcome instance of it deserves a little ceremonious thought. She was willing to mourn him in that sense, as abstract man; certainly not as an individual man, for there had been neither greatness nor goodness in him.

Then a great sound of trampling and shuffling came from the corridor, a good many men, with that peculiar low sweet tone of voice which the deadness of the dead seems to inspire in everyone, even Germans; and a solemn knocking and bumping and clumsiness as they brought the corpse around narrowly from the sitting-room door into the corridor and down it, away, away forever.

The instant it began Alex started to his feet and toward the kitchen-door, to watch it; and Leda, unusually alert, also rose and started after him. Mrs. Helianos managed to catch him by the arm and to hold him back; how often, how often, that had been her maternal function! But now she was tired out, and with Leda misbehaving along with him, it was too great an effort; and then it occurred to her that she need not rely on main force alone this time.

"No, Alex, no," she said. "There will be nothing to see now. They have him covered up on the stretcher. I dare say they have taken one of my good sheets to cover him with."

"Mother, what is a stretcher? I want to see what it looks like."

"It is a sort of little light portable cot with handles at each end," she answered. "But Alex, if they see us peering down the corridor, it will anger them again, they will come and worry me to death again. You have grown up, my Alex, and you must think of things like this, cleverly, as grown-ups do."

She decided that she might as well tell him the whole story. "Alex, they accused me of killing Kalter. I expected them to arrest me and take me to prison.

What would have become of you then, alone, with Leda to look after, I cannot imagine! Dear, do you remember that old major who lives with the Macedonian couple, the one who accused you of stealing the dog-food?"

He made a sound that was half a laugh, half a snarl. "Of course, Mother. I will avenge you if he arrests you."

"No, no, it is the other way around, it was he who prevented the other officer from arresting me. He gave me the benefit of the doubt; and here I am, you see, as free as a bird.

"He is a comical old man; he would have made you laugh. He spoke of how nicely we wrapped the food up in little packages and delivered them every evening; he seemed grateful to us. He has promised to protect us, and perhaps he will help to get your father out of prison."

"Mother, do you believe him?"

"I don't know, I don't know. They talk nonsense a good deal of the time, Germans. We shall have to wait and see. Sufficient unto the day is the evil thereof, as your father used to tell us."

After a pause Alex said, "Anyway, I am glad you told me, Mother. I want to behave well, the way you ask me to, and it's easier for me when I know things."

They sat in silence for a while, all three tired out. Now there was no more tramp of Germans, no movement of death, in the corridor. Not one of them had come back to the kitchen to bid her good-bye. On the whole, all things considered, Mrs. Helianos thought, they had been fairly good to her. She really did not know how good or how bad. She would have to wait and see it manifested in her own grim life in the next few months, one way or the other.

The children on the cot beside her were whispering, that is, Alex was whispering, close to Leda's ear, very softly; something evidently not intended for his mother's ear. But she leaned a little nearer to them, over them; she held her breath and listened. "Maybe Father escaped from prison and climbed up from the street to the balcony outside the major's room and shot him through the window," he whispered.

Mrs. Helianos drew back a bit in order to see his face. The imaginary gleam in his eyes was heavenly; the false conviction in the dramatically hissed sentence, fantastic. Oh, he was mad, this beloved son of hers, mad; And Leda, her little subnormal daughter, believed every word, with her too simple smile like some loose flower smiling at the sunlight, and whispered to him to tell it all over again; and he did.

Then, for a thrilling unreasoning moment, Mrs. Helianos herself believed it, she wanted to believe it. She rose and started out of the kitchen toward the balcony to see if there was any evidence of Helianos' having been there.

But of course she stopped herself after a few steps in the corridor, and came back, disappointed, alarmed about herself again; perhaps she was going mad. If this lunatic war with its constant coincidences and mystifications went on long enough, it would drive her mad.

So once more for a moment, but abjectly, hanging her head, almost ashamed to go back into the kitchen and sit down beside her children, she took stock of herself. She was dead-tired and her nerves were in bad order. She had a bad heart, a broken heart; literally and figuratively broken, literally and figuratively bad. All her introspection since they took Helianos away had been bad for her; and in any case in his absence she was only half herself, half a human being.

She need not have worried; there was no real weakness in her. The years of lunatic war and the shocking blows just lately, had only worn her down to rock-bottom where there was no use in her worrying about herself, illness or wellness, madness or not-madness; where it scarcely mattered. Not even Helianos' absence, not even the Germans—dead but still deadly Kalter, and the other living major who perhaps in his way was worse, who certainly mystified her more—none of it had really incapacitated her for what she had to do; just now, for example, a little more housewifery and motherhood until the day was done.

Back in the kitchen she began preparing an evening meal of sorts; and she persuaded Alex and Leda to help her, and she kept talking to them, trying to calm them and to distract them from what had happened. She inquired what they had seen in the street by the playground while they were waiting for her; what they were planning to do next day; what their favorite games were at the moment, and which neighbors' children they liked to play with. But she was not surprised at their scarcely replying to any of this; their jaded minds wandered.

So she did something that as it happened she had

never done before; she told them two or three of the simpler myths of antiquity. She could not think of another sort of story to interest them, and she felt that this would please her antiquity-loving Helianos.

She told them about the bed of the brigand of Eleusis, Procrustes; how, when it was a tall traveler who lay on it he cut his legs off, when it was a short traveler he stretched them, so that it was a perfect fit for all who came, willy-nilly. She said that it was her own folding cot there in the kitchen which reminded her of this. She and their father were so uncomfortable together on it that she was afraid they might wake up one morning and find themselves misshapen forever.

This amused Alex intensely; and for a joke he slipped around behind her and whisked up her skirt and pretended to have discovered that she had a crooked leg. She gave him a make-believe slap for this, and smiled at him.

Then she told them about the day-mare, or demon of midday; the ancient personification of sunstroke. She confessed that one day she herself had been seized by it, standing too long at the kitchen-window in the blaze of summer, and suddenly losing her wits for a moment, suddenly talking nonsense at the top of her voice, weeping about nothing, and cursing no one in particular. She warned them against it: when noon came they were not to play games in the middle of the street but to keep back on the sidewalk where the buildings cast a shadow, and above all they were never to take naps in the sun.

Evidently Alex found it hard to imagine her falling

into any such disorder as she described; he gave her a skeptical look. As for that warning which was the moral of the story as she told it, they had heard it every day or every other day all summer long all their lives; and he assured her that as a matter of fact they never forgot it; and he informed her of their favorite shadowy place, in what was left of the stairway and cellar-way of the ruined building adjacent to their playground.

Then he wanted to know whether a midday demon was the same thing as a Fury, and whether it might have been a Fury that had caused their German to kill himself.

No, she said; the Furies pursued men for the crimes they had committed against others, especially against anyone near and dear to them, such as father or mother or brother or sister. The rage against yourself, the sickness of yourself, which prompted suicide, was a far more evil thing, she explained; and as for the punishment of the Germans for the harm they had done others, that had not started yet.

Suddenly she observed how Leda was shivering, as if in a fever, with her eyes closed and her fists clenched; and she realized that these were worse tales than Alex ever told her; and she was ashamed. So she took the little one and put her to bed, and lay down there beside her and caressed her until she fell asleep, then fell asleep herself; and that night Alex slept on the cot of Procrustes.

15.

It took an entire day to clean up the sitting room to Mrs. Helianos' satisfaction, with the help of a neighbor woman. Alex insisted on accompanying them as, with two poor scrub-brushes—the neighbor woman having brought along her own—an assortment of rags, a broken broom, and a pail of water, they entered the fatal chamber. He promised to compensate for his curiosity by being a real help. Mrs. Helianos was pleased to observe that it disappointed her young romantic. There was no profusion of gore, nor charnel odor, nor anything worth his asking for and keeping as a souvenir.

Lieutenant Frieher's henchmen evidently had been careful and skillful. For example, they had managed to get the big body lifted down from the armchair, couched on the stretcher, without drops of blood on the floor. The neighbor woman commented upon this. Alex wanted to know how they had managed it: had they swaddled the head in cloths, or would it have ceased to bleed by that time? For which ghoulish curiosity of course he was reproved by his mother.

One henchman, a good German indeed, had wiped off the desk-top. However, a little of the German life-blood was dried into the grain of the wood, which required a prolonged scrubbing. A worn old leather-ette blotter-holder once dear to Helianos bore a stain. Mrs. Helianos decided to throw it away, and the less squeamish neighbor woman asked to have it, forestall-ing the words on Alex's lips by two seconds. Under the desk there was a bad, small, still sticky puddle.

They had removed all the late major's modest martial belongings from the desk and the chest of drawers and the closet. The more removal the mistress of the house noted, the better she liked it. They had observed a certain probity in not taking what was not his, except for an old valise which happened to have been left on the highest shelf of his closet. It was marked with her name but no doubt they really needed it, for odds and ends that could not be fitted into Kalter's bags; and she did not begrudge it for so good a riddance of such bad rubbish, as she ex-pressed it to the neighbor woman. She could not see that they had overlooked anything, except his tele-phone and his reading-lamp. She resolved to have the former taken out with the least possible delay; and she compromised as to the latter, that is, she wanted it and kept it. After all, she said, in Helianos' vein of humor, reading was a good thing in itself.

Meanwhile Leda in the other room, Mrs. Helianos thought, probably was pining away. Alex had ceased to enjoy himself, and his assistance was slight; so she excused him from it. Then the two women talked at their ease. Grateful for neighborliness, and anxious not to fall into any of her own way of thought in the circumstances, the proud merchant's daughter and publisher's wife expressed herself to her neighbor in a much more commonplace way than was her wont. On the whole she did keep from the indulgence of her imagination. She did not flinch or romanticize or exaggerate, even when actually on her knees under the fatal desk with her hands in the slightly reddened scrubbing water—except once, when she recalled something Helianos had told her: the belief of horrible ancient Greeks that having killed a man, the thing to do was to lick up a little of his blood and spit it out, to prevent his soul from pursuing you later on. She quite wisely reflected that a precaution as extreme as this must not have reassured anyone much; and in any case there was no easy way of putting the Germans off one's track.

This neighbor woman was the one whose small daughter had wandered with Leda past the municipal market into the side street heaped with slaughter; long ago, when Leda had her first bad attack of apathy. Meanwhile the daughter had died, the husband also, and the lone creature was extremely poor; but in spite of tragedy she had a happy nature, thoughtless and energetic. She was a tiny peaked woman with strong hands and absurd great feet.

She asked innumerable questions about Kalter's departing this life, questions almost as shocking as Alex's; and Mrs. Helianos shrank from them, wanting to forget, forget! But with the kind and effective help she was getting, she could not fail to answer. Then she found that it did her good to talk to this unimaginative, unintimate person. So she went on and gave a version of the whole story, the entire year, and managed to cheapen it and belittle it, to disinfect and disenthrall her memory somewhat. At one point and another as she told it, the neighbor woman would throw back her head and laugh: a clear, fearless, useless woman's laughter like a bell. It made Kalter's victim and narrator shiver a little but it pleased her.

When they got around to the adjoining bedroom Mrs. Helianos was pleased to find that they had not commandeered any of her bedclothes for a winding sheet. Only someone had flung himself down on top of the bed and dirtied the coverlet with his boots: perhaps Frieher while waiting for the stretcher-bearers; perhaps Kalter himself at some point in his suicidal agony. Someone had smoked a cigar; there were ashes in odd places.

She found that the mere scrubbing of the blood did not content her. She wished to eradicate everything having to do with Kalter alive as well as Kalter dead; the least residue or reminder of the entire year. She attacked every little dust with her broken broom as if it were ghostly; she shivered at his fingerprints and footprints, as you might say, his spoor. Thus by easy stages she and the neighbor woman undertook a kind of general housecleaning. There was no necessity for it except in spite and as a ritual. She and Helianos had gone over the apartment thoroughly during Kalter's absence in April: how long ago that seemed!

Next day the kind strong-handed clumsy-footed one came back with another neighbor, and helped Mrs. Helianos with something that was a great pleasure, the changing of the beds all around: the double bed into Kalter's bedroom where it belonged, Kalter's bed and the kitchen-cot into the children's bedroom side by side. Alex declared that the cot was perfectly comfortable. Perhaps, his mother thought, this was some fancy derived from the legend of Procrustes. In spite of his stunted growth he was precocious; now there was a decided shadow of little hairs on his lip. So perhaps he was glad to have any old bed to himself; perhaps it troubled him to lie beside Leda although she was so familiar and unattractive.

The double bed was one of the oldest pieces of furniture in the apartment, brought in from Psyhiko; and the dearest. Cimon had been born in it. Mrs. Helianos was deeply moved to be back in it although oddly, in its wide and reminiscent space, she did not miss Helianos as badly as she had done on the sagging truckle-bed where he had made her uncomfortable the night through, all year long. Back where she belonged, the first night, she dreamed that she was a widow, but it was a kind of abstract foolish plot with no affecting particulars, no furnishings of everyday reality. It bore little resemblance to her life, except that, as she was a wife, she might indeed be widowed. The foolish part was that the dream-husband in question was someone she had never known; and therefore there was no melancholy or warning in her dream-bereavement.

Then one afternoon to her surprise one of the Helianos cousins came to call on her. It was not one of the heroes; it was the opposite. It was Demos, the black sheep of the family; an unkempt, emaciated, sallow, small old fellow who had wasted all his inheritance on discreditable women, and borrowed from everyone for years. A number of his male relatives had always been indulgent toward him because he told funny stories. But ever since the occupation of Athens he had been in disgrace. He promptly made friends with all sorts of German officers and went about with them in the most obviously friendly spirit in public places. His own amorousness had abated, no doubt, as he was well on in years and not in perfect health; but he had not lost interest, and he had a great acquaintance and competence in female circles. Therefore it was presumed that he made himself agreeable to his new friends as a pander.

The respectable women of the family had been vexed by him for years. It was almost a gratification to have him seem guilty of something worse than his lifelong untidiness, ribald small talk, obscure libertinage, so that at last they could speak their minds about him without their husbands' calling them prudes. He did not ask any of the husbands for financial help any more; and while that was a good thing in a way, as they were no longer well off, they had to admit that it aroused their darkest suspicions.

Nevertheless Mrs. Helianos felt glad to see him. None of the patriot Helianos' had called on her since her husband's imprisonment. They were a discreet family, they had to be now, with prices on so many of their heads. Perhaps they thought that in poor cousin Nikolas' plight at present, a display of their sympathy might impress the Germans unfavorably and make matters worse for his anxious wife. But with a point of pride and womanly inconsistency, she resented this discretion a little; she remembered how in 1941 she and Helianos had been criticized as to their patriotism; she welcomed Demos the more warmly. To his surprise and indeed her own, she kissed him on both his unpleasant old pale cheeks.

It was not his intention to come in and sit down. There on the threshold, he turned his worn-out hat upside down and took out from beneath the greasy hat-band a small package or wad of little papers, saying, "This, dear cousin, is a letter from your husband."

She gave a cry and snatched it from him and began to question him.

"No, I will not tell you how I came by it," he said. "Neither are you to mention to anyone that you have received it. Now good-bye!"

Whereupon he turned and opened the door and started away.

But in her great emotion she grasped his old hand and drew him back inside and went on with her questions, until with a sudden assumption of absurd dignity and ferocity he exclaimed, "Dear Cousin, hush! I must go, immediately. Stop holding my hand, stop asking me things."

"Demos, you're as bad as some German militaryman, with your stop this and stop that. I want you to tell me the news of Helianos. I will not let you go."

"I will be as German and military as I please. You shall not bully me, I tell you. I have run risks enough for you two."

Then with his watery eyes slipped down a little amid crow's-feet, he fixed her with a great glance, as it were a concentration of his will power. "And not one

word to a living soul!" he said, and lifted his fore-
finger to his lips in the gesture of keeping secrets,
keeping silence.

"Don't you see, the role I have assumed in this
damned war depends on my not having anything to
do with the rest of you, all you patriots! I spend my
life with Germans," he added, with a very cynical and
ancient chuckle. "Germans, Germans, morning, noon,
and night!

"You must understand. Your husband is a good fellow and all that; we were great friends when he was a
boy. But about this trouble he has got into now, and
his arrest and imprisonment, the attitude I take is the
German attitude. I may tell you that your husband
himself understands this perfectly. Good-bye."

In the old-fashioned manner he clasped her hand
and lifted it to his loose mouth, and began to depart
once more. But then he cried, "Oh, dear, oh, dear,"
and turned back to her.

"How rattlepated I am! I've forgotten what I came
for. Your blessed letter was just by the way. I came to
give you a bit of a warning. Now, is there anyone else
in the apartment? Where can we sit down comfortably
for a minute?"

So at last she led him into the sitting room; but as
it turned out he gave her no news of Helianos.

"A German named von Roesch, an old major: do
you know the man I mean?" he asked.

"I certainly do. He came here on Saturday."

"Oh, he did, did he? Well, I know him, and I had
a conversation with him yesterday about our Nikolas.
I assured him that he is as innocent and well disposed

toward the Germans as I am, which was not a really dishonest way to put it; just misleading!

"Of course the Helianos' have a great reputation, a bad reputation. It does not seem to surprise the Germans that there should be one pro-German in the family, myself; my well-known vices all my life having brought me to it. But two of us, your Nikolas tagging along after me, is perhaps a little more than they can swallow. Old von Roesch gave me a look, I tell you; suspicious! I suppose they will catch on to me one day."

Thus Mrs. Helianos learned that Demos was a hero too. Would wonders never cease, never cease? she murmured to herself.

"He told me how his friend Kalter came to his sticky end. I never knew Kalter; a bit too strait-laced for my friends, I gather. Now tell me, when was it that he did himself in; was it Friday?"

"Saturday, Saturday afternoon," Mrs. Helianos answered.

"Oh, Saturday; Saturday was the twelfth... Ay, ay, he mustn't have been pleasant to live with all year, that one! It's a comfort not to have him around any more, alive and kicking—though, I must say, evidently he resolved to make a nuisance of himself after his death as well."

Mrs. Helianos did not want to hear all this talk of Kalter. She began to regret having urged Demos to stay and talk to her. She wanted to be left alone with the letter from Helianos, the strange letter. She had unfolded it a little while he was talking: bits and pieces all covered with a minuter version of Helianos'

dear script than she had ever seen before; prisoner's
script. She held it in the palm of her hand on her lap,
where she could steal glances at it. She did not want
to be impolite to old Demos, as he had so kindly and
perhaps dangerously brought it to her.

"You know, dear cousin, you are extremely lucky
not to have been involved in that affair of Kalter's
death yourself," he went on. "He more or less pointed
an accusing finger at you, so von Roesch told me; an
accusing dead finger!"

In illustration of which he pointed waveringly at
her.

"Yes, von Roesch explained it to me too. Kalter left
a letter there on Helianos' desk." She pointed back
over her shoulder at the desk. "In it he gave all his
reasons for killing himself; but he also suggested that
some German bigwig named Sertz be notified, so that
it should be made to appear that we had killed him."

"That was it, that was the idea!" Demos said. "Sertz
is a fiend, I may tell you. Von Roesch went to him and
threatened to testify in your behalf."

"He promised me he would. And, you know,
Demos, I heard him arguing about it with Sertz's
young lieutenant; he thought I did not understand
German. It was a kind of blackmail; von Roesch has
some evidence of their dishonesty, bribes and so on."

"Ay, so that was the way of it," Demos cried gleefully. "Thank you for telling me that, dear. How
clever of you to find that out! I knew they had it in
for each other. Rivals, and opposite types: the old
Junker versus the young up-and-coming Nazi."

She hated this chatter about Kalter and von Roesch

and Sertz, all fiends. She was prepared to endure whatever they might still do to her but she would not bore herself to death thinking of them in advance. She pressed Helianos' letter to her bosom and stood up.

But then Demos said, "So now you have von Roesch after you, dear Cousin," in a small sorry frightening voice. "That's what I came to warn you about."

So she sat down again, and asked him not to hint and joke, but to tell her the worst at once, and clearly, because she was a woman, not very brave or very clever.

"Well, you see, von Roesch is firmly persuaded that your spirit is broken, my dear. Is it?"

"No, it is not," she replied simply.

"That's good," he said. "Anyway, you're going to have to see more of von Roesch, perhaps a good deal more. Not right away; he went off to Constantinople on some mission this morning. He'll be away about a fortnight. Then he will call on you, to pay his respects and express his sympthy about Helianos' being in prison and so on. Then he will ask you to give him some information about the rest of the Helianos family.

"Do you see what I mean, dear Cousin?" he asked earnestly.

"God help me, yes, I see," she answered.

"Yes, you're in a fix, and you hold some of the rest of us in the hollow of your hand. As it seemed to me our best bet was to explain it to you and put it up to you. Try, dear Cousin, do try not to give von Roesch information. Talk nonsense to him. Think up things to tell him, make a game of it."

He spoke very rapidly, with his dissipated but sharp eyes glancing up, glancing down; his old fingers weaving around and around the brim of his hat.

"Don't underestimate him. He's very keen against us Greeks. Not cruel like Sertz but more intelligent. He'd be the boss here, probably, only his politics aren't right just now."

"Also he is indiscreet," Mrs. Helianos interrupted. "It was foolish to let me overhear everything he said to Sertz's lieutenant."

"Perhaps he liked you. Perhaps he was showing off for you," Demos said with a smile.

Mrs. Helianos blushed.

"In any case he wanted you to think that he liked you. You see, he and Sertz have a quite different policy. Sertz is a really vain brute. All he thinks of is quantity of victims, not quality. Therefore it would have meant something to him to catch even you, if you don't mind my saying so, my dear. . .

"Von Roesch has more sense. He doesn't believe in victimizing women and children. What he believes in is using them for pawns and as bait. Perhaps he was indiscreet intentionally, to show you how far he was prepared to go for you; how he defied his fellow-officers for you. He means to arouse your feeling of gratitude, so that you will confide the family secrets to him. I suppose you'd better let him think that you are grateful."

"All right," Mrs. Helianos said dully. On so short notice she really could not think or feel much about this new problem, with half her mind on Helianos' letter.

"All right," he repeated after her. "I must go now. I hope you have a strong character. But after all I have not a strong character, and I manage. There is something in me, something else; perhaps in you too. You see how it is: we're not in a position not to have confidence in you. Either we depend on you or we kill you; and, you know, I can't quite imagine our doing that."

The old fellow rose to go. "You will take care of my reputation, then, will you? I especially am at your mercy. After all, Petros and Giorges and the others can flee away to the mountains. I can't, my little work is here. But I have been a good cousin to you, haven't I? I did bring you your blessed letter; I didn't read it either, although curiosity is my besetting sin...

"Now I must run like the devil, I'm such a chatter box. It's why I didn't want to come in and sit down in the first place. Oh, they'll catch me, some day, while I sit gossiping with some charming woman."

She followed him out into the stairway and hung over the banisters, watching him trip unsteadily down, listening to his thin footsteps out of sight diminishing like a phantom's; and her heart was stirred by respect and also by a little laughter.

16.

HELIANOS' LETTER WAS A LONG STRANGE DOCUMENT, written on four or five different kinds of paper in fifteen or eighteen bits, most of them small, enclosed in one fairly good-sized piece of thin wrapping paper. She took it into her bedroom and sat down on the floor and spread it all around her and read until the children came home, then locked her door quietly and hastened to them and gave them their little supper, without mentioning it to them. As soon as she could get them to bed she went on with the reading. She still had Kalter's reading-lamp and a very little oil for it; she put it on the floor and held the wearisomely small writing up to the light.

What she happened to read first, all on the piece of wrapping-paper, frightened her. It was as if Helianos had lost his mind or his character in prison; or as if the Germans had tormented him into thinking in their way. It appeared to be shameless pro-German propaganda in the form of disjointed notes with, here and there, a fantastic sentence enclosed in quotation marks. Suddenly she realized what it was: a résumé of Kalter's political discourse in the last ten days in May. She herself had heard most of it, kneeling amid the old shoes and under the stuffy suspended garments. Now it vexed her so and bored her so—to think of Helianos still somehow bewitched by all that boastful nonsense!—that she put it aside and took up another piece. She expected Helianos to explain why, knowing her prejudice and her boredom, he had troubled to write that down for her.

The second piece she took up, several similar pieces to be exact, looked easier to read; and to her surprise she found that it was simply an account of his last conversation with Kalter, of which she had heard only the uproar at the end, when the blows and kicks began.

Evidently he had not heard of the grief-stricken and hysterical man's death. But he gave this opinion: *"Although at the time his threat of suicide impressed me as mere German romanticism and rhetoric, now, having thought it over, I conclude that he may do it someday; or he may go mad. There was a crazy sincerity in everything he said that afternoon. It is well known: there is often a suicidal streak in the German nature. Unfortunately they will always take as many of the rest of us as possible along with them to their deaths."*

It was not easy to read, after all; it made her so angry that her eyes flickered out of focus. How she wished she had come to her listening-post a few minutes earlier to hear Kalter threatening, promising, to kill himself! She would have believed it, wanting to believe it, and she would have sensed Helianos' peril. Poor Helianos, he never had been able to distinguish between the truth and the nonsense in anything his wicked major told him, she thought. But then she blushed, remembered how she herself had half believed the other major, the good major.

Then she found a page which was more like the usual letter; that is to say, it was not propaganda and it was not a narrative: *"My dear, a woman's love is never very respectful, naturally not. She sees too much of her man's weaknesses, his incompetence and impotence, and how life has worn him down. Please forgive me for all that, now that I am absent, and forget it as much as you can. I need your respect just now. I have to tell myself that I have it, in a kind of self-flattery that I could not live without. It is my necessary medicine.*

"I have tried never to be pretentious in the intellectual way. It is not good for a man to show off his worldly wisdom and culture in the bosom of his family. But I have some wordly wisdom; please believe it! I have been a great reader in my day, and I have known many brilliant men; and even now, past my prime, this recent experience of having Kalter talk to me frankly so many evenings about the German character and the German dream has been extraordinarily stimulating.

"Perhaps the shock of being arrested and the loneliness and hardship here have excited my mind. In any case I have been very thoughtful these days, and I do want you not to suppose that it is all foolishness just because you know me too well. I implore you to try to take it seriously."

This apologetic prefatory page made Mrs. Helianos weep heartbrokenly. Next she picked a small scrap

[227]

that might have been the start of this strange epistle, which as a whole seemed not to have any formal beginning or any definite conclusion. The small scrap read: *"Oh, I have so many things on my mind and in my heart to tell you! Sometimes they keep us very busy here, with their questioning and so forth. I do not always feel quite well, and of course I can only write when no one is watching. But I am fortunate in that I have a tiny window, and in the prison-yard there is a strong arclight, which is to enable the guards to see that we stay where we belong; and all night it gives me a little light.*

"That old rascal my cousin Demos has been here, and he said he would come again. He gave me these scraps of paper. I wonder where he got them. He has a friend here. I think he will be able to serve as my message-bearer to you."

A series of bits of grayish flimsy tissue like toilet-paper began: *"This is what I want you to do to please me. See my cousins, old Giorges and Petros, whenever you can; especially Petros, if it is safe for him to come into Athens now.*

"You do not like these cousins, I know, they frighten you. But you must be patient and not blame their violence too much; it is the tragic time. They will be good men again when it is over, I swear they will, if they survive.

"I want you to tell them all our story: the life our German led us last year, and the great change in the month of May, then how it ended. One thing that has made me lonely here is my not being sure that you know the very end yourself; and not having had a

chance to talk that over with you. My recollection is that you did not feel well and were lying down; is that true? So perhaps you don't know how he broke down and wept, and how I happened to say what I did, in sympathy. When you came to the door, before he locked you out, there behind his back I puckered up my lips for you to see: it meant a good-bye kiss, but I think you were too frightened to notice. Tomorrow night or the next night I shall try to write a little account of that last scene for you."

Whereupon Mrs. Helianos re-read the little account, angrily again, and as if it were against her will; and she felt how Helianos' mind in prison against his will must be going over it and over it, the memory of his entire relationship with Kalter like a squirrel-cage for him, turning and turning; and she shivered with a little fear of his going mad in prison.

Then she took up the grayish tissue-paper once more: *"It makes me happy now to think that you were listening in the closet on the other occasions—Alex gave away your secret, you know, but don't blame him, he worried about you. I am glad that you have a good memory. I want you to tell my cousins everything you heard Kalter say, as much as you can recall of it. I shall try to make some little notes, to remind you; and then I want to write down certain thoughts which have come to me here in prison: things I should talk to them about if I were free to do so."*

She paused and took the piece of wrapping-paper with the little notes of odious propaganda all over it, and crumpled it up a little and threw it away across the floor under the desk. She identified and sorted out

Helianos' own political thoughts, and postponed reading them until next day because she was afraid of not being able to understand them.

Then she read another bit of the flimsy paper: *"Don't show the cousins these wretched little pages. They are too hard to read—a man of action like Petros would lose his patience—and they are badly written, in my style which is naturally pompous. Only a loving wife would have the courage to decipher this tiny handwriting. It has to be tiny or I shall run out of paper. This is a German pencil and it is the worst in the world; Demos had it in his pocket. I have to sharpen it with my teeth. I implore you to make as much sense of my scribbling as you can; then just tell the cousins everything in your own words."*

Of course she could not make sense of it all but of course she had the courage to decipher it all. Once in a while she grew discouraged and was tempted to put it all away in a box or in a drawer as a mere keepsake, unreadable. But then she would come upon a passage of his old familiar eloquence which charmed her whether it made sense or not, which carried her mind away with his mind wherever it went, even in his contemplation of death without a tremor.

"I will tell you how it is when one contemplates dying," she read. *"I do not speak of my own death, dear; only this is a place where you cannot help thinking of it in general. A part of your spirit loosens away from you, it turns unearthly, and some of your mind keeps wandering. What you want more than anything is to have your friends and family informed of what has happened to you. At the thought of losing the*

bodily life you can't help it; you begin to consider how, without a body, you might still have another kind of existence in their minds; as if you were a ghost making his little plan to haunt someone.

"I suppose this is one reason I want you to talk to my cousins. I shall be happier, and it will help me to bear things with good grace and patience, if I know that they are aware of my little adventure, how it came about, and what my opinion of it is. You need not try to make a good story of it; just the facts. No matter if they feel no great admiration for the way we have behaved; no matter if there is no inspiration in it for them, no particular moral—so long as we are not forgotten! While there is memory there is hope."

On three irregular pieces of the same relatively good paper which obviously belonged together, there were certain reflections inspired by his experience of Kalter. The first read: *"It is in the nature of Germans to change every so often; to appear to change. At the end of a war—or it may be, as in the case of our Kalter, before the end—suddenly they grow tired of war, they love culture, they feel sorry for those whom they have made miserable. It is all sincere; that is what makes it so dangerous for us. We have been taught to care more for sincerity than it is worth.*

"In time of peace they are so likeable. Their emotions are so warm and their minds so cultivated; they are so comfortable in friendship, they take such pleasure in doing little kindnesses; and they are so absolutely convinced of every kind of idealism: there is great charm in knowing them.

"Even in wartime; even Kalter was likeable some-

[231]

times. I know, dear, you never felt it, because he made things too hard for you personally; and your instinct about it was right, as it has been again and again, all our lives.

"But I felt it; I had my moments of liking him, now and then, in the month of May. My prejudiced unreasonable wife, yes, you did warn me. But no, no, I was the good-natured and reasonable and judicious one, I would not listen. I forgave him, especially one midnight. I was sorry for him, especially that last afternoon. Therefore now here I sit in an evil old prison writing you a long, illegible, impotent letter. That is my story. I think there are millions of men as foolish as I, in every nation; and I want them to know what I know now.

"It is something for us to beware of: the good moods of Germans, their suddenly reforming and seeking to please, the natural changes of their hearts. That is the moral of my story.

"In fact the likeable and virtuous ones are far worse than the others as it works out, because they mislead us. They bait the trap for the others."

"Von Roesch, von Roesch, von Roesch," Mrs. Helianos whispered to herself, letting this piece of paper slip out of her fingers on to the floor. Likeable von Roesch saving her from arrest and promising her strict German justice, misleading her into his little trap; Demos Helianos warning her of it after she was in it; changeable von Roesch coming back to spring it in about a week... It was as if her Helianos knew everything that had happened to her. He did not know, he could not know, he had written it in his prison. She was not really afraid of the trap, she was not afraid of anything now, except Helianos' absence; she was lonely. So there she sat a while in a stupor of loneliness that was like laziness: the wife of Helianos, with his letter strewn around her on the floor, as if she were a most commonplace poor housewife with an overturned waste-basket that she was too lazy to pick up.

After a while, on another small crumpled piece—it was the torn flap of a small envelope—she deciphered this: "*Naturally there will be forgiveness after the war, it is the natural thing. People will like them again: at least the Anglo-Saxons will, it is their predilection somehow. But I tell you, liking or not liking doesn't matter, doesn't matter! The important thing is never to trust them. With a mature mind one can like people, or even love them, without a blind confidence in them; cannot one?*

"*But sometimes it seems to me, having been childish myself all my life, that all the good-hearted men and women on earth are children, and only the evil ones have mature minds; and then I despair.*"

Now she had only two distinct sets of little pages left, and she began the one that seemed less minutely written, because it was late at night and her eyes were tired. "*As to Greece in particular, our present calamity and the prospect in the near future,*" it began, "*I do not altogether despair as I hear other despairing. I suppose the loss of life, and the abuse of children, and the ravages of famine and disease, have been worse here than anywhere else. But a nation can recover from all this in time, I think, if it is given time.*

It is the factor of time and the world-prospect that especially worry me. None of the nations will be able to withstand the cumulative effect of one of these German wars every twenty years, every ten years. They will be able to speed up their rate of attack, as the nations exhaust themselves in so-called victories over them, letting them have the peace each time just as they want it, their breathing-spell; and of course in future wars more and more nations will suffer as we have suffered. . .

"Our good old Dr. Vlakos takes a desperate view, of the case of Greece in particular. I did not repeat what he told me at the time because I so wanted you not to worry. Now I am not afraid of your worrying. It is better to consider all the possibilities and accustom ourselves to all the truth. It is not safe to shut our eyes, for then suddenly they are forced open and it drives us mad. I confess to you, dearest, that when I first came here there was a time when I was afraid of madness.

"What Vlakos told me was that the birth rate in Greece has fallen to almost nothing. Greek men have become impotent, Greek women have ceased to conceive. But I suppose that there is a great deal of mystery and miracle about a thing like the birth rate. You would expect a doctor to understand that, but they are so much concerned with matters of fact; and sometimes they discourage themselves unduly, for lack of imagination.

"I do not believe that the children of Greece are irremediably, incurably sick; not all of them. They are like Leda. I have been thinking and thinking of

the poor little one here in prison. She is not really psychopathic, I have decided. She is only horror-stricken and paralyzed by fright, and no wonder. I believe that if the war does not go on too long, she will recover from it. She will be cured by a miracle, and perhaps the very declaration of peace will suffice. She will breathe the wonder of it in the air. She will sense the difference in all of us, and wake up. Remember my telling you this, my wife, when you despair about her.

"So it will be for a fortunate portion of the race of Greeks in general. I do not believe that the virility and the motherhood of our people can have fallen into a real decline. They have all been too tired and disheartened to feel their natural passion, and whether it is their conscious thought or not, unwilling to bring children into the world as it is just at present. But all that will change when peace comes. A part of what has happened to us has been only torment and mutilation and destruction; which is a different thing from a decline or a sickness, the effect in the long run is different. Whatever is strong enough to rise from torment, whatever is left over from mutilation, whatever happens not to be destroyed, will be healthy enough. I told our good doctor so and we had an argument about it.

"Dear, do you remember my old Macedonian grandmother, what great flocks of sheep and goats she had? I think I have not often spoken of all that because she was rude to you when we first married. Did I ever tell you about the autumn I spent up there in her high valley when I was a little boy? I made friends

with one of her shepherds. One night—it was a lovely cold night, the pastures were beginning to frost, the moon rose brilliantly, and all the wild hills were softened down like a cloud—I helped him divide the flocks and drive them where he wanted them; and then he put the rams in with the ewes. He explained that his sheep would not breed until those frosty nights came; then their excitement and potency began as if they were bewitched. His best rams, he said, would beget as many as a dozen lambs in a single night. All my life I have recalled it as a similitude of all that strange great rule of nature; in my thought, almost a religious thing.

"So it will be with all of Greece when peace comes. When I told Vlakos this it irritated him beyond endurance. He said it was indecent and incongruous to liken men and women to animals, in this solemn time of the death-agony of the nation. No wonder the birth rate is falling, I answered, when even doctors grow too solemn for such things. He said that I reminded him of some irresponsible silly modern poet that I used to publish.

"I swear that it is not silly. There will be a great passion in Greece when the Germans depart, there will be wondrous children: children, O my darling, like the Cimon of our youth, faultless and promising! There will be a little new generation begotten in a night, the progeny of bravery and pain and hunger.

"But this is the sad part of it—tell Petros!—it will be in vain, unless the nations develop a greater intelligence and precaution than they have shown so far, especially the great nations. For every few years the

*Germans mean to come back, to bludgeon our new
generation into a psychopathic stupor, to set up their
slaughter-houses all anew, to batten on us. Dr. Vlakos
cannot help that; Greeks dying in battle to the last
man cannot stop it; it will take the nations all together
to prevent it; tell Petros. They will let us come up
again for a season; then when the time is ripe for
them, mow all our lives down again in a disgusting,
useless harvest like this."*

Oh, these written words, Mrs. Helianos thought,
were worse than anything he had ever said in the
nights on the kitchen-cot when she had put her fingers
in her ear to keep from hearing. She was not so sensitive and shrinking now, but even now she could not
bear this. She rose, and left the bits and pieces on the
floor, and went to bed.

It was a bad night, sleepless half the time, and worse
when she fell asleep, with the nightmare of still reading, and still failing to grasp or to reconcile herself to
what she read. Then her dream changed from reading
to listening: his beloved voice so long-winded disturbing her sleep: terrible talk of Leda reborn and of
Cimon re-killed, in a second battle of Mount Olympos
all over again; incomprehensible talk of rams and
slaughter-houses. Then she dreamed that her curiosity woke her, to find out whether he was talking to her
or talking in his sleep; then she actually woke and
found out only his absence and no more dream-voice.
Miserably she flung her arms around the mere space,
pressed her face into the vacant pillow.

This fondness turned to bitterness. For then, wide
awake, she stopped to think of the desperate impru-

dence of his writing her pages and pages denouncing the Germans there inside a German prison, of his entrusting them to foolish old Demos. It was as if he did not care whether he ever got out of prison or not. Oh, was there a more foolish mortal on earth than this Helianos to whom she had given all her love; was there a more useless, helpless intellect than this great one to which she had entrusted her life? It had brought about his downfall in the first place. For one weary hour she had deserted her post in the clothes closet; whereupon out he had come with his fatal opinion of the Fuehrer! Arrest and imprisonment: it was his own fault, it served him right, but it did not serve her right! It was a kind of infidelity, his not taking better care of himself, his letting his tongue slip, his putting his foot in the German trap. He was a child. Indeed their children, even wild Alex and witless Leda, had more sense of self-preservation than he. Then the wife of Helianos felt a kind of maternal exasperation with him; an impulse to catch him and shake and slap him.

Once in their youth when she really had been bad-tempered, in the middle of the night she had scratched him like a cat and struck his face and beat his chest with her fists, bursting into tears finally; and gently making fun of her, he had dried her tears upon one corner of the bed-linen, and drawn her body close to him, soft and helpless with her temper spent, and holding her arms and then her legs in his hard young hands as he wanted them, peacefully made love to her. So now in a dream incongruous enough at her age, she relaxed and fell asleep again.

Next morning she sent the children out to play early, in order to finish her task of reading the letter. There were five pieces left on the worst paper of all, with the faintest smallest writing. *"Now this is what I want Petros to do:—I want him to think about all these things; then I want him to go to America and talk to the people there. He is the only one of us who is a good talker, simple, with no embarrassed style; convincing, with his virile personal charm.*

"I want you to persuade him of it. Do not say anything about his own safety; that will only provoke him. Although indeed he has grown somewhat too famous in our small warfare under the Germans' noses; his exploits are too much discussed! One day in the market-place I heard a cluster of gossips; he had been in Athens that day, and they knew all about it. Presently he will endanger the lives and curtail the activities of the men under him; so he may go without a bad conscience.

"It is an odd thing: I really know nothing about Americans except that spiteful stuff Kalter told me. Only I feel sure that they will be most important again when the war is over. Probably the Russians are ruthless, but the British have too much sense of honor and sentiment for the job that is to be done; and the Americans can influence the British.

"It is important for them to be told what we have learned from the German rule and misrule. I want Petros to tell them. For if we all continue to take our cue in world-politics from the Germans as we have done—in reckless appreciation of them when they are on their good behavior, only fighting when they

[239]

choose to fight, and pitying them whenever they ask for pity—sooner or later they will get what they want: a world at their mercy.

"Tell Petros that this is my prophecy, even if it seems to you intolerable or foolish. He is a younger man, and a man of action; let him judge of the folly of it. I am afraid that men of his type, the best we have, are all so absorbed in their heroism of the moment that they are not giving enough consideration to the future wars that the Germans are planning, and how clever their plans are. It is not a question of the far distant future. Petros and even old Giorges will have another fight forced on them in their lifetime. Even you and I may live to suffer it all over again, though I should prefer to die, and to have you die.

"Tell Petros to warn them beyond the sea that it may happen to them too, before the century is over. Nothing is too difficult for these great mystical, scientific, hard-working, self-denying Germans, possessed of the devil as they are, and despising everyone else.

"I do not suppose that the Americans are indifferent to their fate and danger. I think that their worst mistake must lie in their hope of getting peace established for all time, as if it were a natural law needing no enforcement, so that they can relax and be frivolous and forget it. When they see that this is not possible then they lose hope altogether. They give it all up as a bad job and yield to their cynicism and fatalism. It is what happened after the other war. I want Petros to speak very strongly of this, because it is a terrible folly.

"What on earth do they mean when they speak of

[240]

*peace forever? Naturally it can only be a little at a
time, with good luck, and with an effort and great vig-
ilance and good management, day by day, year after
year. Life is like that; everything on earth is like that;
have the Americans and the British forgotten? Tell
Petros, whenever he hears foolish political men bab-
bling about permanent peace, to ask them: what
about permanent life? Do they believe in that too?
What about permanent love, permanent health, permanent talent?*

*"When we are sick and we go to see a doctor, do we
expect him to promise us immortality? When he pre-
scribes some medicine, do we have to be persuaded
that it is a panacea, an elixir, before we take any of it?
Dear wife, you have never liked my little witticisms
much, I know. But this is a good one, useful and sug-
gestive. Please don't be scornful of it, Petros will see
the point of it."*

That was the end of the letter; not a real ending.
Perhaps just then, if it was the midnight hour, sleep
had overcome him; or if it was the daytime, Demos
had walked into the prison-cell, or the Germans had
summoned him for some ignominious task or some
juridical formality.

The letter as a whole, although it convinced Mrs.
Helianos more than ever that her husband was a great
man, disappointed her; and when she finished reading
she wept once more. She did not begrudge him his
little note of over-assurance and vainglory here and
there; for in affliction it is good for a man to assert
himself. She did not disbelieve his prophecies. Only
she felt a certain bitter jealousy of the great anxious

[241]

shadow of the world upon every page of it, the nations, the nation, humanity, the cousins; with no message to herself alone, no advice about the children, no comfort in her momentary vicissitudes. It was bad enough, his not knowing what they were; as it seemed in the letter he was not even trying to think what they might be. His imagination had flown away to greater causes, worse tragedies.

There was another bitterness, not at all selfish; and it increased the more she thought of it: this was only the beginning of what he had wanted to write. He would have written something greater and simpler and more helpful to the poor world, if they had not interrupted him with their bother and nonsense, whatever it was.

Next day, with her disappointment still bitter, and a sudden dread of having so damning a piece of evidence of anti-German feeling in the apartment, and some other unknown emotion, she decided to destroy it. She tried to sort out all the political parts, and began tearing them up in smaller and smaller bits until no one, no one except herself, perhaps not even she, could ever have reconstituted them. But after a few minutes of this sad silly work she felt ashamed, as if it were an indecency or a misdemeanor. She found a little painted box which had been a present from Evridiki years ago, a handkerchief-box, and packed the mutilated epistle into that, and hid it on the high shelf of the closet in the children's room.

What she had not taken into account was her mind's eye as it was now, like a lens; her new faculty; her inability to forget. The various textures and odd shapes of that correspondence-paper of prison, no two pieces alike, of course facilitated this strange turn of her mind. Whenever she wished, and often when she did not wish, shutting her eyes, in the darkness of her eyelids, she could re-read any paragraph or series of paragraphs perfectly, with every imperfection of pencil, slight defilement of dirty prison-cell, misspelled word, or word left out. Without even taking the letter itself out of its keepsake-box, she puzzled over the changes of Helianos' calligraphy from piece to piece. She worried about the trembling of his hand here and there; she recognized his firmest convictions by the dig of the German pencil into the pulp of the bad paper, trying to re-construct for herself his daily life and mood in confinement, in hell. She learned to love it, not merely as a remembrance of the man she loved, not only for its own sake as a slight well-meant contribution to the problem of the world, but as if it were music that she could hum, odd and unmelodious.

17.

THREE DAYS AFTER HIS FIRST VISIT DEMOS CAME TO SEE
her again. Then by the ugliness of his old face, uglier
than ever, and his preliminary silence and embarrassment, and his anxious inquiry about the children's
presence or absence, and the look of relief on his face
when she replied that they were absent, she knew that
he had bad news. Again he refused to come in farther
than the corridor, and this time his refusal was too
solemn for her to argue against it. He hung his head
like an ashamed schoolboy, standing on one leg and
shuffling the other foot up around his ankle; and tormented the brim of his hat more than ever.

"I am in a hurry," he began, "I have some news for
you about the fix you are in."

"What is it?" she asked bravely.

"Tell me first," he asked, "what did you say the
other day, what was the date of your major's suicide?"

"Saturday, the twelfth."

"Well, then, the day before, Friday the eleventh, he
marched down to Sertz's bureau and made arrange-
ments with him to find Helianos guilty of everything
under the sun."

Mrs. Helianos lifted her hands and reached out on

[244]

either side toward the narrow walls of the corridor.

"He explained to Sertz that he was about to be re-called to Germany and transferred to active service on the Russian front; therefore he would not be here to help with Helianos' case. Therefore they drew up a kind of affidavit against Helianos: Kalter's testimony signed and sworn and sealed, dated June eleventh.

"Von Roesch saw it the day he had his little row with Sertz about you. I knew this, dear cousin, when I came to see you the other day. I didn't mention it because I hoped it would all blow over."

The wife of Helianos held her breath, and frowned so that she could only half see.

"What a ghastly devil!" Demos cried out in a sort of despairing tone. "He planted his hatred of poor Nikolas to take effect after his own death the way we put explosives under bridges and things with a time-fuse, in order to be miles away when they explode."

The desperate woman sighed.

"You are taking this very well, dear cousin. You are a better woman than I thought. Shall I tell you the rest now? Would you like to hear the bad news all at once, like this, alone with me?"

"Yes," she answered.

After all, it was news that she might have broken to herself any day, for days and days, only she could not bear to be the one to break it. She might have known it, except for a fantastic exercise of her poor mind not to know it: except for just enough confusion of her thought with her heart's desire to enable her to put off the blow from day to day; except for the folly of

[245]

her love: love which is an act of imagination and often entails other kinds of imagination and fictitiousness and blindness to fact.

This was the news, the fact, the blow:—"They shot Helianos yesterday," Demos said.

The widow of Helianos said nothing. She did not even brace herself against the wall or stir her head or make a face.

"I suppose that was the compromise," Demos said. "Von Roesch wanted to keep you, so he let Sertz have Nikolas. When he gets back from Constantinople he will tell you that if it had not been for his enforced absence he might have saved Nikolas for you. He will express the profoundest regret about it."

Demos went on talking in a kind of drone, of the particulars and the details, as if he could not stop.

"Kalter had borne witness to his guilt in having uttered an insult to the chief of the German state, and acted insubordinately toward an officer of the German army of occupation, and indulged himself in anti-German opinion and a rebellious attitude generally. His fate had been decided at once. They reprieved him two or three times, as a stimulation and an encouragement to him to give them the names and pseudonyms and descriptions and present whereabouts of the rest of us."

It was hard for Mrs. Helianos to listen to Demos talking like this, but she could not summon up energy enough to stop him; and he meant well; and in any event she would want to know it all eventually, so she might as well listen.

"Then there were the days of waiting to be questioned, and the days of the questioning itself; and in the nights he stayed awake, I suppose, to write you his letter. It all followed a certain German routine; nothing out of the ordinary, except that some inefficient underling left his name off one list of the condemned and put it on the next list; and at the last minute there had to be another postponement of twenty-four hours because the officer commanding the firing squad happened to fall ill. At last, yesterday, they delivered him to death—and they delivered him from themselves—along with four or five men and one woman accused of one thing and another."

Demos Helianos was a strange man, Mrs. Helianos thought. She remembered how well she and Helianos, especially Helianos, had behaved when the news of Cimon's death in the battle of Mount Olympos came. She resolved to behave no less well now. She said, "I must go and lie down. Go away now, Demos. Thank you."

But then Demos like a fool, with that extreme stoic mentality of those who have lived as outlaws in the familiarity of death a long time, thinking to console her, added: "You must not mind too much. It was a blessed deliverance for him. It is hell to be questioned by those fellows, they are so extremely merciless and expert, and against the mind as well as the body. Surely he was glad to have it over with. As a matter of fact I do not believe that he answered any of their questions."

Then she swooned at his feet. It was the thought of that young psychiatrist, the great genius, the author of the great treatises, the one who was to have been

Leda's savior—science all things to all men!—which flashed through her mind at the last instant, and struck her down like a lightning-flash.

Her swooning distressed Demos extremely. It would not have been safe for him to go in search of a doctor. He thought of the telephone and trotted all around the apartment looking for it, but Mrs. Helianos had had it removed. Women's distress had always demoralized him and he had no notion what to do when they swooned. But he was a good creature. He put a pillow under her head; he set a cup of water on the floor beside her; then departed, leaving the door open. He wandered around the block and here and there, and found the playground, and finally found Alex and Leda, drew him away from her, whispered to him what had happened, and gave him the responsibility, as the head of the family from now on.

The boy and the girl ran home as fast as they could. Afterward Alex tried to remember whether or not he had repeated Cousin Demos' tragic announcement to her as they went—he could not remember, but he must have, or it was a case of her abnormal infant clairvoyance; she knew.

They found Mrs. Helianos on the corridor-floor coming to her senses, trying to reach that blessed water which the cousin had provided. Alex tried to help her drink it, but spilled it all over her face. The fact that she did not complain at all, or even grimace, warned him of the gravity of her condition; therefore he did not waste time apologizing.

By gestures she indicated that she wanted to get up off the floor. When she had managed it, leaning against the wall, she noticed Leda and with particular tenderness lifted one hand to pat her shoulder; but happened to feel a greater giddiness just then, and involuntarily rested some of her weight on the little one. The little one with her cloudy but good instinct rose to the occasion, drew closer, and tried to bear more weight.

Alex drew close on the other side; and thus they began the little trip down the corridor, through the sitting room, to the bedroom, the good bedroom. It was a hard trip. For one thing the corridor was narrow, with the mother's arms held out upon her young props; the team of the three of them harnessed across, of necessity, by their mutual weakness. For another thing Mrs. Helianos' weakness was extreme; now and then for a few steps she had to use them as if they were crutches.

When at last she reached her bed and fell on it, for a moment she minded nothing except not being alone. She did not know what it was or why it was. It was no lack or lapse of her tenderness toward the children; on the contrary, she was to remember it ever afterward as a moment of adoring them. Nevertheless she could not endure their standing beside the bed, figures of consternation and pity.

She found it hard to speak. She had to save up breath and consciously direct it from her mouth in a few words at a time, blowing them. "Go away, children. Away a minute. Go away."

Alex responded instantly, "Yes, Mother, I am going, and I will run and I will bring back Dr. Vlakos."

But she forbade him to go just then. "No, not yet.

First, wait, in your room. Wait a few minutes. Come back first, before you go," she said to him in her strange blown whisper.

For this was the great pain, the pain that all the other pains had been promising; the pain like a large fish-hook perfectly inserted in over, and in back of, and around under her heart, the pain like a heavy fish-line solidly attached and pulling with absolute even power, no nonsense, nothing like sewing, no piercing or wrenching: simply that perfect cruelty including her entire heart and that steady pull affecting her whole body. Therefore her spirit went down, down, as if it were a fish instinctively seeking deep and dim weeds to wind itself in, great rocks to brace against, to fight the pull in the only way possible, by weight and depth and quiet. Then it broke. She was not dead, therefore she presumed that it was chiefly deathly sorrow, not really deadly sickness. She was all right. Only she was cold, with a cold enveloping her from head to foot, and washing her inside and out.

Then, according to her request, Alex came back before going to get the doctor. She heard him gasp, perhaps in the supposition of her death. Slowly, with an effort she opened her eyes, to reassure him. He was scarcely able to hear her say, between her teeth set in pain, between her lips just slightly rippling with mortal nervousness, "Take Leda away, keep her away now. If I should get worse, it would frighten her, one of her fits. Two of us, too hard for you, take her with you."

By which Alex understood that she expected or half expected to die. Therefore it was imperative to run

[250]

for the doctor. If he took Leda with him he would not be able to run. What should he, what could he do with her? It was the usual problem, graver than ever.

He took her by the hand and gently pulled and pushed her along and put her in the water-closet. He did not have time to wheedle her or explain to her. He hurried her so that she did not have time to weep. Realizing how he must be frightening her and hurting her feelings, in the instant of closing the door he bent toward her and gave her a kiss; he had never done that before.

He took the key out from the inside and turned it on the outside and forgot to leave it in the keyhole; with it in his hand, sprang out of the apartment and down the stairway and along through the hot streets, tripping and falling once and skinning his knuckles, and in exasperation about that, uttering some curse-words that he had known a long time but never used before, with not enough breath to curse well; then arrived at Dr. Vlakos'. Fortunately he was there in his office. But he was busy setting someone's broken wrist, so Alex did not wait; he ran back home ahead of him.

One more of the poor small miracles of the Helianos family had taken place. The door of the water-closet stood open. Leda was not there. Thinking that perhaps his mother had risen from bed and unlocked the door, or perhaps his mother was dead and some-one else had been in the apartment, he scurried to her bedroom. She was not dead; indeed her face was of a less deadly color, less crooked, more like a mother's face. "Mother, Mother, where is Leda?"

She did not know; she shook her head. He went

back to the water-closet. He looked for the key, and found that without noticing, he had put it in his pocket. "Leda, Leda!" he called.

No answer. He ran to their own bedroom and to the kitchen, and thinking that she might be hiding somewhere in fright or in anger, he looked under the beds, in the clothes closets, in the fuel-box. Then he returned to the water-closet, and then noticed that it had not been unlocked; it had been forced. The fixture, wrenched out of the wood of the door-jamb, lay on the floor. How Leda could have done that with her small weak hands he could not imagine.

In his haste as he came in, he had left the front door open. Now through it, approaching up the stairway, he heard Leda's voice in short sharp notes as if she were a bird in a panic, with footsteps, not only her footsteps. He ran to peer down the stair-well, there she came, and this was the miracle: she was fetching the neighbor woman to nurse their mother. She was pulling the small breathless creature, hurrying her but getting in her way, drawing her up faster by fistfuls of the folds of her skirt now and then, from step to step first on one side and then the other, in exalted excitement, with infinite expression in her face.

Finally, for the last flight of stairs, the neighbor woman picked Leda up and carried her, although she was burdensome and although she kicked. In spite of the sorrowful emergency this made Alex laugh. He took her from the arms of neighborliness into his arms of extreme kinship; and very soon she calmed down, and then turned and gave him a smile of uncanny contentment. Obviously she knew that she had done an extraordinary thing and the right thing.

Afterward the neighbor woman described the little one's startling arrival in search of her. Evidently memory and instinct had brought her wild small feet straight to the right block, the right cluster of old tenement-buildings; but then she did not know which house, which doorway, which stairway. So there in the street she screamed, "Maria's mother! Maria's mother!"

Maria was the name of the little girl who had accompanied her to the massacre, who had died more than a year ago. Another neighbor came and cleverly made out what Mrs. Helianos' poor child wanted, and led her to Maria's mother's door. There Leda had explained the emergency quite clearly, except for punctuation of tears and panting, "My mother fainted, my father is dead, my mother is dying!"

18.

BUT MRS. HELIANOS LAY AT DEATH'S DOOR THREE DAYS.
Old Dr. Vlakos came morning and evening. The
neighbor woman stayed in the apartment, and proved
to be a competent nurse as well as an energetic house-
keeper and a kindly nursemaid. She slept in the single
bed with Leda, and, poor lone female, doubtless enjoyed having her dead daughter's little simple-minded
friend to fuss over. Apparently Leda's miraculous
effort had tired her, but that was all; she did not fall
into her apathy or her tearfulness.

Alex was not happy to have the neighbor woman
living with them. As it seemed to him her presence
was too commonplace and cheerful for this turning
point in their lives. But he kept a sufficient civility.
As he well knew, he could not have managed his little
household by himself. He obliged her to help him
move his cot back to the kitchen, and oddly enough,
made her promise not to tell his mother.

On the fourth day Dr. Vlakos told Mrs. Helianos
that she was out of danger. As to her heart-trouble and
her general health, if she would stay in bed a fortnight
and rest, she would not be much the worse for the
shock and tragedy of her husband's death. Before long
she would be able to live as before, to keep her house

and go marketing and do the cooking, and care for the children.

When he had given the good news and departed, she reminded herself that—while her lot in the last two years, her fate in the war, had been hellish indeed, like other people's—still a portion of a kind of good luck had been mixed in with the rest. In the next few days as she lay there, presumed to be resting, she counted certain of her blessings.

For example, how fortunate it had been for her to have had, in the series of violences of those months of May and June, some practice in extreme emotion! Even Helianos' preliminary absence, while he lived and she hoped: now that his absence was forever she had to admit that it had been a blessing. Her mind, without knowing it, without admitting that she knew it, had had time to take in the possibility of his never returning and to adjust itself a little: so that it did not take her by surprise and kill her.

Vlakos wanted her not to talk. She had nothing to tell the good neighbor woman in any case. She began talking to herself in her old way. Now nothing about herself would ever surprise her, she thought; and then heard her own whisper, "I know myself well, my strength and my weakness, my good qualities and my faults. I am still alive; here I lie sick; I have lost my conceit; I have forgiven myself. But without Helianos to give me a sense of my importance with his love, I am of no interest to myself; and in the circumstances that is a blessing."

How fortunate she had been, in that the news of Helianos' death had been a divided blow. Half of the great pain had been only in her imagination: this had saved her life. Her body had borne half the brunt of her sorrow: that had saved her sanity.

Then, having lost interest, she ceased to whisper in soliloquy; she spoke to Helianos instead.

"Helianos," she whispered, "let me not be too sure of myself, especially as to my sanity. Without you to warn me or comfort me, your steadying influence, I must be careful. I will be careful. For years I have worried you in this way, even when I was fairly young and our life was not so bad; now I am older and my life is worse. Forgive me, Helianos, for worrying you about nothing. You will have to forgive me if I go mad now, when I have good reason to."

Then she quickly fell asleep. A poignant thought of Helianos often swept her away to some dream in which there was a chance of her forgetting that she had lost him.

When she woke she said, "Helianos was a proud man; he would have been ashamed of me if I had lost my mind. No matter now, he will never know it.

"But shame on me for saying: no matter!" she added almost aloud. "In spite of death there is a point of pride; and so long as I feel obliged to live, I shall have, I ought to have, a sense of duty. Helianos' widow is not to play the fool even in grief. Helianos' children's mother must keep her wits about her, for their sake."

It seemed a good thing to talk to herself like this. She thought it would arouse her courage to get up soon and resume her life, her half-life. She could not lie there much longer. She had a great deal to do in the next few days or the next week or two. She began making plans, with a sense that they might cover all the remainder of her days; she might not have any life beyond what she saw so clearly.

In her planning and looking ahead naturally she addressed herself to Helianos her husband: she had done so always. "Helianos," she whispered, "I am in trouble with that major, the one you do not know, the one with the dog, the one with a golden eye and a mouth like a piece of broken whip, the likable one. He is coming to see me one of these days, and I am afraid.

"He is coming, coming, to ask me to inform against your cousins, Petros and Giorges and even Demos, your old rascal. Demos said that you refused to answer their questions in prison. I will refuse too, I promise. I do not know what they will do to me if I refuse. I am not afraid.

"But if it comes to that, if I too must be a martyr to keep our Greek secrets, then I want all your family to know what is happening. If they are concerned about me it will help me to bear it well. I want them to be grateful to me if I do bear it well. Perhaps they will be sorry for me if it is more than I can bear.

"Yes, Helianos, I know, you told me, Petros is the head of the family now that you are dead. I will tell my trouble to Petros.

Then she forgot all about that matter of von Roesch for the time being; and when she next found energy to whisper, it was about the less desperate aspect of her mission to Petros.

"My dearest, forgive me for tearing up a part of

[257]

your letter. I was lonely. I was jealous of your addressing it to Petros. There was no farewell to me in it. It was the political part that I hated. All my life I have hated what I could not understand.

"But do not mind, dear, it is no matter. I know it by heart. I can close my eyes and read the small torn pieces, and open my eyes and copy them for Petros. I will give him all your letter, although it is the only thing I have on earth that I love. I will explain it to him if he is not as intelligent as you think. I understand it now.

"I will tell him our story. Perhaps it will interest him. He is a fighter, and I think he must know only those lives that he is fighting with. Whereas our life, though a poor thing, is what he is fighting for.

"If it interests him, and he has time to sit and listen, I will tell it all. I will remember to put in the little things to make it interesting: the borrowed bed, the old dog eating our dinner, the child sucking its own blood, the perilous window, the lost key, the major's dead brain like a tongue stuck out down his dimpled chin, the blaze of summer in the major's dead eye, the cup of water spilled in my face on the floor in the corridor, the fish-hook hooked in my breast, the children when I had to use them to walk with like crutches.

"That is the kind of little thing that you used to put in your stories, Helianos, to make them interesting. Sometimes I can discover some such thing for myself, now that you are dead. Whenever you came home, you had some story to tell me; which is a good trait in a husband. I love you."

Sometimes the neighbor woman heard her whispering and, not unamiably, laughed at her for it. It was well that she was a little deaf; she would have misunderstood everything. Now she happened to hear the words, "I love you," and she shed tears, which embarrassed Mrs. Helianos.

Vlakos had asked the neighbor woman to keep the children out of the sick-room, and it was a part of Alex's grievance against her: she enforced the doctor's orders in a way which seemed to him loud and presumptuous. One afternoon, in spite of her, he slipped in. She came hopping after him in half a minute, all righteous indignation.

He appealed then to the sick woman herself: "Mother, she says that it is too soon for you to see me. Tell her that it is not so. I will be cheerful. I will behave well."

It happened to be an afternoon of pain; Vlakos and the neighbor woman were right; it was too soon. Sickly, she began to try to tell him so. It might hurt his feelings badly if she had succeeded. But she was unable to speak: her lips broke and shook, her voice frayed away.

Alex stood staring. He heard her wordless mumble, and he saw how she looked: her ivory skin now a kind of soiled pallor like a mushroom; and under her eyebrows the hollows strung with little wrinkles in which her eyes burned and turned; and her mouth pulled down as if by an ugly finger in each corner; and her hair in dark serpentine locks upon her temples, not one gray hair.

Alex turned then and asked the neighbor woman to

[259]

excuse him and with a manner of pitiful good sense, left the room. In spite of her sickness and her emotion his mother observed how he had grown up in those few days, as if they were weeks or months.

When she woke a little later in the afternoon, she found herself whispering to him: "Forgive me, forgive me, Alex. I forgot about Cimon, I burdened you with Leda, I could not bear to see or hear your hatred. I have had to learn it all the hard way.

"Alex, do not expect too much of me from now on. Your father was a tree and I was his vine. They have cut the tree and taken it away. Therefore I am misshapen, wound around the space, stretched out toward nothing, half on the ground."

Toward the end of the week Demos came to see her again. Alex let him in, but Dr. Vlakos happened to be there and at first would not admit him to the sick-room. In general he wanted his patient to have no conversation at this stage of her illness; and in particular he despised Demos as a pro-German. The neighbor woman came into the sitting room then, with a broom in her hand whether by chance or for effect; and added a certain hue and cry to the doctor's remarks, broom up in front of the bedroom door.

Finally Mrs. Helianos uttered feeble cries from her bed, and by pretending to lose her temper, which would have been bad for her, got Vlakos' permission to confer with her cousin-in-law upon an urgent family matter having to do with Helianos' death for five minutes, only five minutes.

Demos was sorry and indeed embarrassed to find her so ill, but they had no time to waste on that subject. He wanted to know whether she had seen von Roesch. The report was that he had returned to Athens; whereupon he had vanished into thin air; and Demos for one did not trust him.

Then Mrs. Helianos told him she wanted to see Petros, Petros.

He replied that they expected him to come into the city any day now, certainly within a week.

She pointed to the drawer in the night-table where she kept the keys to the apartment-building and the apartment itself, and made him put them in his pocket for Petros, so that if it suited him he could come in the middle of the night. She slept lightly; it would not frighten her.

"What do you want to see Petros for? Why isn't it enough for you to see me? It's safer to see me."

"My poor Demos," she whispered back, "you are not intellectual enough to advise me. Neither are you man enough to stir up my courage. You know, you know all that."

"Ay, my cousin, you are sharp. Do you mean to make us all jump, now that you have von Roesch up your sleeve? What have you to do with Petros, if you please?"

Naturally she said nothing about the story of their lives, or Helianos' letter, or a matter still more romantic that she had in mind. She said that she wanted Petros to tell her what to say to von Roesch. It might be possible to turn the tables on von Roesch somehow. She wanted to give him false information, useless to him, disadvantageous to him, or even fatal if they had good luck. If he intended to use her as bait in his trap to catch any of them, well, then, let him beware! For she intended to take the trap and change it and re-set it for him to be caught himself. Perhaps Petros or some other important Greek would let her make a rendezvous for him somewhere, as it were to be captured by von Roesch's men; where a sufficient number of Greeks could lie in ambush for the would-be capturers. "I think this a good idea," she whispered, "but I know nothing, I cannot work it out in detail. Petros will know everything; and there never has been a Helianos who lacked imagination: even you do not lack that, Demos."

He said, "You are mad, my cousin! You are as mad as your young Alex, as mad as your little Leda. You are a terrible family. Your Nikolas had no sense of self-preservation whatever. Now it appears that you have none either. You frighten me."

But in his old loose woman-crazy eyes she saw a shrewdness and an admiration that she took for a good omen. Then Dr. Vlakos opened the door and would not be denied. Demos had to go, but in his pocket were the keys.

Suddenly it occurred to her that if Petros approved of her plan, it would mean pretending to be pro-German. Then she would be teamed up with Demos, misunderstood and condemned by the family as he was: the broken widow with the old libertine. Helianos was a proud man, and she was glad that he would never hear of this. But in the present plight of Greeks, she reminded herself, they must not be proud.

After that she began, in her whispers, rehearsing her discourse to Petros. This was what she chiefly wanted of him, she personally:—"Petros, I want you to take my son Alex to work for you in the underground. He is young, and he is undersized because he has been undernourished, but he is brave and clever, with the Helianos imagination.

"Petros, my husband told me, and Demos told me, that one thing you do is to place explosives in buildings occupied by the Germans, and perhaps bridges and perhaps railroad-trains: I do not remember everything they said.

"Now, this is a kind of work which my Alex could do very well. He is an attractive boy with a sunny smile, and so small: they would not think any ill of him if they observed him wandering here and there. We can wrap your explosives up neatly, to give him the appearance of any ordinary street-boy delivering a package. If I knew more of the details of your warfare I could suggest other little tasks. He would make a good messenger-boy.

"Please understand that this is not a thoughtless offer, Petros, no, not thoughtless. I do not underestimate the Germans any more. I can imagine the risks my son will have to run, working for you. I have considered the cost to myself, as it may turn out in the end."

All that afternoon and the next morning, she went on whispering the same theme, off and on, clarifying it in her own mind:—"Do not blame me, Petros. I know myself and I know my son. He has never really

[263]

loved anyone except my other son who died in battle on Mount Olympos. Ever since then he has been suffering from an inexpressible hatred. Now that they have slain his father as well, he needs to do something. For two years he has not had any life except the care of his little sister, Leda, whose mind is weak. Now I will not have him shut in here any longer, wasting his life on us two. Our lives as they are now are not worth it.

"It would be a great comfort to Leda and to me if he could still live here, at least a part of the time. I could advise him against his worst fault, which is imprudence. I could make sure that he understood your instructions. But if you think he would be more useful shifting for himself in the street with the other street-boys, very well. If you prefer to take him into the mountains, very well. In my proposal I make no reservations.

"Let me bring him to see you. Question him and see for yourself what his feeling is, and what he is like. Try to think of a way to make use of him. It is his dearest wish to give his life against the Germans. Nothing else interests him. My husband warned me of this long ago. In those days my only thought was to prevent it. I was frightened and ignorant. Now in my present misfortune, alone, helpless, and sick, I believe that I could prevent it. For in spite of his hatred he is kind. But now I feel that I have no right to prevent it. I have no desire to prevent it. Furthermore he will never be good for anything else.

"Petros, please accept him. I am a poor widow, a woman of no more worth, but with a strong and terrible heart. I have nothing else to give, and unless I give something I shall go mad."

There was no make-believe about this. It was her firm resolution which she would recite to the hero of the family when he came; and if he would not help her she would find some other way. Alex might have a way of his own. She could tease Demos with talk of von Roesch, von Roesch, until he at least took her seriously. She grew impatient to be well.

On the ninth day she felt almost strong enough to get up, but still had the patience to obey Vlakos. The first time she got up was in the ensuing night, that is, just before the dawn of the tenth day. Helianos had appeared to her in a dream, which had pleased her; but when she woke it startled her so to find herself alone that she could not recall any of it, which was a little false loss like a mockery of her bereavement.

The furniture in the room, even the four walls, in a kind of unhealthy pearly light, anæmic blue, looked insubstantial. In spite of the filth and ailment and murder in Athens, the air coming in the window was sweet, like a child's breath. Then she felt a nameless emotion. The beginning of her recovery of health had only increased her sadness. Probably from now on it would be measured only by her strength; as much as she was able to bear, so much would she feel. Now as it seemed, it thrust her heavily out of her bed and lifted her to her feet and held her up straight, although she was weak from the time of her illness.

Her instinct told her where to go, through the sitting room, down the corridor, softly past the open doorway of the room where the others slept, back to the kitchen. Then upon the threshold she stopped in dismay, finding the folding cot back in its place with the small figure of her son on it. No one had warned her of this. She felt an instant of superstition. No, no, it was only one of those excesses of little pattern in her life that she had had to accustom herself to. She went on into that strange bed-chamber which, now, Alex had inherited.

With her eyes feeling their way into the shadow, with cautious hands, she took an old stool out of its corner, and sat down beside the small boy doomed to heroism; the slight Helianos that she had left. She liked to be near him now that she had thought of a way to prove to him that life had taught her to understand and love him. He lay curled up close to the wall with his hands under his chin, his knees drawn up, somewhat in the position of a child unborn in the womb.

Oh, she sighed, unless Petros impressed her as an honest hero and a good man, she would not give him up; there was time to change her mind once more. But it was only a sigh; she did not really expect to find any such poor excuse, or any way out of her decision. She had Helianos' word for Petros' heroism and goodness.

It was time she asked Alex himself what he thought of it, although she knew his answer. His only hesitation would be his love of Leda. Was the little one to be a millstone around his neck always? Perhaps not; he had so perfectly enslaved her heart to him, she so delighted to do whatever pleased him: he might make use of her even upon deadly errands, or at least let her tag after him to keep him company. Stranger things than that had been seen in this war.

Meanwhile outside in the martyred city she heard a delicate whisper: the restlessness in its sleep preparing to get up presently. Then if she had cared to, she might have taken another look at the Acropolis, the temple in a blur, the hill in a black veil, her great reminder, her worst keepsake. She consciously kept her back turned to the window.

Before long she would come back here to cook famine, to sew rags, to clean havoc and contamination. It had occurred to her that the neighbor woman would be glad to stay and serve her forever. No, if she and Alex were going to work for Petros, they could not have this guileless talkative one so close to them. When she took over the housekeeping again, she meant to keep the curtains drawn close against the Acropolis, and work in a half-light.

Alex, restless, stretched himself out on the cot full length, and happened to push the pillow away from his face so that it slipped to the floor. His mother knelt and took it and for a moment sat on the floor with it in her arms. She found the warmth of his breath in it in one place. She let herself down from her knees and put her head on it for a moment's rest, and then—thinking a dozen vague words in a row: life worth thinking about, interminable war, loving hearts—fell asleep.

A little later, when Alex woke and wanted his pillow, he saw her and exclaimed in fright; but at his cry she woke instantly, smiled, and apologized. "I couldn't sleep, I do as I please when you are all asleep,

[267]

I came to look out the window, I didn't mean to fall asleep here."

He told her how foolish she was, and in an affectionate voice but with a little pretentiousness of manhood, ordered her back to bed where she still belonged.